THE ARMAGEDDON CHORD

Jeremy Wagner

kRP

kNight Romance Publishing

This is a work of fiction. Names, characters, places, and incidents are products of the author's imagination or are used factiously and are not to be construed as real. Any resemblance to actual events, locations, organizations, or person, living or dead, is entirely coincidental.

kNight Romance Publishing
Port Richey, Florida
http://www.knightromancepublishing.com

Copyright © 2011 by Jeremy Wagner
ISBN-13: 9780983129776

Library of Congress Control Number: 2011928257

Cover art credit: Chris Jones
Author photo credit: Chad Lee
Editors: Jennifer Safrey
Polish Editor: Kate Richards

kNight Romance Publishing

PRAISE FOR

The Armageddon Chord

"Jeremy Wagner is an up-and- coming voice in the realm of horror fiction. His talent shines through this debut novel, and I can't wait to see what his next offering will be. A real page-turner, The Armageddon Chord strikes just the right note!"
-Yasmine Galenorn, *New York Times and USA Today Best Selling Author*

"The Armageddon Chord is like The Da Vinci Code with a heavy metal soundtrack! An epic underworld, odyssey, 'The Armageddon Chord' meshes an insider's rock'n'roll erudition with a creative, compelling, historically tinged tale...making for a sinister, provocative page-turner."
-Katherine Turman-*Co-author of Louder Than Hell- An Unflinching Oral History of Heavy Metal (Harper Collins 2011)*

The Armageddon Chord is a wild phantasmagoric thrill ride that will satisfy lovers of the darkest fantasy fiction and the heaviest metal."
-Peter Blauner- New York Times Best Selling Author

"With The Armageddon Chord Wagner combines a world of classic adventure and intrigue with a dash of rock 'n' roll mystique for a unique take on the thriller format."
-Joel McIver – *Best Selling Author of Justice For All: The Truth About Metallica*

Coming Soon

Hard Cover Special Limited Collector's Edition

Dedication

For Mom and Dad. And for Kym: I love you forever.

Acknowledgments and thanks

Thanks to: Lori Perkins—my guardian agent and dear friend, Dawn Dowdle, Tracey Mitchell at kRP Publishing—onward and upward, Sara "KS" Wagner, Peggy Wagner, Tyler and Zoe Affinito—you make life wonderful, Vince and Pat Foglia—much love, Vinnie and Anthony Foglia, Jack and Dorothy Jigante, Frank Mastalerz and Master-Wag International for always believing, Jeremy and MWI, Frankie Nasso and NOVA Entertainment—you rule, Yasmine Galenorn—my amazing friend, Katherine Turman—you always rock, Scott Creekmore, Tom Brandner, Joel McIver, Matt Masciandaro and ESP Guitars, Tory Abel, Cevin Bryerman, Howard Stern and Richard Christy for daily laughter and for inspiring me to aspire, Peter Blauner—you are the greatest, Brian Griffin, Chris Barnes, Eric Greif, Albert Mudrian and Decibel, Vince Linguano, John Boden—my missing twin, Ken Wood and Shock Totem, Brian Keene, Bob Booth and NECON, Shroud Magazine, and Cemetary Dance.

To my amazing editors who make me shine: Jennifer Safrey, Kate Richards, and Ed Stackler.

I wish to salute the following writers, for they have either had profound effects on me or I just dig them and adore them all for one reason or many: Stephen King, Thomas Harris, Peter Blauner, Mario Puzo, Cormac McCarthy, Colin Harrison, Peter Benchley, Nic Pizzolato, Elmore Leonard, Peter Straub, Jack "JA Konrath" Kilborn, Dan Simmons, Dennis LeHane, Dean Koontz, Michael Crichton, Joyce Carol Oates, Chuck Palahniuk, Jack "Dallas" Ketchum, Philip Roth, Justin Cronin, Marquis De Sade, J.R.R. Tolkien, Rex Miller, Yasmine Galenorn, Harold Schechter, David Morrell, Gillian Flynn, and Richard Preston.

"It is impossible to translate poetry.
Can you translate music?"
Voltaire

Jeremy Wagner

Chapter 1
Dream Evil

The bedroom, black with night and cold, was illuminated by the glow of a digital alarm clock with red numbers. It read three-eleven a.m.

Kirk Vaisto sat up among the down pillows and silk sheets scattered on his island of a bed, his body slick with sweat. He trembled, trying to calm himself. Minutes passed before he realized the nightmare was over.

The bad dream burned fresh in his mind as his eyes adjusted to the dark and his heart rate slowed. A chilled knot of fear remained in his chest. As it subsided, Kirk was thankful the nightmare wasn't real.

He had passed out early the night before, drained from working marathon hours in his recording studio, trying to finish his solo album.

The nightmare that interrupted his calm slumber was terrible. He remembered flashes of sexual dreams filled with swimsuit models and hot tubs. Then the visions in his sleep turned darker and he found himself being chastised and beaten by demon-headed men wearing Egyptian robes. The demon-men forced him onto a stage where a satanic heavy metal band was performing. The band looked and sounded so evil, Kirk thought the group made Slayer look like Justin Bieber. A demonic guitarist handed him a blood-soaked guitar, and the demon-men made Kirk play it against his will.

Kirk played a diabolical song, the music possessing and infiltrating his being like an unholy parasite. As his fingers worked the fingerboard, he found himself on top of a pyramid, gazing down upon the entire world. To his horror, he saw the misshapen and obscene legions of Hell unleashed upon the world.

With a thunder crack, Kirk popped back to the stage, but it was now some crazy stage-turned-battlefield. He saw himself standing between charging armies of divine light and monumental darkness. He wielded the unholy guitar and realized it was a weapon—a weapon of musical mass destruction. He didn't know what it was for, but he riffed on it, and the more he did, the more terrors erupted to claim the mortal world. Unclean spirits and cacodemons, the inhabitants of pandemonium, came on like an infernal storm to meet the illuminate troops of piety. Toothy and spiky, red and winged—Kirk watched these loathsome things with dread as they brought torture and agony to all. He bore witness as Satan's spawn did a million unspeakable acts to mankind.

The presence of evil saturated his thoughts and filled every airborne molecule in his nightmare. The song Kirk played spoke without a shape and with countless tongues, arousing a dark and indescribable force. Somehow he knew the song was Satan himself, in musical form. Satan now owned Kirk, and the guitarist found himself a helpless pawn to evil—since he'd induced the end of the world.

Christ appeared as a glowing and weeping form in the midst of the nightmare. His hair and beard long, His body emaciated and scarred, Christ floated before him and spoke into Kirk's mind. "Kirk Vaisto, you've failed and damned this world. You've failed mankind and all that is the heavens. Above all, you've failed as a guitarist. Unpitied and unreprieved, everything and everyone you love is slaughtered and destroyed before you...by your hand."

There was nothing Kirk could do to stop the unseen and malevolent hand that forced him to play the insane and hellish music on the guitar.

The world of man burned away and Heaven fell. Hell was triumphant as Kirk serenaded Armageddon. The frenzied playing came to a violent end as he hit a power chord that rang and reverberated through every mortal and immortal level of existence like a nuclear explosion.

Kirk woke up when the chord sounded in his mind.

The terror felt so real that it rocked him to his core. He jumped up in bed and tied his long black locks back into a ponytail with shaky hands. He turned on the lamp on his nightstand and drank from a glass of water as his mind relaxed.

No more Thai food before bed, Kirk thought as his body and mind cooled off and found peace.

Kirk sighed and turned off the lamp before laying his head down. Within minutes, he fell into a deep sleep full of gentler dreams. He forgot the nightmare as soon as his eyes closed, and when he awoke later that morning, Kirk Vaisto no longer remembered the nightmare at all. But before long, he felt a foreboding he couldn't explain. He sensed darkness, as if horrors were in wait just around the corner.

Chapter 2
The Discovery—Aknaseth's Secret

"*Ficken!* You broke it! You sand-eating bastards have ruined my artifacts for the last time. I'll tear the hide from the next asshole who so much as looks at a piece of pottery wrong," Helmut Hartkopff said, kicking sand and berating an Egyptian laborer in a form of broken Arabic, German, and English.

Helmut paused in his tirade, seeing the American archeologist emerge from the pyramid and into the bright sunshine of the Egyptian afternoon. He noticed the short, round, and bald Barkley wiping sweat from his brow. Helmut wondered where Barkley's partner was. He figured the other man, Tom Morgenson, was below ground.

Helmut didn't like these two American men from the city of Chicago who were hired on to assist him. They annoyed the shit out of him. The world's chief Egyptologist didn't need anyone in his way or trying to steal his thunder. But these extra hands were here because the boss, that *arschloch* Festus Baustone, wanted them here. Helmut knew he couldn't do a goddamn thing about it. *Not now, anyway.*

He thought of Barkley as a desert hog, watching the American donning a fedora and a pair of shades as he walked out of the pyramid, looking quite hot and uncomfortable. Helmut watched Barkley with disgust; the American pig stopped to pant, holding his considerable belly as his desert garb soaked up sweat.

Turning toward Helmut, Barkley waved and cried out, his high-pitched voice cutting through the desert air. "Helmut! We have something for you."

"What the hell is it?" Helmut felt his anger rising.

In his seventies, Helmut had bid farewell to his patience decades ago. He didn't tolerate anyone other than Festus Baustone. He didn't take any shit from anyone and didn't have to. At this age, he was lean and mean and held his own in every bar brawl he instigated. He took pride in being an intelligent, full-blooded German, full of muscle and sadism.

Though his body appeared younger than it was, his face gave no indication of age, as it was burned into a melted deformity—the result of a childhood accident during World War II. He'd thought of this incident every day since 1942.

Helmut took comfort in his appearance, knowing himself as *hackfresse*: ugly, with a mutilated visage. His face was a mask of melted skin with a stump of twisted flesh for a nose. Yellow teeth poked out of a taut, lipless mouth, forming a fixed grin across a face devoid of expression.

"Tom and I opened up a burial chamber on the bottom level. It's large and packed with items."

"It's about fucking time you earned your brass," Helmut said, his disfigured mouth marring his words. "You've wasted a week mapping that passageway. Let's see this chamber."

Barkley led the way back to the pyramid. At the entrance, he flashed a laminated ID card at two Egyptian guards.

Helmut didn't wear an ID laminate. The soldiers guarding the pyramid and perimeter, as well as the countless laborers and archeology crews, all knew who he was—and Helmut knew they all feared him.

Barkley asked, "Is it really necessary to have all these gun-toting thugs everywhere?"

"Festus paid the Egyptian government a great deal for the rights to this site. Security's a priority." Helmut patted the revolver in his shoulder holster. "If he wants to build a hundred foot wall around this site, he will."

Helmut and Barkley descended into the stairway system leading down to the burial chamber where Tom waited. Helmut felt a chill escaping the burial chamber. He heard the tomb groan as Barkley stepped in before him. Amused, Helmut watched Barkley, the nervous pig, jump at the deep and unexpected sound. The rotund archeologist hesitated and gave Helmut a startled look over his shoulder.

"Move your fat ass." Helmut pushed Barkley inside.

Inside, Helmut saw everything illuminated by Tom's lights. A large sarcophagus surrounded by a cache of Egyptian heirlooms caught his immediate attention. He inhaled, knowing this chamber had remained undisturbed for more than three thousand years until this day.

"What have we here?" Helmut scanned the lighted tomb through his sunglasses.

"The 'glyphs in here are strange," Tom said. "Unlike anything I've ever seen."

"Probably cryptic writing. Hiding something important," Barkley added.

"Festus certainly got his money's worth out of you two Einsteins, aye?" Helmut spoke in a long, drawn-out breath, wanting to bury these men right here. He thought of the men as the Laurel and Hardy of Egyptology. The hairless and plump Barkley contrasted Tom Morgenson, who stood tall and thin and wore a long white-haired ponytail. "Okay, I think you're correct, *mein* Barkley. Let's get a look at the sarcophagus."

The three men walked to the middle of the tomb room, strewn with statues and solid gold artifacts. Helmut worked his way around vases and the Canopic vessels he knew contained the viscera of a dead pharaoh.

The large sarcophagus filled up most of the chamber. Helmut ran his fingers over the lid of the granite necro-vault, reading the strange hieroglyphics chiseled into the stone.

Helmut had never encountered writings like this before, but he knew he'd break them down. After all, he'd learned from the best years ago, participating and assisting with countless digs and excavations from childhood to now.

At times like this, he prided himself to the point of arrogance with his knowledge of all the pharaohs and all the dynasties; he could read and decipher the most technical hieroglyphics, and knew how to break the toughest of cryptic writings. Over decades, he read countless coffin and pyramid texts and memorized the *Book of the Dead*, knowing every spell and incantation. He recited every myth, could name all of the gods and deities by heart, and learned to speak the languages of the ancient Egyptians, even the most obscure tongues.

"Peculiar, yes?" Helmut studied the symbols. Then he realized something, and suddenly gained a complete understanding of the hieroglyphics. An immediate flush of excitement hit him. "Look out, you sows. I'm going to get the lid off this monster."

"You can't be serious. That lid's made out of solid granite. It must weigh at least two tons," Tom said.

"All three of us couldn't budge it if we tried," Barkley said.

"You're the best Festus sent from the Field Museum?" Helmut's knowledge surpassed these American fools. Festus handpicked them, imploring Helmut to use them in order to expedite the dig. With contempt, he used them at the site of his discovery, letting them dig and report to him like swine in a hole. "Watch and learn."

Helmut walked to the head of the sarcophagus and moved his hands around the carvings on the granite slab. He paused for a moment, intent, studying another new series of hieroglyphics. Then, with a gentle push, Helmut depressed an etched hieroglyph. It sank into the sarcophagus with a clicking sound. In place of the hieroglyph, a solid gold lever with a baseball-sized sphere of gold attached rose straight up.

Helmut studied it, finding it ancient and beautiful and phallic all at once. He grasped the gold sphere and pulled the lever down like the handle on a slot machine. More clicking sounds echoed in the tomb—with the moan of grating stone, the sarcophagus came alive.

Tom and Barkley jumped back as the granite lid rolled off, moved by some unseen mechanical force. The two-ton cover came to a precarious stop with a large overhang. It seemed to float in the air.

Helmut peered into the open sarcophagus as Tom and Barkley kept their distance. A hissing blast of ancient air hit him in the face and the immediate carrion stench of old death filled the burial chamber.

"Mein Gott." Helmut examined the contents of the sarcophagus. Inside, he found a most unusual mummy. He estimated the wrapped cadaver to be more than eight feet long, with the shape of someone with a large build. Helmut studied the unwrapped head and tried to identify whether the mummy was male or female. He couldn't determine the gender—the head didn't give it away.

Even with his old and seared eyes, Helmut knew the mummy wasn't human. It was, he thought, not of this Earth.

Helmut noticed the scaly, red, and leathery embalmed head was twice as big as a normal human cranium. The mouth was agape, twisted into a silent scream. The desert-dry lips drew back from a bottom jaw jutting out six inches from the face. The jaw was packed full of numerous long, pointy, and misshapen teeth. The toothy palate extended a few inches and merged with two flaring nostrils into an unnatural snout. Helmut identified half-dollar-sized ear holes without lobes on the head, and as for the eyes—there weren't any. It looked like the corpse of some kind of lizard monster.

"What is *that*?" Barkley said.

"It looks like a mummified crocodile or something," Tom said. "I don't feel safe in here."

Helmut ignored them. He focused on two objects in the sarcophagus shining under the tomb's man-made light. The first was a gold uraeus on the mummy's head. The headband was solid gold and featured a gold cobra fastened to a band etched with odd Egyptian symbols and inverted ankhs. Helmut regarded it as a satanic crown. He'd never seen such a thing. He knew no records existed of such an artifact, but he had heard the legends.

Helmut felt an overwhelming sense of evil while staring at the monstrosity and the heirlooms in front of him. The malignant dread filling the chamber didn't frighten him. He felt invigorated by the impious vibe and embraced it.

Resting on the mummy's chest was an ancient book. Helmut took it out. It felt heavy; the pages were made of papyrus and bound in solid gold. Helmut found the hieroglyphs on the golden covers of the coffin texts to be strange, much like the 'glyphs on the sarcophagus. He'd seen coffins texts written on scrolls, but never anything resembling a massive, gold-bound book. It only took a cursory glance at the hieroglyphics on the papyrus pages to know this was beyond mere funerary spells.

Almost nothing made Helmut excited or emotional—unless it was the opportunity to take his violent anger out on some unfortunate soul. Nothing else stirred his feelings. But now, Helmut moaned with excitement as he read. He closed the gold-bound book and held it tightly in his shaking hands.

"What is it?" Tom said.

Helmut didn't reply as he put the coffin texts back into the sarcophagus. Then he stood straight, turned, and withdrew a stainless steel .357 Magnum from his shoulder holster. He aimed the gun at the two archeologists.

"What are you doing?" Barkley said.

"You're not leaving this pyramid alive." Helmut clenched his sandblasted teeth together. "This is severance pay."

"You're insane." Tom pushed Barkley ahead of him. "We're leaving."

A gunshot sounded, echoing through the pyramid's chambers and hallways, but likely drawing no attention from anyone outside.

Helmut watched the bullet enter the back of Tom's skull and blast his brains out through his left eye. Tom fell onto the floor face first.

"Tommy," Barkley said, standing over his colleague. His voice turned into an escalating wail, bouncing off the chamber walls.

Helmut walked up to Barkley and pointed the revolver inches from his head. "Now, you going to be a good pig? Eh, Barkley?"

Barkley looked from Tom's body to Helmut and back twice more with wide, teary eyes.

"Get down and crawl back into the chamber, swine."

Barkley dropped to his hands and knees and crawled while Helmut followed, watching his chubby hostage scuttle among the chamber's treasures. Barkley crawled into a corner and curled into a shaking ball.

Helmut glanced into the open sarcophagus. "Hell on Earth. *Mein Gott*, you're so fucking beautiful."

He put his revolver back in its holster and picked

up a small canopic vessel, emptying the dry-aged entrails onto the floor.

Satisfied that the vessel was empty and clean of debris, Helmut pulled out a double-edged knife from his combat boot.

He approached Barkley with an inward grin.

"Good pig."

Helmut kept Barkley alive for another twenty minutes while working his American pork chop over. As with the gunshot Helmut fired off earlier, Barkley's cries drew no attention from above.

Chapter 3
Festus Baustone the Third

On the fiftieth floor of the Baustone Building in New York City, Festus Baustone the Third—heir, chairman, and CEO of the Baustone International Corporation—sat in a large, leather chair behind an immense, handmade cherry wood desk in his office.

Festus lit a cigar and walked to a window, cursing the pain in his legs. He stared through the glass and let out an angry puff. He was long out of patience for Helmut Hartkopff's call. Festus found a sliver of peace as he studied the city outside his office window. It was, he liked to think, a Baustone city.

Looking to the Manhattan street below, he smiled, knowing he owned three entire city blocks down there. The blocks below his feet were filled with company office buildings and warehouses. He stood in his main building, which hosted a museum and his corporate headquarters. This was where he worked and lived. If New York was the Big Apple, then Festus Baustone the Third was the city's biggest maggot.

Festus smiled, thinking of how well the year was going. His net worth increased at an average of thirty-five thousand dollars per minute as Baustone International stock climbed to a market capitalization of sixty billion dollars.

Festus had spent four billion dollars on radio stations and cable programming networks, creating one of the largest entertainment companies in the world, strong in all three of the U.S.'s most vibrant markets: music, electronics, and television.

The *piece de resistance* was Baustone International's entry into the direct broadcast and satellite television markets. Once Festus won a crucial operating license from the FCC to launch his Earth-circling, low-altitude BauStar satellites, his media empire and vision became global. The vast orbiting system now covered ninety percent of the planet, with three hundred satellites.

He felt as if he owned the planet.

Festus grunted in pain and leaned on the windowsill to ease the pressure on his legs. He was fifty-eight years old, his dark-brown and gray hair thin, but not falling out. He stayed clean-shaven and tanned, abhorring facial hair and pale skin. He'd spent his life staying in good physical shape, thanks to workouts in his gym.

Workouts, however, couldn't scare away what was eating his lower limbs. In his custom suit, Festus knew he looked good, but he also knew he was rotting inside. Festus Baustone III was dying of bone cancer, and it pissed him off.

Months ago, Festus felt severe pain in his legs. He assumed it had something to do with the miles he ran on a treadmill every day, or some other workout-related pain. He took a few days off from working out, but the pain continued and worsened.

When Festus's doctor X-rayed him, dark areas in Festus's leg bones led to a three-hour-long bone scan with an orthopedic oncologist. A surgeon performed a needle biopsy on the dark matter in his legs, and a day later, a pathologist reported it was malignant. Festus's leg bones were riddled with a network of cancerous tissues and tumors.

This was one of Festus's worst nightmares. He'd always feared inheriting cells that might carry the seeds of hereditary damage. He feared the cells that divided and proliferated into malignant tumors—the same things that killed members of his mother's family.

Festus's doctors told him that immediate chemotherapy and radiation treatment were necessary, though they felt it was futile. Festus needed his legs amputated at the hips before the cancer spread to his spinal column, then to his brain.

Festus wouldn't have any of it. He didn't want to die, but he couldn't bear the thought of being weakened by radiation—the excruciating needle biopsy hurt bad enough—nor could he fathom life without hair or legs. He allowed his narcissism to trump efforts to aid his mortality.

Against his doctor's wishes, Festus sought alternative forms of medicine. He traveled worldwide, paying great sums for alternative and holistic treatments in many forms, from herbs and shark cartilage to experimental hand healing and witch doctors.

In an act of desperation, Festus even commissioned a team to scour Florida and the Bahamas for the mythical spring known as the Fountain of Youth, but he knew it was hopeless. Nothing could cure his cancer.

He kept his terminal illness quiet. His only child, Mona, knew nothing, nor did his closest associates. If the public found out, his stock and his empire would crumble.

Dying wasn't the only fear Festus had, just the greatest. The thought of leaving his empire to his daughter scared him. He didn't get along with Mona and knew she was incapable of taking over his company. He believed it was a man's world, and he wished he'd had a son.

More than he wished for a male heir, Festus wished he could live forever. He thought if he was immortal, no one could inherit his world, but it was too late for such fantasies. Festus knew he only owned an uncertain amount of time before a painful demise took him away.

Festus returned to his desk chair, his legs offering no relief as he sat. The only thing taking his thoughts away from death was the lost pyramid of Aknaseth. He'd paid unthinkable millions to the Egyptian government for the exclusive rights to excavate—and even more under the table to keep whatever he found. Festus thought of the hefty fee he'd paid to Helmut Hartkopff, the Egyptologist who'd discovered the pyramid and told Festus what it might hold.

Helmut remained on Festus's payroll for almost a decade, digging up rare objects in Egypt for Festus's collections, like the new and exciting finds at the Aknaseth dig. But Festus hadn't heard from Helmut in days and was feeling most annoyed with this lack of communication.

As he adjusted the phone on his desk, it rang. Festus pressed the speakerphone button. "Yes?"

The voice of Festus's secretary filled the office. "Mr. Baustone, I have Helmut Hartkopff from Egypt on the line for you."

"Speak of the devil. Put him through."

The phone crackled for a moment, and Helmut's voice came through the speaker. "Festus, you there?"

"Yeah, I'm here. Been here." Festus was irritated with Helmut and his leg pain now made his disposition worse. "Where the fuck've you been, Hartkopff? You're supposed to report your progress to me every day."

"I've got reasons."

"You better have something good to tell me." Festus heard the sounds of dance music and voices in the background. "Where the hell are you?"

"An Egyptian bar...inside of a tent. It's late here and the locals are getting loose."

"Aren't you blacklisted from every watering hole out there? You're lucky you haven't been lynched yet. You beat up too many locals."

"No one cares what I do when I have your money. There's been a major breakthrough with the pyramid."

"You'd better tell me you've found the pharaoh's tomb."

"Oh, I have, but the real find is what's inside the sarcophagus of Aknaseth."

"You'd better tell me you've got the mummy."

"Yes, a mummy. A very strange mummy."

"Strange?" Festus blew cigar smoke.

"*Ja*. The mummy's large, over eight feet long, with a large frame. It's got a deformed head. Doesn't look human."

"Is it ugly as you?"

There was no response from Helmut.

Festus waited.

"*Hackfresse? Ja*, like me." Helmut paused. "Can I explain why Aknaseth's important to us?"

"I'm listening."

"Aknaseth was a powerful and highly respected royal priest and advisor to the heretic pharaoh, Akhenaten. But there was a problem with their relationship."

"Sounds like you and me. Go on."

"Religious beliefs were a sore spot. You may recall that in Egyptian mythology, Horus—the sky god representing all that is good—was in perpetual combat with Seth, the god of famine and drought who represented evil. Seth was Satan, you could say. It's said Horus ultimately castrated Seth, symbolically depriving him of power."

"Ouch."

"Aknaseth believed Seth's castrated genitals contained the essence of his power and evil. The genitals transformed into a monster god called Sethis—the god of darkness and evil. Both are Egyptian devils, the gods of all fevers and plagues. They are one in the same. Unholy beings. Evil incarnate. Seth and Sethis are tagged as Legion, Satan. The names differ from millennia to millennia."

"Yeah, yeah. Beelzebub, Lucifer, the Beast. I'm with you. Just tell me why it matters."

"The heretic pharaoh refused to believe in any of the Egyptian deities. He considered Sethis an absurd concept, even though his royal prophet, high priest, and advisors all told him Sethis was a real entity. Still, the pharaoh believed in only one god, the Aten."

"A difference of opinion?"

"Right. But Aknaseth argued that if Aten was the symbol of light and goodness, then Sethis must exist to represent darkness and evil. Without Sethis, there's no Aten. There isn't life without death."

"Ah, the old yin and yang theory. Can't have good without bad, or light without dark. Cut to the chase. This disagreement came to a head?"

"*Ja*, it did. Aknaseth broke with the pharaoh, creating a cult around Sethis."

"So these guys basically established themselves as competitors, holy and unholy pharaohs, right?"

"Essentially, the pharaoh found God and Aknaseth found Satan centuries before the rise of Jewish and Christian beliefs in the devil. Also from Aknaseth and the Egyptians came the idea of an end time."

"A guy I hired years ago, who failed to get the Dead Sea Scrolls for me, said the Book of Revelation was influenced by the mythology of Egypt, Canaan, and Babylon."

"Oh, the influence didn't stop there. Over the centuries, Aten and Sethis developed into God and Satan while the end of time became Armageddon. Nothing's changed but the names. I've spent the entire day and night translating large, gold-bound coffin texts from the sarcophagus of Aknaseth."

"I trust," Festus cut in, "that you've placed this under security?"

"Not to worry, *mein* Festus. I'm personally looking after it. Now, according to the text, Sethis is a monster of many shapes and many tongues, often portrayed as being reddish in color, the same hue as the sands that covered Egypt's farmlands."

"Ah, a real red devil, huh?"

"Yes, a red devil called by many names. Sethis was bound to a bottomless pit by Horus, or Aten, or God— call him what you will. But his power and presence lingered at the edges of the settled world, primarily the desert. The devil operates in darkness and places unseen."

Festus pushed his pain back, exhaling cigar smoke while tapping his ash into a Tiffany ashtray. "What's all this mean to me?"

"I'm getting to it. Sethis came to Aknaseth in his dreams and promised to make him a dark prince and commander of an underworld army if he could summon Sethis back to the world of men."

"And?"

"Aknaseth swore himself to the task and proceeded to try to raise Hell."

"How did he go about doing that?"

"Shortly after the pyramid was built, Aknaseth dreamt that Sethis told him to spill the blood of the five thousand Hebrew slaves who served him. The next day, Aknaseth ordered his soldiers to slaughter the slaves."

Festus sat back in his chair. Helmut's tale almost entertaining enough to get his mind off the agony in his legs.

"The soldiers did their job. They butchered more than four hundred people per hour." The excitement in Helmut's voice registered through the speakerphone. "The following night, Sethis visited Aknaseth again. He was pleased with the sacrifice and told Aknaseth to travel into the desert to retrieve a special uraeus and musical tablets."

"A uraeus and musical tablets?" Festus asked, specifics catching his interest.

"Aside from being a prophet and a high priest, Aknaseth was also a fine musician. He played some sort of six-stringed, guitar-like instrument. A strange fact, since the only stringed instrument of the time was a lyre, which predated the actual guitar by thousands of years. Aknaseth's instrument was acoustic, but the sound, the actual timbre of it, was said to be unnaturally powerful, as if amplified by an unknown source. Also, the color was special."

"Special how?"

"It was stained red like the merciless desert sands. The pigment came from the blood of the Hebrew slave children Aknaseth's soldiers murdered."

"That's a nice story, but get to the point."

"Aknaseth began to perform the music given to him by Sethis. He'd go days without eating, drinking, or sleeping until he'd successfully performed and written down the music. He said the music in his mind was so intense that if he didn't exorcise it through his instrument, he'd go mad."

"Sounds like he was already out of his skull," Festus said.

"There was a reason for his actions. Aknaseth believed his music would unleash Sethis from his imprisonment in Hell, giving him freedom to walk the Earth. The music would also open Aknaseth's soul, allowing Sethis to enter and instill his power in him."

"You're saying Aknaseth wanted to become possessed by Sethis?"

"*Ja.* Eventually Sethis was to put a piece of himself in Aknaseth, like an infecting virus. That was another reason why Aknaseth was to go to the desert. He was to become physically and spiritually transformed by Sethis's darkness entering his body, possessing and transforming him into a twisted version of demon and man. The music was to be a battle cry heard around the world and throughout Heaven and Hell. It would summon and release Sethis and call out his dark legions to destroy all those who had light in their hearts."

"Kinda like that angel who comes down from heaven and blows a horn to kick off Judgment Day?"

"Actually, this is to be a kind of prelude to Armageddon. The music will give Sethis, or Satan, a head start against the good of mankind. A foothold from which to battle God."

"My Dead Sea guy said Armageddon was supposed to take place in a part of Northern Israel called Megiddo."

"Actually, Megiddo's where the armies of the world are to gather. The actual battle between good and evil is to take place in Jerusalem." Helmut produced a whistling sound through his exposed teeth. "But the Bible has also defined Armageddon as the place where the kings of Earth will do battle. Armageddon could happen anywhere."

Festus paused, thinking himself a king of Earth. "Okay, so what about that uraeus?"

"Whoever wears the unholy uraeus on the day Satan is unleashed by the music shall become immortal and lead the armies of Hell."

The word *immortal* rang through Festus's head and an outlandish sense of hope crept through him. It all came down to some ancient headband? "What are the odds of finding this uraeus?"

"The odds are very good, *mein* Festus. I'm holding it as we speak."

Festus chewed his cigar and considered his next words. "Listen to me carefully." He tried sounding at ease. "I want to make sure you take care of that uraeus and the coffin texts, and I want you to get them to me, pronto. You've got some very rare and valuable Baustone property there. God help you if anything happens to them."

Helmut's breath was the only sound on the other end of the phone.

"You still there, Hartkopff?"

"You need not worry about your precious treasures. They're safe and secure. You'll have them soon enough."

"Good boy. So whatever became of our friend, Aknaseth?"

"Aknaseth disappeared with ten soldiers when he went into the desert. He was gone for a month. During that time he butchered and cannibalized his soldiers for sustenance."

"That's resourceful. Clever, even."

"Aknaseth emerged from the desert dust and heat and went into his temple. In one red claw he held the tablets, and in the other, he gripped the guitar-like instrument. He wore the uraeus upon his demonic head."

"Demonic?"

"Something happened to Aknaseth in the desert. He returned taller, larger. His hands and feet were scaly claws, and his head was horn-covered. When he emerged from the desert, he struck pure terror into the hearts of his followers."

"No doubt."

"Aknaseth's remaining soldiers guarding the temple and pyramid didn't recognize his abnormal form, and they attacked him. The Aknaseth-demon had incredible strength and killed many of the soldiers, but they eventually overpowered him. The instrument and tablets were destroyed during the fight. Aknaseth died and was later mummified in his demon state. His royal scribes reassembled the tablets, rewriting the entire tablet text onto papyrus, copying the musical hieroglyphs of Sethis to paper. They bound the papyrus pages in solid gold and put the coffin texts, the gold uraeus of Sethis, and Aknaseth's mummified body into a huge and elaborate sarcophagus. After the funeral rites were finished, all of Aknaseth's loyal followers and soldiers granted Aknaseth's final request."

"Which was?"

"They all committed suicide. Aknaseth instructed them to kill themselves immediately after he was laid to rest."

"Now *that's* loyalty."

"What happened after that is unknown. I suspect Akhenaten and his people tried to erase all evidence that Aknaseth ever existed, just as the pharaoh Akhenaten's own son, Tutankhamen, destroyed most of the effigies and tomb paintings of his father's single-god worshipping rule."

"Well, this has been a helluva story, but I don't think I want to put too much stock in this tale. I'll put my faith in something else."

"I already know where your faith lies, Festus." Helmut's tone sounded impatient. "I've heard legends about Sethis and Aknaseth since I came to Egypt as a boy. I've dreamed of finding Aknaseth's mysterious pyramid for most of my life. I believe this text and the music it contains holds a key to unlock the actual Biblical Revelation. The song must be played. This music possesses a great deal of power."

"Power?" Festus acted as if everything he'd just heard was hogwash, just to keep Helmut off balance. "I'm an empiricist, Helmut. I'd have to see some proof before I believed in this satanic crap."

"*Ficken!* I've got *proof* here." Helmut's voice was rising. "The mummy and the texts of Aknaseth are proof. The song Sethis provided is proof."

"I understand your interest, but *my* interests are to pack up the contents of that pyramid and put it all in my warehouses and my museum." Festus mashed his cigar into the ashtray.

"Listen to me. Aknaseth never had a chance to perform the music. If we're able to play this music—if we can find a guitarist good enough to do it—then we might just find out what power is out there."

Again the word *immortal* screamed in Festus's head, but he kept the coy act going. "Tell you what. Get those coffin texts together, along with that unholy uraeus and mummy. Okay? Get to New York immediately, and I'll decide what to do. If it looks good, then we'll search for a musician, a guitarist who can play that song."

"This is good, Festus. I'll expect a Baustone private jet to take me to New York tomorrow."

"See you soon. Don't forget anything."

"I won't overlook a grain of sand."

Festus remembered a matter he almost forgot. "What about those boys I sent from Chicago? They dig good, but they'd love to get their paws on my shit for the Field Museum. You keeping an eye on 'em?"

Quiet filled the line for a moment before Helmut

answered. "They've...disappeared."

Festus picked up something wrong in Helmut's delivery. "You mean they quit, right?"

"*Ja.* This isn't work for big city Ph.D.s, Festus. Your little pigs need air-conditioning and cable TV. They must be back in the Land of the Free."

Festus remained quiet, thinking of the whereabouts of the two world-renowned archeologists he'd hired to assist. Disappearing without notice sounded too unprofessional for those men. Festus frowned, knowing if they met their fate in the desert, it wasn't by accident.

"Festus, I must go. More work to be done through the night."

He pushed away thoughts of vanishing archeologists. "Goodbye, Helmut."

Festus disconnected and sank back into his desk chair. He held a great interest in all things mysterious. He remembered spending hundreds of thousands of dollars seeking the lost Ark of the Covenant. He'd tried to buy the Shroud of Turin. Years before, he'd even told the then-president of the United States that he'd sign a letter of confidentiality and give ten million dollars in campaign contributions if the prez could get Festus into Area 51 to "browse". Festus felt dissed when nothing came from the commander-in-chief. All of his efforts wasted, and all on a billionaire's lark.

But the story of Sethis sounded different to him. Though it could end up a joke, it also held his last hope for life everlasting. He had nothing to lose. He put powdered tiger penis in his coffee every morning and did everything else possible to rid himself of cancer. Nothing worked. Desperate times called for desperate measures.

Festus believed in evil. He believed Satan was everywhere in various forms. From murderers and child molesters to dictators and cannibalistic psychopaths, evil had multiple faces. Festus wondered what Satan's actual face looked like.

Thoughts and ideas stirred excitement in his mind. He pushed an intercom button on his phone and rang his secretary.

"Yes, Mr. Baustone?"

"I've got a homework assignment for you."

"Yes, sir?"

"It's nothing much. Your son, Jerrold—"

"That's Jerred, Mr. Baustone."

"Jerred, of course. He's how old?"

"Sixteen."

"And he's into music and stuff, right? I think I remember him being in a band."

"That's right, Mr. Baustone. He has a garage band with some friends."

"What're they called?

"Umm, it's not really a pleasant name, Mr. Baustone."

"Go on, Penelope. My daughter listens to a band called Garbage, for Christ's sake."

"Vaginal Octopus."

"Lovely. Boys will be boys. What does Jerred do in the band?"

"He plays guitar and sings."

"Excellent. I imagine he knows a lot about music and musicians?"

"Well, there's no accounting for taste, but yes, he's somewhat of an expert on bands and music. He likes to tell me what sucks and what doesn't."

"I'd appreciate it if you'd ask Jerrold—I mean,

Jerred—who the most famous guitar player alive is. Actually, more than fame, I need to know who's considered the best and most brilliant. Again, living. Hendrix isn't going to help me."

"That's my homework assignment?"

"That's it."

"May I ask why, Mr. Baustone?"

"I'm afraid I can't tell you that. If I did, I'd have to kill you," Festus said with a humorless delivery.

There was a pause before Penelope replied. "I'd be happy to oblige, Mr. Baustone."

"Bring me a CD if your son recommends anything. Remember, I want the best. Now, go home early, Penelope. I'll see you tomorrow morning."

Festus disconnected the phone and decided he'd close shop early. He wanted to get the day done, eager to see what tomorrow—and Helmut—would bring.

Chapter 4
Kirk Vaisto

"Okay. I think I've got it," Kirk Vaisto said, knowing he'd just finished laying down the most demanding guitar tracks he'd ever written and recorded. "I don't wanna do that one again."

"Wanna come in here and see how it sounds?" Grainy, the studio engineer, spoke through the talkback in Kirk's headphones.

"Yeah, I'll be right in."

Kirk took off his headphones and walked to the control room with his guitar in his hands.

He felt happier than ever. He marked this project as a milestone—recording his seventh solo album. He'd performed most of the work himself except for hired hands doing the studio drums, bass, and keyboards for the eleven tracks on the album. He'd kept this album instrumental, with no vocals, just like all his previous solo releases.

He knew he was in the home stretch; only the harmonized guitar solos were left to track, and they'd layer the songs like icing on a cake. Kirk found it to be a challenging endeavor. He knew he was a musician with incredible skill and talent, and also knew he was an anal-retentive perfectionist. In his home recording studio, Kirk was his own worst enemy.

"Let's hear what we've got."

Grainy pressed play on the digital tape recording machine. Soon the control room filled with the sounds of the song Kirk titled, *Beyond*. Though it was a board mix, Kirk thought the song sounded great. Everything fit and Kirk knew his guitar playing was more amazing and dynamic than ever.

When the song ended, Kirk and Grainy slapped each other on the back and let out war cries.

"Hell, yeah! Sounds fuckin' great, man," Kirk said. "Those runs and sweeps were brutal. The arpeggios were a real bitch to lay down four times."

"That's why they call you 'The God of Guitar'."

"Quit kissing my ass."

"Hey, it's true. You're the ultimate guitar madman. I don't work with just any six-string wanker, y'know."

Kirk laughed. "All we've gotta do is finish the harmonies and mix it, and we're as good as done."

"Yeah. I'm thinking we should take a few days off to give our ears a break. Then we can come back here to track the rest and mix this mother."

"Sounds good. Let's see about getting back in here on Monday. That'll give us plenty of time to clear our heads."

"Cool. If you need me for anything, just call my

cell."

"All right, my man. See ya."

They hugged before Grainy walked out into the light of the late afternoon sun. He got into his Porsche 911 and sped off. Kirk waved, then shut down and locked the studio then walked across the cobblestone and tree-filled courtyard toward his mansion.

He gazed at his beachfront house, appreciating what he owned. How far he'd come since his childhood in New York. He loved living in Malibu and enjoyed his fifteen-thousand-square-foot mansion with attached four-car garage filled with four-wheeled toys. The in-ground swimming pool and hot tub were nice, but none of it compared to his recording studio—his pride and joy. A half-million-dollar creative work shed he'd be happy to live in.

He looked at the tall stucco fence surrounding his compound and thought of the numerous fans waiting outside from time to time, often leaving him notes and gifts on the gate.

Kirk owned his dream house and the quiet paradise he'd always wished for. He loved having the whole place to himself. At thirty-nine, Kirk remained single. He'd never been married, didn't have illegitimate children or any pets. Girlfriends came and went like carryout. Guitars were the only permanent and dependable part of his love life. They were the true objects of his affection.

Thinking about his passion for the guitar, he also realized six strings didn't satisfy his desire for the flesh of the opposite sex. Even now, as he walked alone to his house, he longed for the touch and smell of a woman.

Kirk liked keeping himself clean. He chose to never

use drugs and only drank a few beers on a social level. This didn't mean he was without vices. He regarded guitars, performing live, and the pleasures of a woman's body as his addictions. His blood ignited in his veins and his heart pumped with lust at the feel and sound of a new or vintage guitar, the moment he hit a stage in front of a packed house, or the sight, sound, and feel of a woman locked into his every thrust.

As much as he tried focusing on his art and resisting carnal temptations, women made it difficult for him to be good. They threw themselves at him every time he was out. Part of this was because he held celebrity status as the most famous guitarist in the world, and part of it, he hoped, was because most women found him to be attractive. He wasn't a dog. He stood six feet tall, with a thin, muscular build. His hair was long and black and down to his waist. He remembered how his agent once wanted him to try modeling, saying the combo of Kirk's soft and masculine features along with his gleaming, straight-toothed smile and bright green eyes would make great commercials. Kirk wanted no part of it. He focused on music as his sole career.

When the recording sessions for his new album began a few months ago, Kirk stopped getting laid on a regular basis. It was weeks now since he'd been with a woman. He was too busy to drive to Hollywood, where he'd usually go to hang out at the Whiskey, Viper Room, or Rainbow.

Abstinence was proving to be a blessing. Kirk wasn't having any contact with women, so he poured all his tension and frustration into his playing. He played with an intensity and passion above and beyond previous efforts. More focused than ever, Kirk thought it a good idea to put his libido on ice, at least for a little while. For the time being, he wanted to enjoy his love and hunger for the guitar. This appetite was never sated.

He remembered beginning kindergarten as an accomplished guitarist. He soon discovered the music of a man named Jimi Hendrix and a band called KISS. These musical finds proved to be life changing as Kirk went electric in grade school.

Kirk thought of his first electric guitar, a major Christmas gift that ensured his path toward guitar greatness. It was a Sears model and came with a small practice amp. It opened up a whole new world.

Kirk began playing hard rock and guitar solos, by ear. He'd never taken formal guitar lessons before sixth grade, other than the techniques Aunt Mia taught him. People always called him a prodigy.

He never had an interest in sports, theater classes, or school band. Band proved much too simple for Kirk's talents, so his parents enrolled him in a special night class in music at a nearby university.

At the university, Kirk learned to read music. He learned the history of the guitar and how to play different styles. By twelve, he became accomplished in everything from classical to heavy metal. He studied music theory, learning the elements and history of music and musical instruments. He dove into subjects like ethnomusicology and the psychology of music.

His broad influences and heroes ranged from Bach, Paganini, and Segovia to Eddie Van Halen and Randy Rhoads. He held Stevie Ray Vaughn in special regard, along with his peers, Dimebag Darrell Abbott and Yngwie Malmsteen.

Kirk stopped going to night classes at age sixteen and knew if he applied himself after high school he would have nailed down a master's degree at some point. Instead of college, he left New York to teach a special summer guitar course at a music school in Los Angeles.

The summer teaching gig was fine, and the school put him on a small salary from May through August that year. Kirk loved club hopping; he went out every night to check local talent at Hollywood clubs on the Sunset Strip, working the rooms and networking. He got extra work recording material for soundtracks and studio albums. He was young enough to spread himself everywhere without burning out. Kirk was thankful he'd also been smart enough to avoid the traps of substance abuse and fly-by-night agents and managers.

Kirk entered his mansion and seated himself on the expansive couch dominating his living room. Stacked and spread across the large, rectangular coffee table in front of him were thousands of photos along with magazine covers and clippings from his personal press archives. The clippings covered Kirk's career through numerous features from his teenage debut on the rock scene to his most recent *Rolling Stone* piece a month ago. His agent had asked him to pull out all the old press, said it was time to do a memoir. Kirk had laughed at the idea, thinking he was too young to be doing memoirs. He figured these books were for the Sammy Hagars and Keith Richardses of the world. His agent pressed the issue and mentioned that the bidding war for the book was going to reap a huge advance. "Strike while the iron's hot, kid."

His agent also wanted famed rock-book writer Neil Strauss to write Kirk's book for him. This suggestion he refused, adamant about telling his own story his way, even if it meant typing twenty words a day.

Kirk paged through a stack of glossy magazine articles before tossing them down and reclining into the couch. All of the clippings and thoughts of book writing made him weary. They also made him begin to reminisce on his rise to stardom.

He remembered the early days, when he ended the summer school and signed with the Sterling Stars Agency in Hollywood, an agency with an impressive roster of A-list movie stars, best-selling authors, and some of the biggest rock bands and recording artists in the world. Kirk's representative at Sterling was powerhouse agent Rod Yaggerwood, a thirty-year veteran at the agency. As a teenager, Kirk's solid reputation and prodigious playing skills had already elevated him to legendary status as the most famous, most incredible unsigned guitarist in the land. Rod wanted to sign young Kirk to Sterling Stars, intending to make him the biggest guitar hero in the universe.

Yaggerwood. That old shark's still circling. He laughed, knowing he was fortunate to have the tenacious agent in his corner after all these years, though Rod pissed him off more often than not with some of his unscrupulous deals.

A teenage Kirk had reservations about Rod Yaggerwood. The middle-aged, tanned, longhaired, fast-talking, and chain-smoking agent seemed like all the rest: a little too enthusiastic and almost too good to be true. But Rod persisted and wooed Kirk into his office, giving him a full tour of the Sterling Stars Agency. Kirk realized Rod meant serious business and could make him larger than life.

Soon after Kirk signed with Sterling Stars,

Yaggerwood introduced him to one of the agency's biggest clients—the notorious and controversial singer, Jack Slynn.

Thinking of Slynn made Kirk want to abandon thoughts of doing any kind of book at all. He figured Jack Slynn would need an entire book of his own rather than just a mention in one of Kirk's unwritten chapters. Moreover, he didn't have the energy or desire to go down memory lane with Slynn. He knew the trip would be a nasty and ugly one.

Jack was the most famous front man of all time and had been with Sterling Stars since he was a pup. As lead singer and creative core for the hard rock band Cardinal Slynn, Jack was regarded as one of the most outrageous and wild entertainers who ever lived. One part Mick Jagger, one part Iggy Pop, mixed in with bits of Marilyn Manson and Axl Rose, wrapped in a skin of Hollywood horror-glam. Jack was, to Kirk, a rock and roll rebel who lived life like a twenty-four hour a day party.

Out of the thousands of articles before him, Kirk estimated about 90 percent were related to the glory years he spent in Slynn's band. Cardinal Slynn was a mixture of hard rock and serious heavy metal. Before Kirk even met them, the band's first four albums had already sold a combined total of more than twenty million copies worldwide, making Jack Slynn one of the biggest and richest rock stars on the planet.

When Jack's longtime guitarist, Tommy "Bag O' Shit" Boggs, died of a heroin overdose on the road, Jack sought an immediate replacement, and Rod Yaggerwood stepped in and introduced him to Kirk.

Rod wanted Kirk to audition for the spot of lead guitarist for Cardinal Slynn. His plan was to use Jack's band as a stepping-stone for Kirk's career. Once he was in place in Cardinal Slynn, he'd become a household name, though Kirk feared the hazing process would be volatile. His trepidation came from all the crazy things he'd heard about Jack Slynn. Jack set his bandmates on fire, masturbated on stage, and cut himself with razors during songs.

Rod told Kirk not to worry about anything. If Jack made an offer, Rod would guarantee he would be safe and get the best deal possible. Jack Slynn could make Kirk a star, and nothing was more important.

When he showed up at the Cardinal Slynn rehearsal, he felt out of place. The jam spot was full of groupies, women with huge, blonde hair and globe-sized tits. A half-dozen scooter-trash roadies were snorting coke and smoking dope. Others were busy guzzling beer and receiving oral favors from the silicone-boobed, platinum-haired talent. The only other people in the room were Cardinal Slynn's bassist and drummer and Jack.

Kirk remembered the audition as if it just went down. Slynn was in a foul mood that day. Jack wore mirrored sunglasses and cowboy boots along with black leather pants and a black leather vest over his bare chest. He reclined on a couch, smoking a cigarette and sipping on a fifth of Jack Daniels. Slynn's short, tattoo-covered body was strewn with scars and needle marks, his black spiky hair a gel-slicked rat's nest.

"So you're the hotshot gunslinger everyone's been talking about," Jack said in his raspy voice.

"Guess so." Kirk didn't look up as he tuned his guitar.

"Well, I've tried out every axe-strokin' motherfucker on the planet for this gig and none of 'em has made the cut. Shit, you're only what, sixteen or somethin' like that? Probably ain't been laid yet."

Everyone in the room snickered.

"That Bag O' Shit Boggs was an ass-kicking guitarist," Jack said. "You're gonna have to pull a rabbit outta your ass if you're gonna top him and impress me."

Kirk didn't even answer. He turned to the other two members of Cardinal Slynn and nodded, ready to play the entire set of songs for the audition.

Cardinal Slynn, including Kirk on guitar, played for forty-five minutes straight. He played every riff, rhythm part, and guitar solo with flawless precision. He didn't miss a beat and tore through the set like a machine-gun. As the band finished, Kirk topped off the audition with a blazing and spontaneous guitar solo. Everyone stared in awe at the teenage Vaisto. He'd blown their minds with the most amazing display of guitar virtuosity they'd ever seen.

Jack Slynn walked up to Kirk. "You want a job, kid?"

"Sure."

"Good. Because if you didn't, I'd've had to put a gun to your head and made you join my band. You're the best goddamn guitar player I've ever seen or heard. I gotta have you in my band." Jack hugged Kirk. "Welcome aboard."

Within months of joining and signing contracts with Cardinal Slynn, as well as signing to the band's record label of Juggernaut Records, Kirk entered the studio and recorded the fifth Cardinal Slynn album, *Beef Kitten*.

Demand for the band was at an all-time high. *Beef Kitten* was met with great critical acclaim and sold more than eight hundred thousand copies the first week of release, an instant number one on the Billboard charts.

Kirk was seventeen and playing sold-out arenas and coliseums to more than twenty thousand people a night worldwide. He was amazed not only at the sea of faces in front of him every night, but also at the massive production. Backstage shenanigans often resembled porno shoots more than casual meet and greets. Jack Slynn instigated many X-rated after-show situations that made Sodom and Gomorrah look like nice family communities.

Kirk was in the biggest hard rock band in the world and it made him a mega star overnight. With Cardinal Slynn he had it all: girlfriends around the world, a band jet, exclusive endorsements, headlining festivals, awards, and free gear from manufacturers of musical products. He even had his own signature line of ESP guitars.

Kirk was thrilled that his music touched millions and influenced many aspiring guitarists. He loved the way he connected with people in the audience when he played live, looking in their eyes and hitting a spiritual chord with them that cut through the heavy metal bombast. The sound of thousands chanting his name was a rush. On the *Beef Kitten* tour, the press and the fans dubbed Kirk "The God of Guitar".

Kirk was also happy making so much cash as a teenager, even after Yaggerwood's percentage. He put most of it into a savings account and stocks. He bought his first car, as well as a condo in Hollywood, and gave his parents enough money to retire.

During the next four years, Kirk toured and recorded three more albums with Cardinal Slynn, forever making his mark in the history of rock and roll.

Then one day the Cardinal Slynn legacy ended when Jack Slynn disappeared off the face of the Earth.

Jack's Ferrari was discovered burning in an alley near Santa Monica. Bullet holes riddled the entire vehicle. Police found traces of Jack's blood, cocaine, and a fired handgun with Jack's prints on it. They never found a body. Investigators searched everywhere for evidence of Jack's whereabouts, but they all came up empty. The press referred to him as "Jimmy Hoffa Rock-N-Rolla".

Some thought Slynn was gunned down in a drug deal gone bad, but Kirk knew Jack was a habitual cocaine user in massive debt to his drug dealer.

Others thought Slynn might've been whacked by one of the many women he used for sex. Between palimony suits, stalkers, and giving some partners STDs, Jack Slynn was public enemy number one with an army of women he used and abused.

No theory held substance. No one knew anything about Slynn's disappearance. Kirk figured it was one of rock and roll's biggest mysteries. Fans refused to believe Jack Slynn was dead. There were more sightings of him than of Elvis.

An entire year went by without Jack Slynn ever turning up. The world seemed to accept he was gone, and a funeral was held for him in Beverly Hills.

"What ever happened to you, Jack?" Kirk said to his empty living room. *Holed up with Morrison?*

Kirk thought of the career that followed in the wake of Cardinal Slynn. He played for a few years with the British group Korncobb, considered to be the UK's version of Metallica. He then went on to form a super group called The Godly. The mega-metal band was made up of four huge, platinum-selling rock stars, including Dizzy Letchfield, former lead singer from Snothole; Cliff "Killer" Kooper, ex-bassist of Plowing Suzy; Davey Lockheed, one-time drummer for the Armored Darlings, and Kirk.

After three years with The Godly, Kirk went solo. Today, with his seventh solo album in the can, Kirk felt happy. He commanded the freedom to express his artistic ideas and maintain his integrity without interference from other band members with swelled heads or record label personnel who thought they knew what it took to make a great song.

Kirk reached over and picked up a guitar mag. The issue was a year and half old and contained a review of his last album. *Guitarland Magazine*, the world's biggest publication for the six-string enthusiast, said of his playing: "Vaisto's phenomenal. Absolutely incredible. Never has there been a guitar artist full of such innovation and technical chaos. His contributions to the worlds of guitars and music are immeasurable. We've just found out what the *Men In Black* have known all along: Kirk Vaisto's an alien."

Kirk knew his solo material wasn't as commercial or straightforward as the songs he once wrote for Cardinal Slynn and The Godly. Regardless, each solo release sold millions of copies, thanks to his large and loyal fan base. He earned the title, remaining the undisputed God of Guitar.

"The God of Guitar?" Kirk spoke out loud and his words echoed into his vaulted ceiling. Something in this nickname now gave Kirk a new sense of unease. But why? He'd lived with it for so long, and it always came as an affectionate, if not rightful, tag to who he was. Yet he couldn't lose the ominous feeling now creeping into his heart at the thought of being this idol, this six-string deity who was only a man.

Kirk suddenly felt the traces of a recent nightmare surface into his mind and flesh. He didn't grasp any details; the nightmare left only dark and apocalyptic sensations behind like foul oil stains in his soul. He felt sure of one thing, though: the certainty of something malevolent coming his way because of who he was. It felt like his god-like status in all things music was going to haunt him and bite him in his heavy-metal ass.

"Fuck this." Kirk got off the couch and made for the wet bar on the main floor. He figured a drink or two might get his head on straight. He wished he had some company. His house suddenly felt too big and lonely.

As he poured himself a shot of Crown, he thought perhaps he'd been working too hard. The solo album was more than a full-time job, and a memoir was a ridiculous thing to even consider taking on. Yaggerwoood always wanted something from him. Everyone wanted something from him, it seemed, and now he was sure something wanted a piece of him.

Kirk tossed back a shot and poured another. For the first time in his life, he thought it might not be so bad being a regular guy, instead of some "god" whom people worshipped because he played guitar so fucking well. If he were a regular dude, people wouldn't pay attention to him anymore.

Maybe he was just having a moment of bachelor paranoia and exhaustion. He wanted a vacation. Hell, he deserved a long one. Maui was a favorite destination of his. Why not? He could begin his transformation into no one special.

Kirk did his second shot and put the glass down on the bar with a bang. He laughed hard, knowing

Yaggerwood would never let him disappear into anonymity. He frowned then, as he thought of something else bigger and meaner than Yaggerwood also refusing to let him go because of his talent. If such an unknown thing existed, he hoped to Christ he'd never meet it.

Chapter 5
Helmut Hartkopff

Helmut stood on an army airstrip in Cairo, watching over a Baustone jet being loaded with artifacts and luggage for his trip to New York.

He smiled, though his disfigured face couldn't show it. He was on the verge of changing the world with his own version of Judgment Day—as long as Festus cooperated with his plans. The long-lost Egyptian legends of the Aknaseth era told of a global apocalypse, the arrival of Hell on Earth, and of blessed immortality. The legends led him here, and he gave thanks to the asshole, Festus, for Helmut knew the multibillionaire's cash also got him here.

Helmut reflected on his birth in Hamburg in 1937. He marveled at how far he'd come, from the only child of Nazi Party loyalists to the world's greatest Egyptologist. And now, he mused, the discovery in Aknaseth's tomb would make him a king over Egypt. A king, he fancied, over every soul on Earth.

He wondered what his parents would think if they saw him now. His mother, Gertrude, died during childbirth, and he thought it just as well. He figured she would be horrified at the sight of his face if she had lived. He'd never met a woman who smiled upon him; he was forced to pay four times the normal amount before any prostitutes would sleep with his deformed ass. The thought of it added another pinch of hate into his already black heart.

What of his dead father's take on his grown-up and old son? Helmut didn't care or hypothesize. He knew Poppa would be unimpressed, caring only about his loyalty to Hitler and alcohol. He remembered his father, Baldus—a captain in the Panzer tank division of the Nazi war machine—as a brutal, unsympathetic disciplinarian who placed Helmut into the *Hitler Jugen*, the Hitler Youth, at age five. Oh, how he loved the German military and his once-high hopes of becoming a soldier.

Then the memory came to him, an almost happy feeling as he reminisced about the rare opportunity he was given in the summer of 1942, when Field Marshall Erwin Rommel was in charge of a *Panzerarmee* in North Africa. Helmut was with the actual Afrika Corps, just a boy alongside German soldiers, Italian soldiers, and Egyptian soldiers with anti-British sentiment moving eastward toward Egypt with Baldus Hartkopff assisting Rommel.

Standing here on this Cairo airstrip brought it all back to him. Remembering Poppa, mighty Rommel, and his short-lived childhood ending right here in Egypt all those years ago. He regarded his first time here as life-changing, full of responsibility.

In North Africa, young Helmut was to run ammunition to the soldiers under Rommel's command. Rommel imprinted his personality upon the German-Italian army of North Africa, and upon Helmut as well. The great Rommel, intolerant of opposition, always restless and urgent. So gallant and gifted in the conduct of war. Rommel led, and his soldiers, including Helmut, followed with blind loyalty.

On the war field, Helmut watched as Baldus was blasted to atoms. Soon after, Poppa was blown away, Helmut endured an explosion that mutated and should have killed him. But he survived and here he was, thinking now of how fate and the gods—ancient and evil Egyptian gods—wanted him here for a greater purpose.

"I am here." Helmut spoke the words to the desert wind. His thoughts turned to himself at age five, when he felt he had nothing left to live for. Such heavy thoughts for a child, he thought now. Life seemed meaningless as a child with no family, no Füehrer, no Desert Fox to follow.

But then Cairo provided his path when the British man, the great Egyptologist, Professor Upton Durban, adopted Helmut. Durban taught the lad archeological techniques and secrets.

Helmut's midnight heart flickered with a small, deep-sea light for a second as he viewed mental snapshots of Professor Durban. He remembered the professor visiting the Cairo war orphanage, meeting other children but embracing this disfigured German boy named Helmut Hartkopff.

Oh, Professor. If you could see me now. I will resurrect you if I can, Helmut thought, no longer fantasizing about his deceased parents' points-of-view.

The professor was intelligent and talented. He taught Helmut to speak English and Arabic. Helmut owed much to Durban for also teaching him to read and write in those languages. Most important, the Professor gave the young German boy hands-on training in the world of Egyptology.

By the time he was a teenager, Helmut was an expert on the culture and beliefs of ancient Egypt. So deep and impressive was his knowledge and understanding of Egyptian philosophies and history, Professor Durban claimed Helmut had turned from student to teacher.

When Helmut was eighteen, the professor passed away and left all of his possessions and teachings to his adopted son. Helmut embalmed Professor Durban himself, wrapping the man from head to toe in linen, as in the tradition of the pharaohs. This was the professor's final wish.

Professor Upton Durban was buried in a tomb at a Cairo cemetery. He'd been kind and patient. Without a doubt, the professor was always an understanding and caring guardian to Helmut. As the professor was laid to rest, Helmut wept. It was the last time in his life he ever cried.

His thoughts turned to the present and to Festus Baustone. Thoughts of the rich man snuffed out the deep-sea light, returning his heart to darkness. Although Helmut depended on Festus's money to fund the dig, he didn't like him at all and knew the feeling was mutual. Helmut thought Festus most pompous and arrogant. He regarded his employer as a spoiled and lazy piece of twenty-four-karat shit.

He now found himself in a tricky situation. Festus's intense interest in the artifacts he'd discovered grated on Helmut's patience. He'd spent most of his life looking for these items. Keeping quiet about the discovery of the uraeus, texts, and song wouldn't have done him any good. He needed to tell Festus everything in order for his plan to work. Only with Festus's fortune could he find a guitarist to raise Hell. In turn, Helmut would wear the unholy uraeus and be transformed into an immortal commander in Satan's army. This part of the plan didn't include Festus.

Helmut was interested in living forever, but more, he wanted to raise Hell on Earth and wipe the world clean. He fantasized about becoming a tyrant who would dwarf Adolf Hitler's legacy.

The fueled Baustone jet was loaded and ready for takeoff. The thought of Festus Baustone the Third turned Helmut's internal smile upside down. Festus was going to be difficult to deal with if he insisted on keeping the unholy uraeus and the Song of Sethis for himself. Helmut wouldn't allow that to happen. He needed to have complete control and possession of the relics.

Helmut couldn't butt heads with Festus over this. They were already arguing on a regular basis, and he didn't want Festus to lose interest in his grand scheme over a pissing contest.

The only way to succeed was to throw Festus a golden bone and keep him quiet and happy. Again Helmut reminded himself that he needed Festus's support to bring the satanic song to life. After that, Festus Baustone the Third would be the first casualty of Armageddon.

Chapter 6
The Cabal

Festus worked a busy morning. He'd been in nonstop meetings since eight and was in excruciating pain as the tumors in his leg bones ate at him.

The phone on his formidable desk rang, disturbing his first moment of quiet all morning. He glanced at the phone's digital display, identifying his secretary.

"Yes, Penelope?"

"Hello, Mr. Baustone. I just wanted to let you know I've got some information for you regarding a guitar player. You might want to look into this one."

"Guitar player?"

"Yes. Yesterday you asked me to find out if my son knew who the best and greatest guitar player alive is."

"Oh, that's right." Festus now remembered the

previous day's events, events that now felt like they happened years ago. "My head's somewhere else today. That last board meeting ruined my morning. What did your kid come up with?"

"Well, Jerred gave me a name."

"And?"

"He says out of all the guitar players in the world, there's only one who's considered to be the absolute, most amazing guitarist ever."

"The name is?" Festus waited for a few seconds. "Do you need a drum roll?"

Penelope uttered a nervous laugh. "Sorry, Mr. Baustone. The guitarist you'll be interested in is Kirk Vaisto. He's referred to around the world as 'The God of Guitar'."

"God of Guitar? I want to contact this Kirk Vaisto."

"Sir, my son loaned me a CD of his last album. Inside the liner notes is a contact phone number and address for the management company representing him."

"Good enough. Bring me that CD, ASAP."

"I'll be right there. By the way, Mr. Baustone, what should I do with Helmut Hartkopff?"

"Helmut? What d'ya mean?"

"He just arrived. He's in the lobby right now."

"Oh, yes." Festus now remembered Helmut was coming to see him. He usually tried avoiding face-to-face meetings with the Egyptologist. This time was different. "Send him in here immediately."

"Yes, Mr. Baustone."

Within minutes, Penelope delivered the Kirk Vaisto CD. Helmut followed and settled into Festus's office.

"How was your trip?" Festus greeted Helmut, but didn't offer a hand. He smiled, feeling unnerved as always by Helmut's disfigured visage. When they first met, the man told Festus how he'd been just a boy running ammunition to German soldiers in North Africa. Telling Festus how two jerry cans full of gasoline exploded in his face with the subsequent fireball blowing the Nazi kid out the back of a burning truck and forever turning his body into a fire-kissed ruin.

"The trip was like any other." Helmut sat in a chair across from him. "Too fucking long."

"So, what d'ya got for me?"

"I brought over the mummy, along with the uraeus and coffin texts. I've got the uraeus and the coffin texts here in this flight case. The mummy's being held in Baustone Warehouse Number Two."

"Good, I look forward to seeing it all." Festus was only concerned with getting his hands on the uraeus but didn't display unnecessary enthusiasm. "We'll take a limo to the warehouse in a few minutes. By the way, I've got info on a guitarist for you."

"Really?"

"My secretary's son is an expert on talented musicians. He claims this guy, Kirk Vaisto, is nicknamed God of Guitar or something. Here, check it out."

Festus slid the CD across the desk. Helmut picked it up. Festus opened an elaborate humidor on his desk. He looked over the dozens of cigars inside and pulled one out. "These are Trinidads. Fifteen hundred dollars a box. Want one?"

"I'd rather puff on camel shit."

"You've got no taste, you know that? This is a forty-dollar cigar." Festus lit up and enjoyed the first, long draw.

"So, are we contacting this guitar player?"

"That depends on what you've brought back for me. Like I said, if it looks convincing, then we'll see if this guitarist has what it takes to play the song. I haven't contacted anyone yet."

"Fine. Let's take a ride in your limo. We'll listen to our guitarist on the way."

Festus phoned Penelope. "I'm leaving the office for the rest of the afternoon. Hold all my calls and cancel all appointments. Get the limo out front."

"Who do you want with you, Mr. Baustone?"

Festus chewed on his cigar, thinking about which security guards to bring along. He always required security. A dozen men worked his day shift, but he didn't need them all. He decided on two guys who were built like professional wrestlers and carried heavy firepower.

"Give me Chuck and Donny."

"Yes, sir."

"All right, Nazi. Let's take a spin." Festus stifled a moan as he rose, his legs killing him in the literal sense.

In the limo, Festus listened to Kirk Vaisto's music as he stared at his two bodyguards seated opposite him and Helmut. To the left sat Chuck—a mountain of solid muscle dressed in a fancy black suit. His head a square block resting on broad shoulders. He seemed to have no neck. His wide chin sported a pointy, dark brown goatee, while his square head was topped with short, brown, spiky hair. He bore a constant frown and his eyes were hidden behind a pair of black sunglasses.

To the right, sat a monster with a long, blond ponytail. Donny was bigger than Chuck. He sat in a crouched position because he had no headroom. He was also dressed in a fancy black suit. The suit stretched to hold in his bulging muscles, which seemed to be on the point of bursting through the material. Festus suspected Donny was a juice-user, fond of shooting up anabolic steroids that tripled mass and made the user's disposition as volatile as the chemicals in his veins.

Festus noticed the black sunglasses covering Donny's eyes and the ragged and deep scars running from his forehead, through his left brow, over the bridge of his twisted nose and across his right cheek, where they ended at his jawline.

Combat knife? I think that's what he told me once, Festus thought. Donny sat, grinning from time to time, displaying a mouth full of solid gold teeth.

"I don't know too much about guitar players, but this guy sounds like he came from another world. Wild shit," Festus said as another Kirk Vaisto track poured into the limousine.

Helmut nodded his damaged head in reluctant agreement. Helmut wasn't a fan of rock or any other form of contemporary music. Festus figured He only appreciated the melodious screams of Egyptian laborers or an archived speech from *der Fuehrer*.

Festus thought the sounds the guitarist produced were phenomenal and distorted. The electrified harmonies and vicious hooks impressed him. He had never heard such roller-coaster time changes in his life. The music moved from hard to soft, then to dark and sensual with graceful fingertip fluidity.

"Let's see that uraeus," Festus said.

Helmut opened the flight case, took out the uraeus, and hesitated before giving it to Festus. It shined in the limousine's interior light and felt light in Festus's hands.

"You sure this thing's made out of solid gold?" Festus turned the object over in his hands.

"No ordinary gold. Remember, the metal is special...it came from Hell."

Festus laughed. "Sure it did. It'll do for my collection."

"It holds a much more important purpose than just collecting dust in one of your fucking museums. It's a vital mechanism, and it plays a very significant role, along with that song, in raising Satan. Let me keep it with the coffin texts."

"I don't think so." Festus gripped the uraeus with both hands. "I'm hanging onto it for a while."

"But—"

"I told you if I see proof that this song can do some weird shit, I'll go all the way with your whacked-out plans. Until then, I'm gonna keep the uraeus with me. I just might wear it to bed tonight."

"But—"

"But nothing. I'll do what I want with it. I own it. All of it. You know this. Don't go getting attached to things."

Helmut didn't argue. He turned away from Festus, stared out his window, and said, "Get me back in the desert. I hate this city."

The limo delivered Festus to his warehouse. He entered the building with his posse in tow. He felt like Citizen Kane as his eyes spotted the many crates of rare artifacts and oddities from all over the globe. The crates filled every space, along with dinosaur skeletons and Neolithic statues, rare cars and odd military vehicles.

"That's one ugly sonofabitch." Festus examined the

mutated mummy of Aknaseth on a stainless steel table in the middle of the warehouse.

Helmut stood beside Festus as they leaned over the ancient corpse, talking and studying while Chuck and Donny stood as still and quiet as the Vesuvian statues wrapped in plastic bubble wrap in the warehouse.

"Now do you see what I was talking about? This was once a man, but he was turned into a monster. Physically formed into a demon by the very forces of Hell. By Satan himself," Helmut said. He pointed out all the mummy's deformities.

"Do you like the name Satan or Sethis better?" Festus wondered what looked worse, Helmut or the mummy.

"I don't have a preference. Sethis *is* Satan. They are one and the same. The names aren't important. Pure evil. They are both the literal root of all evil."

Festus caught sight of his bodyguard, Donny. The word *evil* seemed to make the man grin, his gold teeth glinting in the light. Festus turned and examined the reptilian-looking head of Aknaseth. "Thing looks evil, all right. It's hard to believe there's a man somewhere in this mess."

A sudden commotion came from inside the warehouse. A man ran out from between crates next to the examination table.

"Stop this foolishness at once!" The man's loud voice rang through the warehouse. "You're tempting the legions of darkness."

Festus and Helmut whirled around. Startled, Festus thought the guy was going to attack him. Just as the man was a step away, Chuck and Donny were on him hard.

"Who are you?" Helmut demanded, barking like a

lipless terrier.

The man was tall, old, and gaunt. His head was covered with thin, white hair growing out of an age-spot speckled scalp. Countless creases wrinkled his face. He was wearing a pair of ragged black pants and a black shirt with the clerical collar of a priest.

"I'm Father Antonio Zacharelli." The old man addressed Helmut and Festus with a thick Italian accent. "You are committing a great folly with your ambitions concerning Satan. Stop this madness now before you and all those around you are destroyed by the Antichrist."

Two middle-aged, overweight African-American security guards dressed in Baustone rent-a-cop uniforms ran up to the four men and their elderly captive.

"Mr. B., I'm real sorry 'bout this," the first guard said. "We'd no idea this guy was in here. He musta slipped in somewhere."

"Yeah, we's sorry, Mr. B.," the second security guard said. "We'll get this old guy outta here."

"That won't be necessary, boys." Festus thought of firing the two guards before the day's end. "We've got everything under control. Go back to whatever you do around here. Suck on some doughnuts or something." Festus turned his attention back to Father Antonio Zacharelli and pointed a cigar in the man's face. "I don't know how you got in here, but you're trespassing, old-timer."

Father Zacharelli locked his gaze with Festus and said, "And I looked and beheld a pale horse, and his name that sat on him was Death and Hell followed with him. And power was given unto them over the fourth part of the Earth, to kill with sword and with hunger. He kills with death and with the beasts of the Earth."

"This is the religious rambling of a madman," Helmut said. "Get him out of here."

"Even the kings and the richest men of the world won't be able to flee from the wrath of God. Your efforts to bring Hell on Earth will be all in vain," Zacharelli shouted in Festus's face.

"Back off, old man," Chuck said, putting a choke hold on Zacharelli.

"Hey, this fucker's bleedin'. He's got some heavy-duty holes in his arms," Donny said.

Festus examined Father Zacharelli's arms and found a hole in each wrist. The bloody holes were about the size of half-dollars, large enough to see right through.

"Looks like his ankles are fucked up, too." Chuck pointed to blood pouring out through Zacharelli's socks.

"Christ, get this old dog outta here. In fact, give the Father a nice work over. A good ass kicking will make him think twice about comin' around here again." Festus's spittle spattered Zacharelli's face. "Take him out the back door by the loading dock."

Chuck and Donny both grinned, their expressions indicating to Festus that they wanted to give the old man much more than just an ass kicking.

"Wanna see how far the six-inch barrel of my gun can go up your ass?" Donny said to the holy man.

Chuck laughed. "I'm just gonna bury my brass knuckles in his dome. Got me a new punching bag."

Festus watched the thugs making their way toward the rear of the building, dragging Father Zacharelli across the warehouse floor by his arms.

"Looked like stigmata." Helmut whispered as if it was a secret.

"What?"

"Nothing, Festus. Just observing."

Festus nodded and shook his head, thinking the old Kraut was losing it.

Father Zacharelli yelled out to Festus, "The first angel sounded and there followed hail and fire mixed with blood, and they were cast upon the Earth—"

The warehouse door slammed shut behind Chuck and Donny as they dragged Zacharelli through it, cutting off his religious rant.

"Let's get back to the limo." Festus turned away from Aknaseth's mummy. "There's lots to do. Time to work on gettin' this devil music rockin'."

"*Ja.* I want to commission this guitarist to transcribe the music. We need him now. I want to start working with him as soon as possible," Helmut said. "I think that—"

Helmut's words cut off as the warehouse door slammed open by unseen hands. High-pitched screams sliced the air from somewhere outside the open door. More screams followed in harmonized pain.

"What in the shit's going on here?" Festus said. "That didn't sound like the old man."

"I'm thinking your boys might have a problem," Helmut said.

Striding in rapid fashion, Helmut and Festus made their way to the back of the warehouse and exited out the door with Festus leading the way.

Festus came upon a brutal scene. Father Antonio Zacharelli had disappeared. Instead of finding an old man beaten to mush, Festus found Chuck and Donny. His Baustone thugs appeared to be in a massive world of hurt.

"Mein Gott." Helmut sounded surprised.

Festus saw Chuck on his back, blood-covered and lifeless. Chuck's brass knuckles were embedded in his forehead like an extreme Gen-X accessory.

Festus looked over to see Donny crawling around on his belly, whimpering. The grip of a revolver protruded from the seat of his blood-spattered suit pants. Festus winced, realizing the entire barrel was buried in Donny's large intestine.

"Aw, Jesus!" Donny wailed. "Get it outta my ass!"

The two warehouse security guards came running with their guns drawn. Together they said, "Wazz up?"

"Get an ambulance here. Now!" Festus said. "I wasn't here, got it?"

"Yes, sir," the guards answered together.

Festus turned to Helmut and said, "Let's go."

They walked from the building and got into the limo. Helmut sat across from Festus and said, "Strange events back there."

"Yeah." Festus was shaken from the scene at his warehouse. The pain in his legs started kicking in and he felt miserable. "You tell me what the fuck happened. I'm sure all this weird shit's got something to do with that satanic mummy in my warehouse."

Helmut let out a hard laugh. "Getting a little superstitious, eh?"

"Superstitious? No. Very goddamn curious. I wanna know what we're dealing with. Seems you found something unnatural this time." Festus held the uraeus tighter. It felt like it might bend in his big hands. He wondered what power it might hold, what cure it might provide.

"Dear Festus, I hope you're not getting scared off by

some old man."

"I'm definitely not scared of old men." Festus massaged his legs. "If I was, I wouldn't hang out with an old Nazi like you, would I?"

Helmut stopped laughing.

"You've got to admit, it's very strange that such an old, injured man—a priest, of all things—was able to make his way into one of my guarded warehouses without being detected." Festus now mused on the enigmatic Zacharelli. "And it's even stranger he was able to overpower two of my biggest and meanest bodyguards."

Helmut glared at Festus and gave a quiet nod.

"Well, I'm going to find out who that old bastard is. And when Donny's willing to talk, I'm going to ask him what the hell happened. Chuck's dead for sure. I can't believe it. I've seen Donny break football players in half. Now he's going to make it into the 'You'll Never Believe What I Got Rammed Up My Ass' column of the *American Journal of Medicine*."

"I don't care about your bodyguards." Helmut's words turned icy. "I want to know right now if you will help me bring the Song of Sethis to life."

"I told you before, I want proof before I just go off and invest in a bunch of bullshit. Now I've seen the mummy. Freaky. I've heard your pitch. And, well, the unexplained got my attention. You've got something here. I'm prepared to do what's necessary to bring this song to life. I already said I want to get this music started. Just for curiosity's sake, if anything."

"Good. As soon as we get back to the office, let's work on getting in touch with that guitarist. We can work together to decipher and transcribe this song. I trust you'll give me the support I need?"

"Yeah, sure." Festus acted reluctant. He knew he possessed a habit of being flippant with money. He wanted Helmut to earn this. "I guess I can give you a couple of million dollars to start with. Make Kirk Vaisto a substantial offer for his services and use the rest for equipment and expenses. Anything over a two million cap needs to be discussed. Got it?"

"*Ja*. Not to worry. I'm tight with money, as my work in Egypt's already proved."

"I wouldn't exactly say the fifty million I've spent digging up that pyramid was based on the accounting of a *tight* budget."

"Well, money won't be a concern or a care of yours when Kirk Vaisto finally plays this music. If things work out as Aknaseth predicted, our lives will change forever."

"I hope so." Festus tried willing away the pain in his legs. "I hope so."

Chapter 7
The Hired Gun

All Kirk wanted to do was pass out after spending another extensive workday in the studio. He still felt like something bad lurked behind him, but he did his best to ignore it. He threw himself into his long recording sessions to focus, but was becoming fried as the overtime combined with poor sleep and made him a zombie. He yearned for a real rest, one free of disturbing visions.

He kicked back in bed, longing for sleep to come. His wishes for slumber were disrupted by the sound of his cell phone ringing. Kirk rolled over and grabbed the phone off an end table. He glanced at his caller ID.

"Shit. What's Yaggerwood want now?" Kirk hesitated for a second, then answered. "Hello, Rod. How can I make you rich today?"

Rod Yaggerwood let out a raspy laugh. "Funny you

should ask that. I've got an incredible offer on the table that's just too good to pass up."

"I've heard this before."

"Hey, have I ever steered you wrong?"

"Well…"

"You know how I got to where I am? By taking advantage of every opportunity I could. When I started out in this business, I had to work part time in the mailroom of Sterling Stars during the day and I flipped burgers at night at the local Burger Jerk. That mailroom job was the only way I could get my foot in the door, but it was an opportunity I couldn't pass up. Why? Because it paid off after I met people higher up in the company, and the more big shots I met, the more opportunities presented themselves. Now look where I am."

"You've been telling me this story since I was sixteen."

"Good. Then maybe you've learned something."

"Well, unlike you, I'm not impressed with big shots."

"You might be impressed when I tell you one of the biggest big shots in the world wants to work with you."

"The bigger they are, the harder it is to make me want to do anything at all."

"Does the name Festus Baustone the Third mean anything to you?"

"*The* Festus Baustone?" Kirk said, intrigued.

"The one and only."

"Doesn't Baustone own part of Juggernaut Records?"

"Yes, he does."

"I thought so. What's a multibillionaire want with a little ol' guitarist like me?"

"He wants to hire you for a special assignment. One of his people has been calling me, a man by the name of Helmut Hartkopff. Guy's an Egyptologist who apparently digs up stuff for Baustone."

"Well, if they're after any of my antique guitars, they can forget it. I'm not selling."

"They don't want your guitars, kid. This guy Hartkopff dug something up in the desert. He's got some ancient Egyptian song he wants you to figure out for him on guitar. Needs you to transcribe it from hieroglyphics."

"You must be giving me more credit than I'm worth. I know a thing or two about world music, but I can't transcribe hieroglyphics."

"Not to worry. That's where this Hartkopff comes in. He says he's gonna help you with most of it. Evidently he's already taken the hieroglyphics and transferred them into a computer. He's broken them down into a series of technical vocal tones that he wants you to transcribe and utilize for the guitar. Piece a' cake."

"How much is this piece a' cake?"

"Two hundred and fifty thousand dollars."

"Before or after your ridiculous cut?"

Rod laughed. "That's after my ridiculous cut. Nice chunk of change for doing what comes naturally. Hell, I've seen you transcribe shit for nearly nothing for all those guitar mags."

"That always pissed you off, didn't it?"

"Of course it did. I'm here to make you serious cash, kid, not get nickel-and-dimed to death. So, what d'ya think?"

Kirk wasn't interested in doing anything other than the new album. Plus, transcribing lost its appeal after putting thousands of rare and well-known classical pieces to the guitar.

But the thought of an ancient Egyptian song intrigued him, as did Festus Baustone's offer of two hundred and fifty thousand dollars. It sounded good on artistic and financial levels.

"Okay, I'll do it," Kirk said. "But I wanna do it this week. I've got a small window here. I've got an album I need to wrap."

"No problem, kid. Baustone's people want to get the legal stuff squared away and signed right away. The Egypt dude wants to go to your compound within the next few days. He's eager to start work immediately."

"That's fine. Grainy's not coming back to the studio for a few days. I'll push him off for an extra day or two if I have to."

"Perfect. I'll let Hartkopff know we're in business, and we'll arrange for him to be at your house before the week's out."

"Why would anyone pay so much to have a song transcribed?"

"I guess this song's a major find. Top secret. You're gonna have to sign some confidentiality papers. Festus wants to keep this underground. He's an eccentric, likes having things no one else can. He likes control."

"Cool by me, as long as you don't just accept a flat payment." Kirk was suspicious of his agent. "You wouldn't do that, would you?"

Rod's phlegmy laugh sounded like static over the line. "You know me too well. You get ten percent of any and all profits made from the song as long as you remain the sole musician to transcribe it, perform it, and record it."

"You're a fuckin' shark."

"I've gotta go. Having dinner with a director friend who's just begun working for Paramount. We'll talk tomorrow."

"Yeah, after I meet with Helmut."

"Oh, by the way, don't be surprised if you see your name and Festus's popping up together in papers or magazines soon."

"Wait. You said I've gotta sign confidentiality papers, keep this a secret."

"That's right. *You* do. Not me. I'm your buzz man. Everyone's going to want to know why one of the world's richest men is working with my client, the God of Guitar."

"You're gonna piss some people off. You're a whore, Rod."

"No, kid. I'm a pimp. You're my whore, and I've got your best interests in mind."

"Right. Bye, Rod."

Kirk hung up and sat on his bed. He was intrigued and eager to see what this project would bring. He wondered what Festus Baustone hoped to get out of ancient Egyptian music. With the amount of money Festus was laying down, he could've bought the publishing rights to a song by the Beatles or Elvis. It was big money for something that might yield nothing.

Kirk knew money made people do crazy things. He figured music made people do even stranger things.

Chapter 8
Guest of Dishonor

Kirk sat at his kitchen table, feeling rested and prepared for his visitors. Since agreeing to work with Festus Baustone and Helmut Hartkopff, Kirk had spent the last three days signing papers with Rod Yaggerwood and prepping his studio for guests.

Kirk's day maid brought him the morning paper. He ate waffles and laughed as he read about himself on the front page. *Bastard's quick,* Kirk thought, impressed at how fast Rod Yaggerwood leaked the story.

He looked at the shot of himself next to a picture of Festus. The information in the article was vague. Sources reported Kirk Vaisto would be working on a top-secret project with Festus Baustone the Third. The article revealed nothing more.

Kirk finished breakfast and went upstairs for a

quick shower. After showering, he went downstairs and saw a black stretch limousine pulling into his driveway. He glanced at a medieval-looking clock in his large living room. It was around ten. His guest had arrived earlier than expected.

Kirk walked outside into the misty Malibu morning. The first two men out of the limousine looked huge and scary. One owned a scarred face that hosted a pair of black sunglasses and a blond ponytail. His black suit looked ready to bust open. Kirk noticed the man walked with an odd limp. The brute looked to be in pain, as if every step hurt.

The other man had ebony skin and a bald head. He wore the same sunglasses and black suit. Kirk saw a bulletproof vest beneath his jacket.

"Is one of you Helmut?" Kirk asked.

The men didn't answer. The blond man pulled equipment out of the trunk.

"I'm Helmut."

The voice belonged to a sturdy-looking older man stepping out of the rear of the limo. The man's face was nothing like his body. The melted facial tissues, missing nose, and exposed teeth made Helmut Hartkopff look like a grinning corpse.

Kirk looked past the disfigured face and extended his hand. "Nice to meet you. I'm Kirk Vaisto."

"The pleasure's mine." Helmut shook Kirk's hand.

Helmut's scarred hand felt like rough leather. Kirk said, "And these guys?"

"They're just a couple of Festus Baustone's helping hands. This is Mr. Jaspers." Helmut gestured toward the black man with the bulletproof vest. Mr. Jaspers stood as quiet and motionless as a guard at Buckingham palace. "And this would be Donny."

Helmut nodded at the ponytailed thug. "Donny had a little accident a few days ago. He just got out of the hospital. You might say his handgun *backfired* on him."

Kirk detected an inside joke somewhere. The humor didn't seem lost on Donny, who gave a pained, gold-toothed grin at the comment.

Kirk wasn't sure what to make of the group. They made him uneasy. "Can I help you with anything?"

"No, we're fine. My baggage handlers will take care of everything."

"What's in the luggage?"

"Computer equipment and a very ancient and valuable songbook."

"You can set everything up in my recording studio. That's where all the work will take place."

"Good. I've much to show you. I trust you've signed the confidentiality agreement?"

"Yes, I signed everything I was supposed to. Follow me and we'll get started."

Inside the studio control room, Helmut and the thugs opened the padded, shockproof cases and set up the computer equipment. A fancy-looking computer tower and monitor were placed on a table with some extra gear.

"Do you guys need anything else? Something to drink?" Kirk asked.

"No, we don't need anything. I just need you to get a guitar and sit with me," Helmut said. "We're almost done setting up."

Kirk walked to the house to retrieve a guitar. Reaching a high-tech security door on the first floor, he entered a series of numbers and opened the security lock.

Of the fifteen rooms in his mansion, Kirk entered

his favorite: the guitar room. The space was the size of two racquetball courts and was filled with guitar gear Kirk had collected over the last thirty years. The room was temperature controlled like a giant humidor. There were no windows, and Kirk forbade smoking anywhere in the room or in the house.

He gazed at the hundreds of guitars hanging from the walls. Many of the instruments were stock models Kirk received as gifts from numerous guitar companies who courted him over the years.

Gotta clean this place up, he thought while looking over his impressive collection of rare and valuable vintage and custom guitars and Civil War-era acoustic guitars and banjos. The antiques were locked in the hundreds of custom-made guitar cases and flight cases scattered and stacked in disarray inside the room.

Aside from the guitars, Kirk viewed his mess of a tube-amp collection. More than fifty hot-rodded amp heads were stacked on top of one another and took up most of the room. The remaining space was filled with a plethora of rack-mounted effects and speaker cabinets mixed with miscellaneous guitar toys and accessories.

Kirk made his way through the maze of gear. He walked up to a stack of guitar cases and pulled one out. The case was labeled, "Kirk Vaisto: ESP Custom Signature #1." Kirk valued this instrument above all others. He held it close to his heart because it was the first Kirk Vaisto signature model made by ESP guitars. He also treasured it as a personal favorite because it played with a feel and design far superior to any other guitar he'd ever wielded.

Kirk opened the case and the smell of the electric guitar reached his nose. In his mind there wasn't a smell finer than a mint guitar resting inside a case.

He examined it. This one, like all the others modeled after it for the series, was made to his specifications. From the neck-thru, Strat-styled body to the pickups and ebony fingerboard with metallic *V* inlays, the guitar was Kirk's idea of six-stringed perfection.

Kirk gave the guitar a strum. The strings were a little old, but it was in perfect tune.

Guitar in hand, Kirk walked back to the studio.

"How're we doing in here?" Kirk said, entering the control room. He saw Helmut typing into a computer while Donny and Mr. Jaspers stood a few feet away, looking as if they were ready to pounce on something.

"Everything's up and running," Helmut said, patting an empty chair beside him. "Sit. I want to show you exactly what I've got here."

"Looks like you're using a recording software program."

"It's a new program from Baustone software. I'm still learning how to work it properly." Helmut turned the computer over to Kirk. "I had a crash course to get the basics. I've got my interpretations of the hieroglyphics in the computer now. I don't do well with these New World things. Perhaps you can find your way around it?"

Kirk played with the keyboard. "This is similar to the Pro-Tools software I use. The audio files you've recorded are in basic waveform format. I can work with this." With a click of the mouse, he pressed the play button on the program toolbar.

The sound of Helmut's voice came through the PC speakers. His recorded voice was interpreting the hieroglyphics as different tones. Helmut was singing what sounded like a dark and unknown chant. It wasn't words at all, just sounds made by the human throat, duplicating the musical value of each hieroglyph. Helmut's voice sounded rough, but Kirk implemented a voice tuner, corrected the pitch, and determined the keys of each recorded vocal tone.

The recording ended in five minutes.

"Sounds kinda weird and moody. Wide range of notes. There's an evil, nasty tone to it. How'd you decipher this stuff?"

"I've been reading 'glyphs since I was a boy," Helmut said. "I can read any form of Egyptian hieroglyphs, from the Rosetta Stone to the most cryptic and obscure writings."

"Is there a meaning to this song?"

In the dim light of the control room, Helmut's face appeared more ghoulish. Shadows seemed to add more detail to the textures of his melted facial flesh. Kirk couldn't tell if Helmut was pleased or pissed off by the question.

"I trust you remember the terms of your confidentiality agreement, Kirk?"

"Yeah, yeah. Don't divulge our business or speak of work I do or will do for Festus Baustone, whatever."

"*Ja*. Now, the original 'glyphs I've been working with are unlike any I've ever seen. They're of a musical nature. In fact, they *are* music. These hieroglyphics make a complete song. It's a song written thousands of years ago that has never been performed."

"I'm not sure I follow you. How can a song be written if it's never been played?"

"It doesn't have to make sense to you." Helmut snapped his yellow, gritty-looking teeth together. "You're not being paid to ask about why the song exists or how it was written. You've been hired to transcribe it and play it on a guitar."

What an asshole, Kirk thought. "Okay. I'd like to know one thing, though."

"What's that?"

"How do the hieroglyphics translate into a musical format? How do they represent actual musical notes?"

"Each 'glyph is a symbol. The 'glyphs we're working with are similar to traditional hieroglyphics. With traditional 'glyphs, each individual one represents something important, usually events in the lives of the pharaohs and the gods. The hieroglyphs I'm working with are symbols too, but they represent tones and become music when they are run together."

"You read music?"

"Not standard sheet music. Each of the 'glyph symbols I'm working with holds a musical value that's read as a musical syllable. What you hear on the recording isn't me chanting, but me reciting the notes vocally."

"As in do-re-mi-fa-so-la-ti-do, huh?"

"*Ja.* Similar concept. The process wasn't easy. It was a challenge to break the 'glyphs down, but I managed to turn them into musical vocal syllables. You're going to turn my vocalizations into guitar music."

"Sounds like the concept of *solmization.*"

"Solmization? What's this?"

"Solmization is a system of assigning syllables to different musical pitches. An Italian monk named Guido d'Arezzo invented it, along with inventing the musical staff."

Helmut said nothing as Kirk continued with his facts. "Guido adopted the basic musical scale of the six-tone *hexachord* to help choirboys remember the scale and assigned a syllable to each note of the hexachord. The four-line staff he used is still used for writing Gregorian chants."

"Italians. *Ja.* Hitler would've been better off without them." Helmut snorted as the words left his lipless mouth.

"Oh, *hell* no." Kirk's voice rose as he became angry. "Don't be talking shit about Italians because you're looking at one. I'll kick your fascist ass outta here."

Donny and Mr. Jaspers took menacing steps toward Kirk, but Helmut, eyes flashing with surprise and anger, stopped them with a wave of his hand. He took a deep breath and exhaled through his bare and yellow teeth with a slow hiss.

"I'm an old man who's from a world long gone," Helmut said, his tone calming. "Sometimes my mouth gets the best of me."

"I don't care where you're from or what you think. I'm just here to do a job, the sooner the better."

Kirk tried to cool down. He turned his attention to the computer and played with the keyboard. "It's easy enough to use. I can hook up the computer's digital soundcard to my studio board and outboard gear. I'll use my MIDI system to play and record the song. I'll also transform your vocal wave files into actual notes, then I'll transcribe it all to guitar."

"Be sure to note the recording I've made for you is layered with multiple tracks. This was one of the most challenging sets of 'glyphs I've ever translated. The ancient music is highly technical. The hieroglyphs were written so the tones and notes overlapped each other."

"Got it. I can see and hear it all. I'll pull chords and scales out of this garbage. Good thing you got me. This is no easy job for a first-time studio engineer like yourself."

"*Ja*. I can't afford to fuck up, *mein* Kirk."

"Since no one's heard or played this music before, how do we know how it's to be performed? The timing, et cetera?"

Helmut paused. The vibe he gave off induced a sudden chill Kirk felt floating across his flesh. He detected a sinister smile, a ghost grin he couldn't see in Helmut's expressionless face. It made him feel as if Helmut was holding something back. Something, perhaps, Helmut didn't want to show, but at the same time, wanted to blurt out for him to hear. Kirk felt sure he didn't want to hear anything now.

"Oh, you'll know when the time comes. That's why we hired you," Helmut said. "You'll figure it out. Play it with all the passion you possess. I'm confident the song will show you the way."

Kirk frowned, not finding one ounce of solace in this statement. "I'll do my best."

"Before I go, do you have any other questions I can answer?"

"You sure it's all right to ask something?" Kirk couldn't resist playing the smartass. "I know I'm not paid to do anything but transcribe and play."

"Ask whatever's on your fucking mind."

"Can you show me what the actual hieroglyphics look like?" Kirk was happy to irritate Helmut. "I'm curious."

Helmut sat back in his chair and sighed. "All right. I'll show you the work. I hope you appreciate this because there isn't anyone alive who's seen the actual texts aside from Festus and myself. Mr. Jaspers, bring me the coffin texts."

Kirk watched Mr. Jaspers hand Helmut what appeared to be a heavy-duty suitcase.

Helmut opened the case and revealed a book with gold covers. "This is the coffin texts of Aknaseth." Helmut pulled it out of the case. "It contains Aknaseth's biography and the complete song."

"Is there a name for the song?"

Helmut showed off the strange designs of the hieroglyphics written on the ancient papyrus pages. "I call it the Song of Sethis."

"Is this thing bound in solid gold, or what?" Kirk marveled at the craftsmanship.

"Yes, one of the finest pieces of gold work I've ever come across."

"It must be worth—"

"Worth more than a fortune."

"Now I know why you've got these two with you." Kirk nodded at Mr. Jaspers and Donny. "One other thing. How do you know if this song's meant for a guitar? I know they didn't had guitars in ancient Egypt."

"*Ja*. This is true. But Aknaseth intended to perform the song on an instrument of his own creation. It was a six-stringed, fretted instrument that supposedly gave out a loud, amplified sound."

"Must've been quite an invention, since it would've pre-dated the creation of the first real guitars by thousands of years."

"That's Aknaseth for you. An amazing man."

"What happened to this ancient guitar?"

"It was destroyed."

"And Aknaseth?"

"He was also destroyed."

"How?"

"Perhaps I'll enlighten you some day." Helmut stood. "I need to be on my way back to New York now. And since I won't be able to supervise you in person, I've asked Festus's daughter, Mona, to drop by daily and monitor your work."

A flare ignited in Kirk's mind. "That's not cool. I don't need anyone to watch over me. In fact, I work better when I'm alone, without distractions."

"This time you'll have to make an exception. We retain the right to have representatives of the Baustone International Corporation call on you day or night, to supervise your work until the job's completed to our satisfaction. You might want to consult your agent about our agreement."

"I don't need to talk to my agent." Kirk knew Rod had duped him into another awkward situation for a quick buck. "I'm sure I've signed my life away."

"Like I said, you might want to review our agreement so we don't have any further misunderstandings."

"I'd do what the man says." Donny spoke for the first time with a golden grin.

Mr. Jaspers nodded in agreement.

Helmut said, "Your agent's got my number. I look forward to hearing that song soon."

Kirk didn't shake hands. He walked out of the studio and watched Helmut get into the limousine with his two gorillas. As the limo pulled away, Kirk slammed the door and made for his mansion. He wanted to kick Yaggerwood's ass.

Chapter 9
Back From the Dead

"Whoa now," Rod Yaggerwood said. "Don't go fucking hostile. Just tell me what happened."

"Helmut Hartkopff. That prick came to my place today with a couple of bodyguards who looked like fugitives from a WWE wrestling event."

"Yeah? They threaten you in any way? I'll tell Baustone to shove that song where the sun don't shine."

"I wasn't exactly threatened." Kirk replayed the earlier events in his head. "It was just, Helmut's a real bastard. Telling me to do my job according to their terms and shit."

"Okay, so he's a businessman."

"And Festus Baustone's daughter will be babysitting me to make sure I'm getting the work done? What's up with that? Helmut said any old Baustone rep could come by day or night to check up on me."

"I'm afraid that's part of the deal. But I figured you'd have this project done in a day or so."

"An hour with that Nazi fucker is enough to make me wanna stop now."

"You're making a clean two hundred fifty *K*, plus possible future royalties."

"My dignity's worth more to me than that."

"Sounds like a certain guitar god got his ego bruised."

"Fuck you, Rod. I don't need to deal with assholes."

"Kid, if there's one thing you should know by now, it's that this whole business is full of assholes."

"Especially you."

"Whoa. There's that hostility again. Don't forget, *this* asshole made your career."

Kirk eased out a sigh. "Look, I know your job is to make me lots of money, but this Helmut guy and the whole situation really rubbed me wrong. I got a real bad vibe from them. And I promise it wasn't some reaction to his deformity."

"What deformity?"

"Or injury. Whatever. His entire head is one large burn scar. He doesn't have a nose or any lips."

"Jesus. Did you ask what happened?"

"Fuck no. He might've set his toughs loose on me."

"Definitely a strange bunch. C'mon, Kirk. You've jammed with Jack Slynn, of all people. I'd think by now you'd be immune to the grotesque."

Kirk laughed. "You're right about that."

"Well, kid, what's it gonna be? Are you gonna let Freddy Krueger piss you off and affect your work, or are you gonna finish that song and tell 'em to fuck himself?"

"I'll finish the goddamn song, but you need to start appreciating the fact that I want my privacy and I only wanna work with people who treat me with respect."

"Hey, I do appreciate that, kid. You deserve respect. But I can't always predict how an individual's personality is gonna be. If it were up to me, I'd give ya a gentler, kinder music business."

"Just keep my wishes in mind and don't abuse your power of attorney."

"So, we're cool?"

"Yeah, cool. But there's something else."

"What's that?"

"How many sources got word I was working with Festus Baustone? I just read about it in the paper."

"How would I know? Entertainment news spreads like herpes. Stories turn up everywhere."

"Not that I care, but we might get a lot of flack when Hartkopff and Baustone find out. What if they say I broke the confidentiality agreement and come after the money they paid us?"

"Not to worry. Baustone's got tons of money invested in this project. He's not gonna pull the plug just because the press blew some steam."

"I guess you're right."

"Of course I'm right. Now I gotta go. Keep in touch and let me know how you're comin' along. Let's do dinner at Spago sometime next week."

"Maybe. See ya, Rod."

"See ya, kid."

Kirk tied his hair back and headed for the studio. He played with the computer Helmut left him, and after a few hours, he had turned Helmut's vocal-hieroglyphic syllables into a complete arrangement of sheet music.

Kirk hooked the computer up to a MIDI system in his recording studio. The musical instrument digital interface —MIDI—was a performance information exchange system that enabled the computer's music software to communicate with mixing boards and synthesizers along with rack-effects and other gear. The MIDI program manipulated Helmut's vocal data and converted it into musical notation.

After the conversion, Kirk would read the music and apply it to the guitar, or he could use MIDI to transfer the music score into guitar tablature. He felt it best to sight read and work from the direct score, as the tablature wouldn't provide all the technical aspects of the piece. But first he needed to define the melody, then the rhythm and harmony. After that, he'd play the piece as he wished.

Kirk finished at dusk and decided to call it a day. He'd tackle the guitar work tomorrow. He left the studio and at the mansion gate, a voice startled him. "Hey, mister, I got somethin' for ya!"

Kirk saw a teenager on a motor scooter waiting at his front gate. "What?" Kirk wondered if it was another fan or a member of the paparazzi.

The teenager waved a manila envelope.

Kirk walked to the front gate. Close up, the kid wore a helmet with stickers of punk rock bands all over it. GBH, The Exploited, and the Sex Pistols plastered the plastic dome. The kid had a waiflike body and wore oversized Jam shorts and a tank top. A stainless steel hoop pierced his septum.

"Want me to take that?" Kirk reached through the gate.

"Nah-uh. You've gotta sign. Here." The teenager handed a clipboard to Kirk. "Put your John Hancock on line number ten."

"Okay, how do you spell *John*?"

The teenager didn't laugh.

Kirk gave the clipboard back. "Are we done here?"

The teen handed Kirk the envelope and examined his name on the clipboard. "You're that famous guitarist, aren't ya?"

"Why?" Kirk smiled. "You dig my shit?"

"No, just curious. Actually, I think you're a fuckin' poser."

The teenager smirked and sped away while Kirk stood at his gate, laughing despite himself.

The only thing inside the envelope was a flier for a place called Vampire Sun, a greasy little Goth bar in Hollywood. Kirk knew it and wasn't fond of the place; it was too dark, the women looked like corpses, and the smell of clove cigarettes made him gag.

He reviewed the week's schedule. Monday was Bauhaus Night, Tuesday was Sisters of Mercy Night, Wednesday was Ladies' Night with "DJ Darkk spinning his sinful Goth remixes", Thursday was The Cure Night, Friday was Dracula Night, and on the weekend anything was fair game.

There was nothing interesting about the flier until Kirk turned it over. On the back was a handwritten note.

Kirk, the last time we saw each other was at our after-tour party at the Palladium. Long time, no? You've gotten on with your life quite well—I've been watching your career for a while now.

The reason I'm risking contacting you is I want to warn you of something.

Go to Vampire Sun tonight at nine and don't be late. I don't care what you're doing, just be there.

Your Beef Kitten,
J.S.

Jack Slynn? Kirk reread the letter. No fucking way. He'd been dead for years. Kirk shook his head.

Was *this* the answer to the rock and roll mystery of the century?

Within thirty minutes of reading the note, Kirk was in his Mercedes Benz AMG and on his way to Hollywood.

Kirk pulled up to Vampire Sun, valeted his wheels, and got out. The sidewalk was filled with a mixture of pale-skinned men and women in black clothing and makeup and street bums begging for change and pushing grocery carts full of trash.

Kirk walked in and paid a ten-dollar cover charge. He noticed people whispering as he walked by. Kirk thought they either recognized him or were concerned since he wasn't one of the undead.

Inside the dark interior, he was hit by the smells of incense and smoke from the clove cigarettes he loathed. With the depressing bombast of The Cure hitting his ears, Kirk felt his way through the club like a blind man until he found a vacant booth in a corner.

He ordered a Heineken from a waitress who resembled Morticia from *The Addams Family*. As she returned, a man joined him in the booth.

"Long time no see." The man looked like an overweight version of producer Rick Rubin. The man sat across from Kirk. He had a black and gray moustache and a long black and gray rectangular beard. His salt and pepper hair was receding. The hairline began on the top of his scalp and hung down in thin, shoulder-length strands. He wore faded, baggy blue jeans and a flannel shirt. Black sunglasses with round lenses hid his eyes.

How in the hell can he see anything in here? "Who are you?" he said, studying the man.

"C'mon, you don't recognize your old front man?"

"Well, I know you're not Dizzy Letchfield of The Godly. He'd never be caught wearing anything but a pair of snakeskin pants and boots."

The man laughed and said, "Yeah, well, Dizzy always was a real bitch about his clothes. Wanna guess again?"

Kirk already knew. The tone of the man's voice was unmistakable. Though he looked nothing like the last time Kirk had seen him, he was the same man he'd had shared many stages around the world with.

"I'll be a goddamned sonofabitch, Jack," Kirk said with dumbfounded amazement. He stood and hugged his former band mate.

"Take it easy, buddy," Jack Slynn whispered and hugged Kirk back. "I'm thrilled to see you, too, but let's not make a scene, okay?"

"What the hell happened to you, man? You've pulled the greatest disappearing act ever known. It's still one of the most controversial events of the last two decades."

"You don't have to tell me. I've watched myself on the *E! True Hollywood Story* and *Behind the Music* on VH1."

"I can't believe you're here, man. What the fuck's going on? You've gotta tell me."

"It's a weird story. Complicated." Jack sipped a beer.

"I've got time. Looks like you've been eating real well."

"Yeah, I've gained a bunch of pounds and changed into a giant slug. Had to change if I was gonna stay alive."

"But you're one of the biggest stars ever. You've nothing to fear."

"*Au contraire*. I had lots to be scared of. Imminent death."

"Why? Yaggerwood gonna work you to death? Crazy fans?"

"Nope. You could've sent all the Mark David Chapmans of the world to my house and I wouldn't have flinched."

"What? Tell me, man. I'm not gonna guess all night."

"What happened was a cunt with a vendetta."

"No shit? I heard a groupie might've whacked you," Kirk said. "Lemme guess—you gave someone VD?"

"Oh, it was more than just giving some bitch VD. On our last tour, I fucked a broad who turned out to be the most dangerous piece of ass I ever laid into."

"Who was that?"

"Mona Baustone."

"Come again?" Kirk blinked a few times. The dropping of Mona Baustone's name hit Kirk like a punch to the chest.

"Come again? No, thanks. The first time I came, I signed my death warrant."

"Funny."

"Sure is. When your life's turned upside down overnight, you find humor in the absurdity of your existence."

"What did you do to make her wanna kill you?"

"I knocked her up."

"You're serious?" Kirk inhaled and tried to recover from these unsettling disclosures.

"Serious as a grand mal seizure."

"When did this happen?"

"On our last North American tour. We were in New York, second sold-out show at Madison Square Garden. After the show there were all kinds of fine-looking sluts hanging around."

"As usual. I remember the show."

"There was one chick who was a real knockout. She was a huge Cardinal Slynn fan. A brunette with a pair of awesome tits, dressed in pretty fine clothes. Not your average groupie look. She wanted to meet me real bad. After signing some stuff and taking pictures with her, we got to talking. We split a fifth of Jack Daniels, then I took her on my tour bus and fucked her like the Marquis de Sade."

Kirk didn't doubt this. "So what happened?"

"I dumped her on the side of the road when I was done with her, but she ended up showing her face at the next seven or eight shows. She was being a regular psycho-stalker." Jack took a swig of beer. "I tried getting her barred from the backstage area, but the bitch had clout. Found out later she was Festus Baustone's daughter. Made sense why she got backstage so easily."

"Right." Kirk felt uneasy hearing his new employer's name brought up in this context.

"I've never kept track of the whores who bothered me on the road. Shit, I been hit with palimony suits, stalkers, and bitches claiming I raped them or gave 'em a disease." Jack shook his head. "I handled this the same way. Blew Mona off hard-style. Came home to a thousand voice mail messages from her. I changed my phone number like ten times, but somehow that little bitch found ways to reach me. Bitch even showed up at my house."

"Uh oh."

"At the time, I was fucking that porn star Britney 'Triple D' Dawson. She answered the door when Mona came-a-callin'. There was a catfight I had to break up. I told Mona to get the fuck off my property before I kicked her ass down the block."

"Sounds like a bad scene."

"Yeah, you could say that. Mona was crying and telling me that she was in love with me. Then she dropped the bomb and said she was pregnant."

"You must've been thrilled to hear that."

"I gave her the usual bullshit. *How can you prove it's mine? You're just a whore after my money, yadda, yadda, yadda.* She threatened to have the kid and get a court-ordered blood test to prove it was mine. After that, she'd nail me for child support and let the press know what kinda guy I am. Blah, blah, blah."

"How'd you work it out?"

"I got pissed and kicked her. In the gut."

"You *what*?" Kirk was shocked to hear this, thinking about the degenerate Jack once was and might still be. "Man, you're some asshole."

"Hey, the bitch was making me insane. Plus, I had to look out for my interests. After I kicked her, I apologized and tried to avoid any more trouble. Unfortunately, as they say, Hell hath no fury like a woman scorned."

A woman scorned? Kirk wasn't thrilled to see Jack anymore. Slynn might've changed physically, but he was still the same fuckhead he'd always been. "Beating up women isn't cool, bro. That shit's way outta line."

"Look, I was never an angel, and I agree, beating women ain't cool. I don't condone it, and I hate myself for a lot of shit I've done." Jack shook his head. "Believe me, I paid for it in the end. After our...altercation, Mona went home. I was wondering how a seventeen-year-old girl was able to track me down and then come across the country looking for me. That's when I found out she was super rich and who her daddy was."

"How's that?"

"She sent me hate mail. In her letters she said it didn't matter how big of a star I was 'cause I wouldn't get away with what I did. She said I hurt the wrong girl."

"Sounds like it."

"She signed her letters as Mona Baustone and enclosed newspaper clippings from the front page of *The New York Times* and the *Post*. Clips of her and Daddy Festus."

"Started to get that old sinking feeling, eh?"

"Kinda. I wasn't really worried at first. It was gonna take a lot more than a multibillionaire to scare me off. The day after I got that letter, I got a phone call from Festus Baustone himself. He wanted to know what happened between me and his daughter."

"Uh oh. What did you do?"

"I totally snapped, man. I was so sicka this bitch and wanted to explode." Jack's voice became angry. "I told Festus that I fucked her in the ass, cunt, and mouth all night until she was pumping jizz through her veins. I also told him if he had a problem with that, he could suck my cock after his daughter got off it. I remember Festus laughing on the other end. *Laughing.* That's when I got worried."

"You ever tell Yaggerwood about this?"

"Yeah, I'll get to Yaggerwood in a minute. You'll be interested in some things I've got to tell you about *him.*"

"God, I can just imagine." Kirk felt his regard for Yaggerwood going down another notch.

"With everything Mona told her old man and what I said to him on the phone, Festus declared war on me. I had shit hitting me from all directions. Festus sicced some thugs on me. And get this, I found out Festus owned Juggernaut Records as a silent CEO. He got access to my confidential files."

"No way."

"Yeah, he found out where I lived, what my Social Security number was, and he fucked with my royalties."

"What about the guys who came after you?"

"They were big fuckers. I started noticing them hanging outside of my house. They followed me around. I didn't know what they wanted at first. They were really fuckin' with my peace of mind. I'd see 'em on my way to rehearsals, at shows, the In-N-Out Burger, you name it. They were always there, watching. I'll never forget. One of the motherfuckers had a mouthful of gold teeth. Always grinning."

Kirk raised his eyebrows, thinking of Helmut's monstrous henchmen, Donny in particular.

"I hired the biggest boys from our road crew to act as my personal bodyguards. They went everywhere with me. But it didn't matter who I was with. I wasn't safe."

Kirk waved down a waitress and ordered another beer. He glanced at Jack, who looked like he'd aged fifty years.

"Baustone's boys tried getting me one night outside the Rainbow," Jack said. "I was with four of the biggest, meanest guys you ever seen. We came onto Sunset Boulevard, and those fuckers who kept following me popped up. Gold-tooth said they were gonna take me away. I told 'em to fuck off and I unleashed my little mob."

"That had to change things around, huh?"

"Those two Baustone guys beat my bodyguards senseless. I couldn't believe it. I had Big Lou, Randy the stage manager, as well as the brothers—Tommy and Jake Douglas. You probably remember those guys."

"Hell, yeah. They were built like tanks. Big Lou was like three hundred pounds."

"That's right. And after those two thugs hit him, he hit the Sunset Strip like a three-hundred-pound bag of horse shit."

"What about Tommy and Jake?"

"Put up a good fight for a few minutes."

"What about you?"

"I ran away as fast as I could. My Ferrari was parked in a security lot near the Whiskey. I hopped in and tore ass outta there."

"They didn't catch you?"

"Not then. The Baustone hit squad was still dealing with my guys. I drove straight to my house, and when I got there, it was trashed. Someone had been there and destroyed the place. They shot my Dobermans as a calling card."

"Jesus. Didn't you call the cops?"

"That didn't seem like a good idea at the time. After years of dissing the pigs on my albums, 911 probably wasn't going to do me any favors."

"So what did you do?"

"I packed my clothes and my Glock nine and went to Yaggerwood's house."

"Rod? That bastard's always acted like you were dead." Kirk felt a new wave of unsettling surprise. "He never let on that he knew all this."

"He had to play dumb. To protect me."

"Yaggerwood really took you in?"

"Fuck yeah, he did. How could he turn away one of his biggest stars? Shit, I made the man a fortune. Anyway, I told Yaggerwood about everything. I told him every gory detail about the things I did to Mona. Told him about my conversation with Festus, the hit men coming after me, all the shit."

"What brilliant plan did he concoct to get you out of trouble?"

"Rod had some good ideas." Jack pulled a hit off his beer. "He offered to do his best to try and act as a liaison between me and Baustone. Y'know, to smooth things out."

"Did it work?"

"Rod made some calls and eventually reached Festus. Rod told Festus that whatever I did, I was sorry for it. Rod told him I was just a hotheaded punk whose mouth got the best of me. He apologized on my behalf."

"Good ol' sweet-talking Rod."

"He seemed sweet enough 'cause Festus said he wasn't pissed anymore and he'd forget everything. It looked like everything was gonna be cool. Baustone said he'd call off his dogs and leave me alone."

"What about your royalties? You said Festus was fucking with 'em, right?" Kirk became curious to see where Jack's story was going.

"Yeah, he fucked with 'em, but when Rod talked to him, Festus said he wanted to straighten that out, too. It was wrong. Illegal. He wanted to wipe the slate clean. But it was a lie."

"What was a lie?"

"Everything. Festus wanted me to go to the offices of Juggernaut Records in Santa Monica the next day so we could straighten out my royalties. I drove out there to find a trap."

"Sounds like he wasn't about to forgive and forget."

"When I pulled into Juggernaut's parking lot, a black sedan came roaring up to me. Those same two monsters jumped out. Gold-tooth yelled somethin' to me about Festus still holdin' a grudge. After that, they opened fire, man."

"They're hit men?" Kirk felt a sense of dread, wondering what quagmire of shit he was into. "You get shot?"

"Not then. I drove like Mad Max through Santa Monica, but I couldn't lose 'em. They were on my ass all the way. I turned into a blind street and got stuck. They blocked me in with their car and started blastin'. They hit my gas tank and the next thing I knew, I was on fire."

"How'd you get outta there?"

"I started shooting like Jesse James."

"There must've been cops coming down on you."

"If there were, I didn't notice. My world was a battle zone. I think I hit the man with the golden mouth in both arms. I know I hit the other gorilla 'cause he fell hard."

"You're not exactly an assassin. What happened to you?"

"Got lucky. Only grazed along my head. Two rounds hit me in the shoulder but passed clean through. I didn't stop runnin' until I found a place to hide."

"Where'd ya go?"

"In a Dumpster."

"Shit. That must've sucked."

"Yeah, it was pretty fucking nasty. I stayed in there for a good eight hours or more, soaking up Dumpster juice. Gag me with a fucking spoon. It was torture in there. Bleeding...fighting off flies, bees, raccoons."

"This'll be great in your memoir someday." Kirk found himself eating up the revelations of the real Jack Slynn story. "And then?"

"Found my way to a pay phone near Venice Beach and called Yaggerwood at his house."

"Bet he was surprised to hear from you, huh? I remember TV helicopters looking for you and your supposed kidnappers or killers." Kirk recalled the chaos surrounding Jack's disappearance. "It was like watching the O.J. Simpson chase."

"Yaggerwood sent a car to pick me up. When I finally got to his house, I got all doctored up."

"What did Rod say? I imagine he was fulla grand plans."

"Not really. Everything was chaotic, happenin' too fast. Yaggerwood didn't know what to do. He thought I was already taking a dirt nap before I phoned him."

"That's Rod for you. Sympathetic to the end."

"Can't say I blame him. With my Ferrari turned into a fireball and my carcass missing from the scene of the crime, I can see why Yaggerwood and everyone else wrote me off."

"What went down at Rod's house?"

"Yaggerwood and I discussed my options and realized I didn't have any."

"I'm sure you could've been put in protective custody."

"Protective custody?" Jack started laughing. "I don't think so, Kirk. Baustone's the richest, most powerful bastard in the world, and he wanted me dead."

"Maybe you could've gone to the press."

"Get real, man. The fucker *is* the press."

"So why would he even bother chasing you down?"

"Because he's a twisted fuck. It was fun for him. After talking it over with Rod, I decided to become a ghost and vanish."

"Where'd ya go?"

"First I went to a plastic surgeon, then I took off to the Bahamas."

"You went to a plastic surgeon?" In the darkness, Kirk couldn't make out Jack's features beneath his massive beard and moustache.

"Yeah, he was recommended to me by Yaggerwood. He was unlicensed, cheap, and worked out of his house. Turned out to be a real butcher. He fucked my mug up real good. That's why I've got this ZZ Top shit growing outta my face."

"Sounds like you went through hell."

"You've got no idea. My face was a mess, same with the flesh on my arms, back, and chest. Y'see, I had that quack remove all my tattoos as well. He used some kinda homemade laser on me."

"Goddamn..."

"Had to do it. I needed to disguise myself if I was gonna start a new life. It was the worst pain I've ever felt, but that's the price I paid to be reborn."

"You were really that scared of Festus Baustone?"

"Fuckin' *A*. Guys don't shoot at you to be friendly, dude. He made it clear he wanted me gone, so I took off. Know what? It was one of the best things to happen to me."

"Why's that?"

"After being on my own in the Bahamas, I realized I

was burnt out on the music biz and being a rock star." Jack looked deep in thought. "Shit, I'd already lived all my dreams. I've played in almost every country and on every legendary stage in arenas worldwide. I've been in all the magazines; I've been worshipped and idolized. I've gone down in rock history with Cobain, Morrison, and Lennon, man. Hell, even got my cock immortalized by Cynthia Plaster Caster."

Kirk chuckled at the thought, knowing Cynthia Plaster Caster as one of the most famous and original groupies in the history of rock and roll. Her plaster molds of rock star genitalia were legendary. Her collection of penis casts included everyone from Frank Zappa to Jimi Hendrix. Some said once you'd been cast by the Plaster Caster, you'd made it. Kirk was happy he made it without submitting his penis to Cynthia's dental mold.

"It was time to quit," Jack said. "I grew out my hair and quit drugs. I got fat and lived on the beach. I changed my name, too."

"What is it?"

"Can't tell."

"Where you living now?"

"Can't tell you that either. Gotta keep my secrets and lie low. I'm outta the loop forever, or at least until Festus bites the big one. The only reason I'm here is to see you."

"What about Rod? Does he still talk to you?"

"No, we parted ways forever right after my plastic surgery and tattoo removal. He hooked me up with my new identity and passport, got me a bank account somewhere. He set it up so my royalties are wired there. Fucker's still getting a percentage."

Kirk laughed, this fact not surprising him. "How's

that work?"

"When I originally signed with Yaggerwood, he took me under his wing. He raised me in the business. Since I had no parents or any other relatives, I made Rod my sole beneficiary. If I died, he got everything I had. I'm surprised the bastard never tried to have me killed." Jack laughed, his hairy face just a shadow in the dim light of the bar.

"Yaggerwood took over your entire estate?"

"Exactly. When I decided to go into hiding, I told Yaggerwood to take control of my assets. Just consider me dead. All I wanted was fifty percent of all the money from my houses, royalties, and savings. I told Yaggerwood to keep everything else. As soon as I was declared deceased, he had complete control of my stuff. From there, he set me up for the rest of my life."

"So, you just live off the money put in your mystery account?"

"Exactly."

"Doesn't anyone recognize you?"

"Not at all. C'mon, look at me."

"Don't you ever miss the music? The shows and fans?" Kirk tried imagining what it would be like to throw away an amazing music career. He couldn't grasp it. He knew he could never do it.

"Fuck yeah. It ate me up for a long time. But then I realized if I would've kept goin', I would've died, with or without Festus Baustone. All that coke and whiskey I was doing. Shit."

"I just hope you're happy, man."

"I'm cool. I'm in a good place now."

"Your note said you wanted to warn me of something. Baustone?"

"Stay away from him. He's dangerous. You slip

once, you get fucked hard-style." Jack's voice was cold and serious. "I always liked you, Kirk. I'd hate to see anything bad happen to ya."

"I appreciate you comin' out and telling me all this. It's good to know what happened to you. It's like a load's been lifted off my mind."

"Maybe you'll start believing in ghosts, now."

"Maybe. As for Festus, I'm not worried. I'm just doing a little deal for his company, that's it."

"Baustone's pure poison."

"Well, it's not like I'm fertilizing Baustone's daughter or anything. I mean, you gotta admit, you really went out of your way to piss him off."

"That's not the point. Festus is a fuckin' maniac. I don't know what he's paying you, but it's not worth it. Get away from that motherfucker before it's too late."

A blend of the DJ's loud Cure remix and heavy clove smoke added to Kirk's growing sense of unreality and unease. He now had numerous questions for Yaggerwood. The first being why he didn't tell Kirk about what really happened to Jack Slynn, and, even more alarming, why he hooked Kirk up with a psychotic multibillionaire who had tried to kill one of Rod's biggest clients.

"I've gotta take a piss." Kirk stood up and stretched in the darkness of the club. "I'll be right back."

"Cool." Jack tipped his bottle at Kirk.

In the darkness, Kirk could see the whiteness of Jack's teeth as he smiled, the only identifiable feature on his former singer's face.

Kirk took a stance in front of a urinal and relieved himself. Seeing Jack after all these years jolted him. Hearing Jack's tale about Festus and Mona Baustone was even more shocking. Kirk's mind filled with a hundred scenarios and more questions.

Kirk rinsed and dried his hands. As he headed for the door, he encountered a tall, gaunt man in the doorway.

"Excuse me," Kirk said, trying to walk past him. The old man stood in Kirk's way, looking at him with a solemn expression. He wore ragged clothes and a clerical collar. Kirk wondered if the old man was a wayward priest.

"I need to speak with you, Kirk," the old man said in Italian.

"Do I know you?" Kirk was surprised to hear the man speaking Italian. He wondered if the old man was a rare, elderly, immigrant fan of his music.

"I'm Father Antonio Zacharelli."

"Father, huh? What d'ya want there, Padre?" Kirk spoke in rusty Italian.

"I'm here to steer you away from the dark and into the light of God's glory before it's too late."

"Padre, if you wanna get me away from the dark, all you gotta do is walk me outta this club. I can't see a thing in here."

Zacharelli sounded adamant. "You cannot see the legions of the Antichrist as they loom around you, but they're here. Satan's pawns will trick you into using your special gift to summon Hell on Earth. They'll try and fool you in order to bring Satan forth. You're going to be the conduit that induces Armageddon. But you have a chance to—"

"I don't have time for a sermon right now." Kirk tried pushing his way past Zacharelli.

"By the grace of God, you must listen to me." Zacharelli grabbed him by his forearm with a hard grip.

"What the fuck?" Kirk was surprised by the old

man's strength. He looked at Zacharelli's arms, seeing dark blood flowing out of large holes in the wrists.

"Like the angels blowing trumpets on Judgment Day, you will sound a cry that will raise Satan and his legions of Hell. But if the light of God is in your heart and His instrument is in your hands, you shall command His will through an instrument that He died upon, an instrument possessing the sonic fury of the Nazarene's wrath. His will shall come from above and be an extension of your soul, and when you sound off, you shall eradicate the evil you unleashed."

Kirk began feeling freaked out and concerned for the old nut. The large, bleeding holes in the dude's wrists called for medical attention. Maybe the man was into self-immolation. "Listen...you need serious help. You need a doctor, man."

"No, my son, it's you who needs help. Your strings are being pulled by Satan's manipulators. If you don't stop now, you'll have to fight the legions, then by God, you'll need to wield a weapon only He can provide."

Kirk broke Zacharelli's hold. "Fuck this shit." He burst from the bathroom and stumbled into the smoke, noise, and darkness of the club. He looked behind him, seeing no one other than patrons in corpse paint.

Kirk paused, allowing his eyes to grow accustomed to the dark. Once he could see better, he made his way back to his seat. When he got there, Jack Slynn was gone.

Chapter 10
Mona Baustone

Kirk's sleep was troubled by strange dreams. He heard Helmut's eerie and diabolic vocal patterns—the foundation of the ancient song—in his head. The sound terrified him. He saw a gathering storm in his mind. He dreamt of Jack Slynn and Father Antonio Zacharelli.

"...then by God, you'll need to wield a weapon only He can provide."

Kirk got out of bed, grabbed some coffee, and got right to work. With guitar in hand, he sat in front of Helmut's computer monitor. The instrument was plugged into a customized amplifier, which was connected to the soundboard in the control room. Everything Kirk played would come out through the studio monitors.

Hieroglyphics were now transformed into sheet

music. Kirk felt the Song of Sethis was ready to be played as a guitar piece. When he clicked the play button, the musical notes would begin moving across the screen from right to left in time with a digital metronome. Kirk noted the music would take five minutes to perform.

He had done the major part of the job. He had transcribed the song in its entirety. Now completed, all of its parts put together, Kirk tuned up, ready to play the entire song all the way through on his signature ESP guitar.

Just as he was about to get the music moving and play the song, a flashing light and buzzer went off in the control room. There was someone outside the studio door buzzing to get in.

Who the hell can this be? He set his guitar on a stand and walked to the door.

Usually the day maid used the buzzer in order to give Kirk an urgent message or to notify him of a real emergency. He hoped it wasn't either one.

Kirk opened the studio door, surprised to find a woman standing there.

"Can I help you?" Kirk looked the woman over from head to toe. The attraction was instant.

"Kirk Vaisto?"

"The one and only."

"I'm here to check on the progress of the project you're doing for my father. I'm Mona Baustone," she said with a half smile and offered a hand.

Kirk took her soft and small hand for a moment and released it. Last night's conversation with Jack came back to him. The psycho-stalker was here. The dangerous groupie with a broken heart was now standing before him, wanting to do business. Kirk hoped she didn't have a vendetta against any of Jack's former band mates.

Kirk's eyes took Mona in. She was about five-six, with black hair in a French braid and aqua eyes. Her lips and long nails were painted the same silvery color.

He noticed her ample chest, nice hips, and great legs. She wore a bright, colorful sundress and high heels. With the subtle scent of perfume, Mona seemed to be a perfect package, but she hadn't talked long enough for him to cast a final ballot.

"Uh, right, right. I was told someone might be dropping by here sometime to check on me."

"Good. Then I wasn't totally unexpected."

"After dealing with Helmut Hartkopff, you're a pleasure just to look at."

Mona ignored Kirk's flirting. "So, can I see what you're working on?"

"Definitely. I was just about to perform the material," Kirk said, showing Mona inside the studio. "How'd you get in here, anyway?"

"I sneaked through your fence gate. My limo's parked out in front of your main gate. I rang your gate buzzer and intercom, but no one responded. Since our contract declares I'm to supervise every bit of your work, I came looking for you."

"That's what I get for having my agent sign contracts on my behalf."

"Don't worry, I'm not going to chuck a wrench into your work or violate your privacy. Unlike my father, I try to treat people with respect. But since I work for him, I've got to see what you're doing and report the progress. Then I'll be on my way."

"No problem. Lemme show you what I've got. Since you're here, you can watch me play the entire song on guitar for the first time."

"Really? You haven't performed it yet?"

"I've only transcribed the music and set up the arrangements and entered the transcriptions into the computer as digital sheet music. I haven't performed all the music straight through. With all the pieces and times changes complete and pasted together in the computer, I can finally play the entire song as it was meant to be."

"You're just going to play it off the computer?"

"That's right. The program will run, and it'll display the musical notes across the screen from right to left. Every note, chord, and intricate run is in there, fully transcribed from hieroglyphics to vocal patterns to actual music. I'll play the music as it moves across the screen by sight reading. Just like a musician in an orchestra would do with sheet music in a symphony."

"I'm eager to hear it."

"So am I. You should know, I was told to use my discretion regarding the execution of the song." Kirk thought of Helmut's cryptic words. *I'm confident the song will show you the way.* "So, with my style and through my rig, the music's gonna sound more like modern heavy metal than old and mummified."

"That suits me fine." Mona smiled at him. "I like heavy stuff."

Kirk sat down in front of the computer monitor with his guitar, and Mona took a seat beside him.

"Once I hit the play button with the mouse, the program will begin running," Kirk said. "It'll give me a four-count click before the song actually starts."

Kirk clicked the button and prepared to perform the song. The four-counts sounded and he began playing.

From the first note, Kirk's fingers were a blur across the fingerboard. He moved his hands with an intense fervor as he executed insane speed runs and colossal power chords along with other dizzying displays of fingerboard gymnastics.

The music carried a heavy and distorted sound. It reeked of everything dark and foreboding. It cried with the anguish of a muse being tortured deep in the underworld. Kirk found it eerie and beautiful and soon found it terrifying. He couldn't stop playing the song.

Kirk found macabre things within the notes. Elements of seductive darkness intertwined with human pain and unholy fury. This all meshed with the tones of eternal ecstasy mixing with the dark desires of his soul. It hit him as satanic, erotic, and extreme.

As Kirk played, the musical notes on the screen morphed into inverted crosses, and soon the digital staff was speeding across the monitor. Before he could question what was happening, he was sucked into the song. Instead of commanding the musical piece, the music commanded him, body and soul.

Kirk's musical passion and attack bordered on sonic insanity. His hands and fingers sped up and slowed down as the music's tempo and dynamics carried him away. Soon his hands and fingers weren't just a blur; they moved with speed that defied the limitations of physicality.

Kirk went into a trance. His breathing and heart rate slowed, his brain activity was overloading, and his eyes rolled back into his head. He had been conscious and sober when he first began playing, but now, as he fell into the music, he played it like an intoxicated machine. On autopilot as he played, Kirk experienced the music he was playing accompanied by the terrible images that came with it.

The song opened Kirk's mind and flooded him with visions of Hell. He saw people indulging in every explicit perversion known to man. He saw a million deaths and tortures. He saw Satan in a million different images, demanding Kirk release him. He saw the souls of billions who'd been sent to the eternal torments of the underworld since the dawn of mankind. Madness.

Kirk's body convulsed with each terrible vision, rivers of blood and fire washing over and drowning Egypt and the rest of the world, himself on a battlefield with an electric guitar in his hand, standing between two charging armies of virtuous good and unholy evil, himself crucified to a giant electric guitar, the headstock and half the neck planted into the ground, the blood-red body of the instrument looming high above, humming with high voltage.

Kirk saw himself naked and nailed to the body of the guitar. Spikes were driven through his wrists, forearms, ankles, and calves. He wore a crown of instrument cables, which were woven in and out of his cranium. Kirk tried to scream, but his mouth was wired and sewn shut with heavy-gauge guitar strings.

Kirk played on, electrified as he performed the song, his body reacting to the music and the guitar as if he were touching a live power line.

In the last measure, Kirk pulled off a malevolent run that ended on a massive power chord. As Kirk hit the chord, the studio shook with a violent tremor that split the studio walls into spider web cracks. The thick glass in the control room and in the isolation booths exploded into thousands of fragments. He watched his guitar amplifier burst into flames and saw the monitors in the studio expand and contract before exploding and sending shrapnel from their cones everywhere. The control room filled with smoke and the deafening sound of static and feedback.

The song was over and Kirk felt the strange spell was broken. He looked down with dismay, finding his beloved guitar smoking from the pickups, strings, and input jack. The instrument fell from his hands as he collapsed on the floor—hyperventilating, covered in sweat, and with bloody fingertips.

He looked through the smoke, searching for Mona. He found her curled against a wall, shivering, with an expression of terror stamped on her face.

Kirk tried to get up, but fell to his hands and knees. Crawling, he made it to the studio door and opened it from the floor. The fresh air of the outside world hit Kirk in the face. He took in a deep breath and vomited.

Mona stumbled outside and fell down next to him. They both gasped and retched.

"What in God's name just happened in there?"

"Not sure," Kirk said, finding the strength to sit up. "Whatever went down in there happened 'cause of that song. It's got some kinda power."

"How's music got the power to do those things? The sounds? The shit in my head? The force..."

"I don't know. Bet your old man and Helmut got an idea."

"When they briefed me on this project, they said the music you're supposed to transcribe is for some old song no one's ever played before. How could they know it's powerful or weird?"

"They know something. This whole thing feels wrong. Smells *bad*."

Mona was silent. Kirk looked at her, but she offered no answers for the visions and emotions that raped their minds.

"I've got a hunch this tune isn't gonna be released as an oldie for shits 'n giggles. I think your father dug up this song for more than listening appeal."

"C'mon. Ulterior motive? There's got to be a rational explanation for this."

"When you cough one up, let me know. Right now I've gotta check out my studio."

Smoke drifted out of the control room. Kirk found it a wreck inside. Debris and glass was spread everywhere. Burning plastic and wire filled Kirk's nose.

"Fuckin' *A*." Kirk moaned and surveyed the damage. His expensive, hot-rodded amp head was now a molten blob of plastic, burnt knobs, and fried vacuum tubes. His monitors were dust, and the sound of white noise and feedback filled his ears. Kirk looked at the molten computer. The song program flickered on the warped monitor.

Kirk stepped over debris and made his way to his rack of outboard studio gear, where he killed the power.

"I'm sorry about your studio." Mona stood in the doorway and waved smoke away from her face.

"Sorry? This studio is fucked up beyond all recognition. Thank God I locked my master recordings up in a private vault. I've got an album to finish here and now that's gonna be put off until this studio's back in shape. Talk about bringing down the house. Shit."

"What'll it take to get your studio back to normal?"

"I don't know. I'm not an insurance appraiser. The studio cost me half a million to build."

"Consider it paid. I'll have a Baustone check made out to you and in your hands by tomorrow. When I tell Dad you can play the song, he'll be ecstatic. He won't care about paying for damages. He spends a quarter million dollars on dinner."

"Now wait a minute, I don't wanna play that song again. The way things worked out, that fuckin' music *played me.*"

"C'mon, let's get you cleaned up."

Kirk looked himself over. The fingertips on his left hand, his guitar-neck hand, were bleeding.

"That hurts." He flexed his painful and bloody digits. "Am I covered by workers' compensation?"

"You're covered by something better."

"What's that?"

"You're going to be taken care of by the fine people at Baustone International." Mona smiled.

"If you're trying to make me feel better, you might wanna say something I can believe."

Mona shrugged. "Your wounds need tending to. Let's go."

Kirk took a last look at his studio and shook his head. He turned away and showed Mona to his mansion.

Chapter 11
Progress Report

"How's that?" Mona wrapped a final Band-Aid on one of the fingers of Kirk's left hand.

"That's fine." Kirk felt dull pain in his fingers. "I can't believe they're so cut up. A needle can't even penetrate the calluses I've developed on the tips over the years. I would've thought the guitar strings would give before my fingertips."

Kirk and Mona were sitting at the kitchen table in his mansion. Kirk was shirtless, and he studied the Band-Aids on his fret hand.

"So, what happened to you in there? What did you see?" he asked.

"I saw some crazy shit...unholy stuff. Hellish images. I saw my deepest and darkest fears. I wanted to scream, laugh, cry, and fuck. Evil."

"Did you happen to catch what I was doin' while I was playing the song?"

"All I remember was when you started playing the song, you went into some kind of trance. Your eyes rolled back, your teeth clenched, and you were seized by convulsions."

"Convulsions?"

"Yeah, you were totally spazzing out. Your hands and fingers were flying across the guitar at lightning speed. It looked insane."

"Jesus, I don't remember any of that."

"That's all I remember seeing of you in the studio. My mind was filled with all kinds of nightmares while you played that music. When those visions hit me, my mind was gone."

"I remember starting the song, thinking how evil the music sounded. That's it. After picking the first few notes, I descended into a terrifying world." Kirk's memory played flashes of the horrific images. "My mind was on a trip to Hell. The music I played...like a soundtrack for my journey. It was all fucked up."

"I don't get this. I mean, music doesn't have the power to make you hallucinate."

"Music makes people do all kinds of things. It's one of the most powerful forces ever. Music makes people cry and dance. It makes people aggressive, and it makes people extremely happy. Music moves people in many different ways." He produced a sly smile. "I've seen music with extremely low tones and frequencies give some people orgasms."

Mona laughed. "Yeah, right. If music can give orgasms, I'd never need a date. I'd just slap on a Type O Negative disc. That's the closest thing to audio pleasure I know of."

"Seriously, there are frequencies, tones, and certain acoustics that can really have an effect on the human body."

"What else, Professor?"

"Well, for one thing, music heals. It helps you get in touch with and identify your emotions. Music opens a door. It can get your emotions across to people and it can also help you understand the emotions of others."

"I guess I never thought of it that way. It's always been entertainment to me."

"Music's much more than entertainment. When I hear music full of emotion, I'm gonna feel that emotion. It's gonna hit me hard and hit me right. Like when I listen to the music of Stevie Ray Vaughn, Paganini, or Skynyrd and old Metallica. It lifts me emotionally."

"It totally moves you. I get that."

"Yeah. It's something you can't quite explain." Kirk gave this some thought. "It's something you feel. Like playing live. For me, it's better than sex or any drug. Music's emotional and spiritual forces touch me. Maybe it's the physics of music that affects me."

"Physics?"

"The frequencies, tones, and acoustics are part of the physics of sound. Physics is all about musical sounds and how they're interpreted not only by the human ear, but the human mind and body as well."

"Music that strikes a chord in us, so to speak?"

"Exactly. I believe people resonate with a chord that's within them. It vibrates in part of their being. Some more than others."

"You mean like guitar chords or something?"

"Well, it's not like you can just point at someone and say, 'She's an *A* major,' or 'He's a *B* flat.' It's deeper than that. I feel everyone vibrates to a chord, and that chord goes through a progression during our lives."

"How do you know what chords are within you?"

"Depends. People are instruments. Everyone possesses unique chords vibrating with their soul."

"You think they affect our souls?"

"Chords certainly have different effects on people. Minor chords alone sound sad, and there are other tones you can add that can evoke deeply rooted emotions in a subtle and hypnotic way."

"You born again or something?"

Kirk laughed. "No, not born again. I do believe in a higher power and the forces of good and evil. But my faith is spiritual and musical. Music's my religion."

"You really think my father knows something about this weird song that we don't?"

"I'm thinking Helmut knows this song has an element of evil to it. Since he's the fucker who discovered the song, only he would know its history. I got a hunch he used your dad to hunt me down because I was the only one who could transcribe and arrange the music to be played on a guitar. I'm sure your old man and Helmut never really believed that this song had any real potential. I mean, it's hard to believe it can do the things it can, but since your dad had the bucks and Helmut had the knowledge, they probably figured, fuck it, and used me for a guinea pig."

"It sounds so farfetched and strange. Then again, my dad's always been a kook." Mona sighed and frowned.

"I've gotta tell ya, I'm best off being done with him. I don't know if that song's a gateway or something else. It's pure evil. You know it, too. I don't want anything to do with it. Look what we've seen and what happened to my studio. Bad juju."

"I already told you we'd pay for your studio."

"Doesn't matter. The same shit could happen again when I play the song. How many studios are you gonna rebuild?"

"Then play it somewhere else."

"I don't know."

"I'll be honest—my father's a persistent asshole. He does what he wants and always gets what he wants. I work for him because he's the only family I've got. I've got to tell him what happened today, and when he finds out the music Helmut gave you possesses an unexplained power, he's going to be hell-bent on having you play it for him. Part of the deal."

"Just tell him I'm giving back the money he paid me and I'll take care of the studio damage myself."

"It's not that easy. You and your agent signed exclusive contracts. My father's paid a lot of money to get this music out of Egypt. If you refuse, he'll come at you with a platoon of lawyers. I hate to think of what else he'd do if you don't work on this project."

"Is that a threat?"

"Not a threat, just a warning. I know what my father's capable of when he wants something."

"Look, no one tells me what to do, okay? And no one gives me warnings." Kirk felt himself getting angry. "I'm not Jack Slynn."

Mona's face flushed deep red. "What the fuck's that supposed to mean?"

"Nothin'," Kirk said with instant regret.

"Nothin', my ass. I had my reservations about coming here because of Cardinal Slynn. Jack Slynn. What a real bastard. I hated him for a long time. He broke my heart and used me. I'm sure you know all about me. Jack probably told you I was a slut. Maybe that I stalked him or some shit. You probably think I had him killed."

"Hey, Mona, listen."

"No. I was worried about coming here. I figured when you found out who I was, you'd have no respect." Mona's voice rose. She shook a finger at him. "You proved my point. I value my reputation and my good name."

"I'm sorry. I didn't mean anything. I don't think of you in any way but professional. I don't like being pushed around, is all."

"No one's pushing you around. You signed a contract and you'll abide by it. Otherwise, we'll see you in court."

Mona shot up from the table, her high heels making loud, angry clip-clopping sounds as she left. When she got to the front door, she turned and said, "Y'know, I don't give a fuck what you think about me."

Kirk tried to say something as he got up to follow her, but before he could utter a word, the door slammed shut.

Good goin', dickhead. He watched Mona getting into her limo. She was gone and his head throbbed. He stretched out on his couch and closed his eyes, hoping his day would get better.

Chapter 12
Daddy's Girl

Mona Baustone arrived at her luxury suite in Malibu and threw herself on the bed. She was on the verge of tears. After all these years, she'd thought Jack Slynn was history. The lovesick, rich teenager infatuated with her idol was long gone. Instead, Mona had grown into a woman who now had her priorities in order. Being smitten with rock stars wasn't one of them. It took her years to get her self-esteem on track. The offhand comment by Kirk Vaisto hurt hard.

She held back the welling in her eyelids and grabbed her cell phone. It was time to call Dad.

Mona dialed Festus's cell phone. After three rings, he picked up.

"Festus," the phone voice said.

"It's Mona."

"Ah, the daughter calls with good news, I hope?"

"Yes and no. First of all, Kirk Vaisto transcribed the song as promised. He actually played it for me for the first time."

"And? Anything happen?"

"I guess you could say that."

"Well?"

"This is going to sound crazy."

"I *love* crazy. Tell me." His voice sounded excited and impatient.

"Okay, when Kirk played the song, we both started seeing and feeling...hellish images." Mona saw the unexplained scenes in her head as she spoke. "It was like nightmares were taking over our minds. Kirk looked possessed. He said the song played him. Get it? As soon as he hit the last chord, the studio exploded."

"Exploded? Anyone hurt?"

"Everyone's fine. The whole thing was nuts."

The other end of the line was silent.

"Dad? You still there?" Mona heard only light static.

"Yeah, I'm here. What's he doing right now?"

"Probably pissing and moaning. He wasn't too happy about his studio being destroyed. He doesn't want to go on with the project anymore."

"He has no choice!"

"He said he's going to return your money and he wants to forget the whole thing."

"You'd better get him back on track."

"I already tried convincing him. He wouldn't budge. We parted on bad terms."

"Then fix it. I didn't go through all this trouble and money just to have this guitarist deny me." Festus paused before he returned with a quieter tone. "It's your job to keep him focused and to remind him of his contractual obligations."

"It's not always easy to persuade the hardheaded. What do you suggest?"

"You're a smart girl. I'm sure you'll think of something. You've always had a way with rockers, haven't ya, honey?"

Anger washed over Mona like a rogue wave. Her day was already ruined by Kirk's earlier jab, and now she heard her own father insulting her.

"You know what?" Mona tried keeping the anger in her voice from erupting but couldn't manage it.

"What?"

"You're a real asshole."

Mona threw her BlackBerry across the room and didn't know whether to scream or cry. She sulked around her suite for an hour before deciding to clean up and reconnect with Kirk. She wanted to get on his good side. This was going to take some creativity.

Chapter 13
Nocturnal Emissions

Kirk woke from a nap, took a shower, and dried off just as his cell phone rang. He walked into his master bedroom with a towel around his waist and picked it up.

"Hello?" he said, holding the phone away from his wet ear.

"It's me, Mona."

"Hey."

"Catch you at a bad time?"

"Nah. Just got out of the shower."

"Oh, should I call you back?"

"No, no. That's okay. What's up?"

"I just wanted to apologize for storming out of your

house earlier. I'm touchy about my past."

"Don't worry about it." Kirk was glad she called. "I was out of line with what I said. I should think before I open my mouth. I don't care about your past. It's not important to me."

"That's good to hear." Mona's voice sounded cheerful. "When we spoke earlier, I didn't mean to imply anything threatening when I spoke about my father's interests. My dad sucks, okay? When he gets a wild hair up his ass, he's relentless. I just want you to do what's comfortable. I know we've experienced something incredible and horrifying. It might be monumental, y'know? I hope you'll reconsider working on this project."

Kirk sat down on his king-sized bed. "Actually, I'm gonna play that song for your old man."

"Really?"

"Yeah, but don't get too excited. I'm only doing this because I'm a man of my word. I fulfill my obligations. After I do it, that's it. I never wanna deal with him again."

"I understand."

"I'm thinking the guy who originally wrote this music was extremely gifted and found a way to open a door to Hell."

"And we walked right in. The music took us there."

"The music gave us a sample of what Hell's like. Imagery and emotion invoked by the music. It took over our minds. There's something the song is trying to tell me."

"Maybe this music's a medium, tapping directly into our brains. Using our minds to exploit our nightmares or to create new ones."

"There are tons of explanations you could come up

with. The music's very technical, and it actually controls the player as he performs the piece." Goose bumps covered Kirk as the water on his body dried.

"I think you're right about Dad. He knows something about the power of that song. He was furious when I told him you were backing out."

"He sounds about as charming as Helmut."

"They're birds of a feather. I've only met Helmut once. That was enough. Yikes."

"I'm not worried about what they want or what they threaten to do if they don't get their way. I'm doing this to honor the contract. I want you here. You're the voice of reason. I need you on my side. Plus, I like having a good woman around."

Mona laughed. "Okay, Mr. Vaisto. You've got me. I'll be here to help you with whatever you need."

"Cool." Kirk was happy to have Mona back. "So, where you at right now?"

"I'm at a fancy hotel in Malibu."

"What's for dinner?"

"Nothing on my agenda at the moment."

"How about coming over here and joining me for some din-din? I've got no one to keep me company."

Mona paused. "I usually don't...but since you're working for us, I'll come over. What're we having?"

"I'm gonna whip up a nice Italian meal. I make a fantastic fettuccine with shrimp and chicken. Pasta, bread, salad. Some wine."

"Mmmm. I love Italian food. However, I'm actually a part-time vegetarian."

"Part time? How's that work?"

"When I'm on my own, I don't eat meat, but when I'm in the company of a handsome, long-haired man, I'll eat just about anything."

Kirk felt something stirring inside him. "I think we're gonna have a good time."

"I hope so. See you in about an hour?"

"Sounds great."

"See you then."

Mona arrived at Kirk's mansion on schedule. They talked and laughed as they ate homemade pasta and drank wine.

"So, what's it like being the daughter of the one and only Festus Baustone?" Kirk wondered what Mona's mouth tasted like.

"It's nothing glamorous. When your father's Festus Baustone, you can have anything in the world, except love."

"Your old man doesn't love you?"

"Not really. He cares about me only when it suits him. I don't think he really wanted children. I'm a bit of a novelty to him. He's a cold, selfish, megalomaniac asshole."

"And your mom?"

"Dead."

"Shit, I'm sorry."

"Don't be. I probably wouldn't know her if she was alive anyway. She was a bit like my father, from what I've been told."

"Did he ever take time to raise you?"

"No. I was raised by my grandmother. My father gave me everything I needed as far as a nice house to live in, clothes, money for my education, and all that crap. But that's as far as his fatherly duties went. He never made an effort to give me the dad connection I needed."

"That sucks. The father-child bond didn't mean squat."

"My dad's always been too busy with himself to care about anything other than money and power. He'd rather buy up Manhattan or collect every rare fossil and weird artifact in the world before spending any quality time with me. He didn't even go to his own mother's funeral. He had an important meeting that day."

"You serious?"

"He had the funeral service videotaped so he could view it at a later time."

"Sounds pretty heartless."

"Yeah, I was plenty pissed. My grandma was such a sweet woman. She was always there for me and I loved her. My dad gave my grandma everything she needed and treated her like a queen, but like with me, he had no real emotional connection with her. That made her sad. But in the end, it didn't matter if my dad loved us, because my grandma and I had each other."

"Family's important. I don't know what I'd do without my parents. They've been my support system since I was born. I owe them so much."

"I wish I could say the same." Mona finished another glass of wine. "The way I see it, my dad owes me. Rich as he is, he'll never cough up enough cash to make up for his absence in my life."

"Can I ask you a touchy question?"

Mona looked Kirk in his eyes. "Is this about Jack Slynn?"

"How'd you know?"

"C'mon, Kirk. I know you're curious about what happened between Jack and me. The comment you made earlier told me you've been thinking about it."

"I'm really sorry about that. I just want to set the record straight. I know it's none of my business, and if you don't wanna tell me, that's cool. You're a good person and I respect you."

Mona grinned. "Well, you're a sweet-talker and I'm a little drunk. I'll answer your question. Shoot."

"Just tell what you want to tell."

"None of it's too nice. You see, I love hard rock and heavy metal, and since my dad owned most of Manhattan, I got into every concert that came to the city. My favorite band was Cardinal Slynn."

"Should I be flattered?"

"Not really. It was just a phase."

"Thanks a lot." Kirk feigned a hurt look.

"Don't take it the wrong way. I actually thought you were the one who carried the band as far as the music was concerned."

"Aw, thanks."

"You're welcome." Mona released a girlish giggle. "I used to have scrapbooks full of pics and pinups of Cardinal Slynn and Jack Slynn all over my bedroom walls. I was obsessed with Jack."

"He was your fantasy or somethin'?"

"Yeah. I worshipped him. My favorite picture of Jack was when he posed for the cover of *Rolling Stone* with nothing but a sock on his cock. Ripping off the Chili Peppers."

Kirk rolled his eyes. "Yeah, I remember that one."

"I started going to every show you guys did in the tri-state area. One night at the Garden I got backstage and achieved my mission."

"Which was?"

"To meet Jack."

"I see."

"My intentions in meeting Jack were purely innocent. I just wanted pictures and autographs. I didn't go there to blow him or anything."

"I didn't assume that. Just wondering why you really wanted to meet him. Most chicks into band guys wanna do 'em and tell their friends."

"I'm not like most *chicks*, okay? I mean, I love sex and all, but I don't just fuck anybody. But when I met Jack Slynn, I was open to anything."

"What happened?" Kirk was ready to square her account with Jack Slynn's side of the story.

"To make a long and bad story short, Jack and I wound up on his tour bus. We were still going at it when the sun came up." Mona shook her head. "Jack snorted a lot of coke and he wouldn't go to sleep. It was daylight and the sun came up and the bus kept rolling. We were somewhere in Pennsylvania."

"Weren't you worried about where you were going?"

"I was rebellious and carefree. Kinda naïve. I thought Jack Slynn really liked me."

"Uh, oh. A groupie's fatal flaw."

"I'm not a fucking groupie." Mona's tone turned sharp. "Never was, never will be. I slept with the sonofabitch because I really liked him."

"I'm sorry."

Mona didn't acknowledge Kirk's apology. She poured more wine into her glass. "I soon found out what an asshole Jack Slynn was. He got rough with me and kept calling me a whore. He was way cruel."

"What did you do?"

"I got pissed off. I was hurt. Jack was done with me and wanted me off his bus. We got into a fight, and the next thing I knew, I was stranded in a parking lot at a truck stop."

"That's cold. How'd you get home?"

"Uh, Long Island was too far to walk, so I called a limo. Luckily, I had Daddy's credit card."

"I imagine you must've ripped all those pinups off your wall."

"Totally. I tore every shot of Jack to shreds. I couldn't stand the sight of that fucker. I brewed about everything. I figured I'd start showing up at some of Cardinal Slynn's other tour dates to give ol' Jack a piece of my mind."

"Sounds like stalker material."

"Call it what you want. I was out to show that asshole he couldn't get away with disrespecting someone like me."

"Were you out to hurt him? Physically?"

"Naw. Just wanted to confront him. Maybe scare or humiliate him somehow. I started skipping school so I could fly out to his concerts. I always got backstage, but once I got near Jack, he had security nab me."

"Was he really worth all the trouble?"

"Hell, yes. He was worth the trouble 'cause he broke my heart and I wasn't going to let that slide. But later, I found out he'd done more than that."

"What did he do?"

"He got me pregnant.

"Really?" Kirk said, faking surprise.

"Yeah. I found out I was pregnant about a month after I met Jack Slynn for the first time. How stupid was I? Not using protection with Jack Slynn? God."

"The shit must've hit the fan, huh?"

"It definitely added insult to injury. I flew out to L.A. to hunt Jack down. Once I got there, I went to his house and got in a fight with some porn bitch he was fucking. Jack got into it with me, and when I told him I was pregnant, he kicked me in the gut."

"Jesus." Kirk was sorry to hear the story again.

"I flew home that day and miscarried on the way."

"Man, he was a heartless prick. It's a shame you met him."

"I was sick for a while after that. My grandmother was beside herself. I told her everything that happened. She wanted to call the police and get a lawyer, but I begged her not to. I didn't want any bad publicity for my family. My dad already did a great job giving us a bad rep everywhere."

"Any contact with Jack after that?"

"The only thing I did was send him hate mail. Told him I was Festus Baustone's daughter. Hoped to scare him with that. It didn't matter. We never had contact again."

"What did you think when you heard of Jack's disappearance?" Kirk was now curious to see where this might go.

"I was surprised. I figured someone else must've found out what the real Jack Slynn was like and let him have it."

"Who d'ya think did it?"

"I know what you're getting at, but I'll tell you I didn't have him killed. Don't look at me like that. I know people out there love to think I was responsible for Jack's death. That's tabloid bullshit."

"I heard your old man had Jack whacked."

"Why would he? He certainly didn't care what Jack Slynn did to me."

Kirk drank more wine and wondered about the circumstances surrounding Jack Slynn's disappearance. He believed Mona really knew nothing about it. Kirk concluded, for whatever reason, Festus took it upon himself to try having Jack Slynn killed, either for vengeance for his daughter or because Grandma Baustone had begged him to do something—or for sport.

Kirk wanted to change the subject. He caught Mona staring at him. Their eyes locked. She smiled and licked her lips. A wave of heat passed through Kirk. He cleared his throat and took a sip of wine.

"So, how old are you?" He studied Mona, wanting her.

"You don't ask a woman that. But since you're curious, I'm actually the same age as you. Thirty-nine, right?"

"Yeah, that's right. You look ten years younger than that."

Mona blushed at the compliment. "Well, aren't you just full of sweet words? You must really charm the pants off the ladies with that mouth."

"I can do more than that with my mouth." Kirk felt cocky and grinned.

"Oh, yeah?" Mona got up from the table and walked around to Kirk. "Why don't you show me?"

Kirk stood as Mona reached him and the kiss was deep. Their tongues danced and Kirk could taste the sweet wine in Mona's mouth. With a gentle hand, he grabbed the back of her hair and pulled her head back, licking her from her jawline down to her cleavage.

"How's my mouth doing now?" Kirk whispered in her ear.

"It's doing just fine. But it can do better. C'mere."

"Moving fast here, huh?"

"Shut up." Mona hiked her black skirt over her waist, took Kirk by his hand and put it between her legs.

Kirk let the uncut fingers of his right hand slip

inside her, and they both hummed with what he found.

"Good," Mona said, moaning, her knees giving way.

"Guitarists are great with their fingers." Kirk nibbled and kissed the nape of her neck.

"You're a dork." Mona backed up and got on her knees. She started undoing Kirk's pants.

"Not yet. Later." Kirk helped Mona to her feet. "I'm not done with you."

Kirk walked her to the kitchen. He picked her up and sat her down on the granite countertop. He spread Mona's legs and placed them over his shoulders.

"You can bill me for these." Kirk laughed and tore Mona's panties off.

Mona smiled and opened herself up a little wider. "You weren't fibbing." Her words were now imbued with a tenor of pleasure. She pulled Kirk's hair and clawed his scalp. "You really can...do other things with your mouth."

Kirk didn't answer her. His tongue and lips worked her anatomy. Mona cried as her legs stiffened and her lower torso bucked with orgasm. Kirk kept his mouth in place as Mona ground into his face. A rush of wetness flowed from Mona, making him ravenous for her sex. He went at her as if he'd never taste a woman again. Mona bucked again on the kitchen counter before pushing Kirk back.

"I want you. Right now." Mona eased off the counter and onto her legs. She took off her skirt and removed her silk blouse and bra. She kept her high heels on, and it made Kirk crazy with lust.

Kirk kicked off his boots and wiggled out of his pants and shirt. He grabbed her around the waist and kissed her.

"I wanna fuck you so bad." Kirk pressed his hardness into her belly.

"Do it already." Mona stepped away from Kirk. She faced the kitchen counter, leaned down with her arms spread and braced. Her high heels clicked as she stuck out her butt and assumed a position. She looked over her shoulder at Kirk and said, "From behind, Guitar Boy."

Kirk came up behind Mona, teasing for a moment before working himself in. He stood motionless, taking pleasure in Mona's hot and wet grip. Then he broke his celibacy with a vengeance.

Mona cried out while Kirk thrust and grunted with all he had. After several minutes, he felt the far-off tingling of the inevitable. He moaned, trying to hold back. He burned and throbbed, swelling and filling. No longer in control, he released into Mona.

Mona squealed and he slammed into her. He cried out with pleasure, looking down at Mona's backside as he did so, wondering what Slynn and Festus Baustone would think if they saw him now.

For the rest of the night and into the early morning, Kirk and Mona fed their hunger for each other. As the sun came up, the two lovers lay curled together in Kirk's giant bed, exhausted and raw.

"This's been a helluva of a first date." Kirk yawned and struggled to keep his eyes open.

"It was fun. Don't think I'll be walking right for a while."

"So, when do I have to play the song again?"

"Today. I didn't tell you this, but I got a voice mail from my dad. He's flying out here today with Helmut. They want to see you play it. The sooner, the better."

"Aw shit, they should've stayed put." Kirk groaned

at the news. "I don't even have a suitable place to perform. With the studio blown up and all, we gotta scout a new location."

"Don't worry about it. Dad'll find somewhere to set you up. My dad was originally coming here to convince you to stick with our agreement. Now all you got to do is play. He'll find a place."

"Was he gonna make me an offer I can't refuse?"

"I don't think he was going to put a gun to your head, but he might've tried muscling you into doing your job."

"Oh, great."

"That's not the issue anymore. Just play the song for those jokers and get it done. As soon as you finish, you'll never have to deal with 'em again."

"And once that's done, where will you go?"

"That depends on you."

"How's that?"

"If you want me to stick around or not."

"I'd like you to hang with me for a while. If you want."

Mona kissed Kirk's cheek. "I want."

Chapter 14
Diabolus in Musica

Kirk awakened to the sound of the front gate buzzer. He looked at the alarm clock. It was morning, just after nine. He'd only been asleep for a few hours.

"What's up?" Mona yawned and sat up in bed.

"Someone's at the front gate." Kirk got out of bed and walked to his large bedroom window to peek through the blinds. He saw a long, black limousine and a black cargo van parked out front. Helmut was out there, buzzing away.

"Looks like Helmut and his partners in slime are here."

"Shit! My dad was supposed to give me a call when he landed at the airport." Mona scrambled out of bed. "He knows we need time to prepare."

"Well, either your old man likes surprising people

or he just couldn't wait to get here. We've gotta deal with him now."

"Do me a favor. Go down and keep 'em busy. I'm going to clean up and look somewhat respectable for my dad. I don't want to give him the satisfaction of seeing me fresh out of bed."

"I'll take care of them." Kirk tied his hair back and slipped into a pair of jeans and a T-shirt.

"Thanks, hot stuff." Mona kissed him on the lips and disappeared into the bathroom of the master bedroom.

Kirk admired her naked backside as she walked away. He left the bedroom and went down to greet Helmut and his posse.

Kirk walked out into the overcast and cool morning, seeing Helmut with his fixed grin at the gate. He wore a khaki outfit and black sunglasses covered his fire-blasted eyes. Helmut held a flight case in his hands, which Kirk assumed contained the coffin texts.

"What's up?" Kirk opened the gate.

"Entertain me," Helmut said. "I want to hear you play that guitar of yours. You've unlocked the song, *ja*? We've come here to listen to what you've got."

"Who's *we*?" Kirk looked at his reflection in the lenses of Helmut's shades.

"Festus Baustone, Doctor Q., Donny, Mr. Jaspers...and myself." Helmut gestured as people exited the limousine.

Kirk watched as a fancy-dressed man emerged. He was tanned and clean-shaven, and looked to be in good shape. A short, gray-haired man wearing thick eyeglasses and a lab coat followed. Behind them came the black-suited monster men, Donny and Mr. Jaspers.

"Nice to finally meet you," the first man said,

coming toward Kirk. "I'm Festus Baustone."

Kirk studied the large man and thought Festus walked funny. It seemed as if his legs bothered him.

"So, you're The God of Guitar, huh? Should I be bowing right now or something?"

Kirk didn't laugh. He felt exhausted. There was no humor in him and he felt an atmosphere of dread among the men who stood around him.

"You know why we're here." Festus lit a cigar and blew smoke into Kirk's face. "You're going to play that song for us."

He glared at Festus. "I've agreed to play the song to fulfill my end of the contract."

"Good. As you should." Festus turned to his entourage. "I know you've met everyone here except for Doctor Q."

Doctor Q. was the short guy in the lab coat. Doctor Q. didn't extend his hand or utter a word to Kirk. He stood still as a robot, as if waiting for Festus to activate him.

"The Doc's what you call a neurophysiologist. He's going to be doing some tests on you while you play that song." Festus smiled. "My daughter says some strange things happened when you performed the music."

"Yeah. You could say that."

"I trust you'll be able to play those same notes."

"Sure, but I won't be able to do it here. My studio's destroyed. I'll need to play the song in a different venue."

"Don't worry about the studio." Festus chewed his cigar as if he was pissed off at it. "I've got a small, empty warehouse outside Malibu for you to play this music for us."

Kirk wasn't in the mood to play the song. He was hoping to put Festus and Helmut off for a while.

"That's fine, but I need time to get some gear in order," Kirk said. "The transcribed sheet music's saved to a disc. We're gonna need a computer. Gonna need my amps and I need to grab a new guitar. My main axe got all fucked up."

"No problem. We're way ahead of you with the computer and a place to play. Donny and Mr. Jaspers can help gather everything else you need. We'll load all of your equipment into our cargo van," Festus said.

"Okay then." Kirk's mouth felt dry. "I'll grab my things and we can get going."

"The computer I left you is damaged?" Helmut asked.

"Last time I checked," Kirk said. "It got fried. Sizzled with everything else. The disc with the music for your song is the only thing that survived. Well, aside from Mona and me."

"Good," Helmut said. "Bring the disc so you can properly perform the piece."

Mona walked up and joined the men. "I see you didn't waste any time getting here."

Kirk saw she was wearing her outfit from last night. Her hair was up in a bun, and she now wore a touch of makeup.

"Business waits for no one, my dear," Festus said. "Tell me, are you now an early riser, or did we miss out on a slumber party?"

Mona glared at him, as did Kirk, who disliked Festus more than ever. He wanted to kick the smirk off the rich bastard's face.

"Get everything together. We have a warehouse waiting," Helmut said. "We must make the most of this day."

"Helmut's right. Got to make progress. Can you hurry up, Guitar God?" Festus prodded.

Kirk hated the whole scenario. "I don't like being rushed. I was hoping to shower and pull select guitar equipment together."

"You can shower later, pretty-boy," Festus said, his voice curt. "Just show Donny and Mr. Jaspers what you need, and they'll put everything in the van."

Kirk sighed. He didn't want to pack up and run, but he didn't want to fight about it. The thought of playing the song and ending his obligation to Festus and Helmut gave him the motivation he needed. "Just follow me to the house, and I'll show you everything I'm gonna need."

"Donny. Mr. Jaspers." Festus waved the two bodyguards toward Kirk. "Time to use those muscles."

Two hours later the entire group was at a warehouse in a small industrial park thirty miles outside Malibu. The warehouse was made out of sheet metal. Kirk smelled old dirt and oil inside. Several grease-smeared windows provided minimal sunlight. The overhead lighting was poor, only enough to illuminate a few spots inside the building, including the table Kirk sat at. An occasional rat scurried in the shadows.

Donny and Mr. Jaspers stood outside and maintained security while the rest of the group circled around Kirk.

He sat in a chair in front of a large folding table that supported all the computer equipment from Kirk's studio. Another table hosted medical equipment set up by Doctor Q.

Kirk was shirtless, with Doctor Q. applying wires

over his chest and forehead. Festus and Helmut explained that the wires were hooked to electrocardiogram and electroencephalograph machines, which would read and display the activity of Kirk's heart, nervous system, and brain waves.

"Don't worry about these medical gadgets. We just want to find out what's going on with your body when the music kicks in," Festus said as Doctor Q. finished up.

"I'm not worried about the medical equipment," Kirk replied. "There's no way this gear's going to show you what I see when that song's played."

Helmut walked up. "I've got all the video and audio equipment hooked up. Are we ready yet?"

"I'd say so," Festus said. "Doctor Q.?"

The doctor nodded.

"How about you, Kirk? You ready to go?" Festus asked.

"Yeah, I'm ready to shred." Kirk checked the tuning of his guitar and fiddled with the computer keyboard. His fingers were still sore from the day before, but he felt confident in his ability to play the song.

"Are you sure you're okay with this?" Mona stood behind Kirk with her hands on his bare shoulders.

"I'm cool, thanks." Kirk mustered a smile.

"Well then, I'm going outside," Mona said. "I don't want to go on the same trip I did before."

"We'll catch up with you later," Festus yelled after his daughter. "Doctor Q., you might want to put on that ear protection we provided for you. I don't want to be responsible if anything crazy happens to your genius mind."

Doctor Q. nodded and placed a headset over his ears.

Kirk strummed a few power chords to test the volume and tone of his guitar rig. The heavy-sounding riffs blasted through the warehouse. He watched Festus and Helmut jump at the abrupt and loud sound, while Doctor Q. didn't seem to notice. Kirk smiled, wishing his riffing would blow the assholes out the door.

Kirk's warehouse guitar rig consisted of four hot-rodded Mesa-Boogie amp heads hooked up to eight Marshall speaker cabinets placed in stacks of two. The stacks were placed near each wall, along with a small rack of outboard gear, adding to the overall guitar tone.

Kirk had brought the least expensive pieces of guitar gear he owned. He hated the thought of any of his amps exploding to smithereens. He also felt anger about his prized and original ESP signature model burning up. Kirk now held an inexpensive stock model, not caring if it was sacrificed.

"The program's ready to run. Prepare yourselves." Kirk used the mouse to click the Play button on the monitor. The four-count clicks played over the PC speakers, then the musical notes began running across the screen.

Kirk began playing the song.

The first measure started with the passion and fury of a man making homicidal love to his instrument. Kirk went into an instant trance as the music took over his mind and body. He delivered each sinister time change and progression with the sonic subtlety of a thermonuclear strike.

Kirk's breathing and heart rate slowed, his eyes rolled back into his head, his teeth clenched, and his brain slipped into a place where the kingdoms of dark and light collided. Though his mind was filled with activity and his hands moved at incredible speed across the fingerboard, he felt his brain registering delta waves like someone in a deep dream.

The music possessed Kirk like it had the first time he performed it. He saw himself crucified on the giant guitar in the battlefield of Armageddon. He saw Helmut and Festus leading armies of evil, while the armies of divine light charged toward their foes. In his dark visions, Kirk turned his face to the heavens and screamed while the music played on like the soundtrack for the End Time.

Kirk felt himself entering the minds of the men in the room. He first saw things through Doctor Q. He knew the doctor couldn't hear anything. Kirk saw himself through the doctor's eyes, feeling Doctor Q. monitoring medical equipment, checking the measurement of Kirk's electrical activity on an oscilloscope and watching Kirk's body doing strange things. He felt the doctor's confusion, Kirk seeing himself convulsing and twisting while his heart rate, breathing and brain acted as if he was asleep. He read the doctor's thoughts as Doctor Q. wondered what diabolic forces were at work, and Kirk felt the pinch of fear in the doctor's heart.

Then Kirk left Doctor Q. as he continued to play. He shifted into Festus's thoughts. Kirk saw himself through the billionaire's eyes, Kirk looking upon himself in wonder as he attacked his guitar with ferocious elegance. He felt Festus shaking with sanity-straining emotions. Kirk sharing Festus's thoughts, knowing Baustone had cancer and knowing the pain in Baustone's tumor-ridden legs had vanished. Kirk, as Festus, was now overcome with fear and a burning lust. Kirk began screaming, forcing Festus to scream, as Kirk witnessed Festus's mind flooding with inexplicable visions.

Kirk's mind jumped from Festus, the guitarist now finding himself entering the horrors in Helmut's mind. He discovered Hartkopff was also on his way into Hell. Kirk saw Helmut riding alongside Festus upon dead steeds of bone and mummified flesh. Kirk saw smoke pouring from the empty eye sockets and nostrils of the Hell-horses as they galloped without touching the ground, leading the legions of Hell into the final battle of good and evil. Kirk watched the two mortals ride, leading hordes of underworld terrors.

Kirk realized the two men made one half of the four horsemen of the Apocalypse. Festus rode a red steed. and he was War, while Helmut, as Conquest, rode a white horse and wore an Egyptian headband as an unholy, golden crown. Kirk experienced Helmut's delight at seeing Hitler, Rommel and his father, Baldus, flanking him along with Festus and the other two black-robed and skeletal horsemen representing Famine and Death on their black and pale mounts.

Kirk returned to himself while continuing his frenzied performance. Through third-person vision, he saw his hands move in a blur of motion while his body convulsed. He saw the speakers beginning to expand and contract. He saw lights and electronic instruments flickering, and felt the warehouse shaking.

Then the guitar music became more extreme, taking on more sinister, inhuman tones. Voices of the damned mixed with the guitar music, becoming audible through the speakers. The voices of Hell harmonized with the notes, and Kirk knew this not as his song, but rather as Satan's guitar music.

Satan, the self-proclaimed "God of this World" *was* the music, note for note. Kirk felt the performance released the great devil and his throngs from whatever Gehenna chasm they simmered in.

In Kirk's mind, the world was going to end as two armies attacked for the reward of Earth. Just as the forces of good and evil were ripping into each other, Kirk ended the song on the same ultra-brutal and catastrophic power chord. He saw everything in this Judgment Day realm turn white and become vaporized.

At the same time, in the parallel mortal world of the warehouse, Kirk struck the final apocalyptic power chord. The three simultaneous notes released a sonic detonation that blew out all the windows and doors of the warehouse and sent small tremors through the ground.

The surge protectors melted as blue lightning shot through the electronic equipment and through all the men inside. Kirk felt the electrodes fly off his body, torn away by unseen forces. He saw it all. Doctor Q. blown across the warehouse. Festus and Helmut picked up by unseen hands and shaken in midair like rag dolls before being thrown into a sheet metal wall. Speaker cabinets and amp heads exploded, while all video, audio, and medical equipment fried out.

His guitar flew from his hands. It soared across the room and *screamed* before hitting a wall and bursting into flames. The power chord rang on with sinister sustain, and Kirk, in his exhausted mind and spirit, felt the presence of pure evil filling every molecule within the room, as if adhering to the dust and smoke in the warehouse.

Kirk fell to the floor and curled up in the fetal

position. He lay bleeding, retching, and covered in sweat. He saw Doctor Q. groaning on the floor and watched as Festus and Helmut, looking intoxicated, attempted to get back on their feet.

Kirk's vision blurred with Armageddon scenes. He wasn't sure if he was still in the warehouse or stuck somewhere between the Messiah and the Antichrist. He realized he was on mortal ground, hearing the warehouse creaking before half of it collapsed. The building opened up, releasing the sound of feedback and clouds of smoke into the clear sky. Kirk smelled electricity in the air. He also smelled the odor of burnt flesh and saw rats littering the floor in dead, smoking piles.

The dust and smoke cleared out, revealing the destruction. Through it all, Kirk's eyes fluttered, and he refocused to see Mona and the two Baustone thugs coughing and sneezing as they entered the building. Mona ran up to Kirk and looked him over. He felt himself falling in and out of consciousness.

Mona helped Kirk sit up. Donny and Mr. Jaspers assisted Festus and Helmut, getting them up again while Doctor Q. helped himself into a chair.

"Well, it seems this song's living up to all the hype," Festus said as he wiped dirt and blood from his suit and face.

"I told you," Helmut said. "Did you see what I saw?"

"Yeah, I saw...some terrible things," Festus said, walking away from Helmut and over to Mona and Kirk.

Mona squatted next to Kirk, stroking his forehead. He tried to speak but only produced moans as Armageddon scenes flashed in his head with echoes of the music he'd performed.

"Is he all right?" Festus said.

"I'm not sure," Mona said. "He's breathing normally. But he keeps passing out."

"Can you revive him?"

"Do I look like a fucking doctor?" Mona retorted, snapping loudly in Kirk's ear. "He needs medical attention. I hope you're happy."

"Oh, I'm happy, all right. Your boy did a fine job." Festus was smiling now. "He doesn't need medical attention, honey. All he needs is a little rest, and he'll be good as new."

Kirk wanted to give Festus a good "Fuck off", but he was too weak to even spit. He watched Festus, seeing the rich man looking around at the burning equipment, studying the damaged walls and ceiling of the warehouse, the still-standing parts appearing ready to cave in.

Festus turned back toward Kirk. He went into a coughing fit before saying, "Let's pack you up before we all die in here. Can't afford that. Not when I've got to use you for so many important things."

Chapter 15
Family Ties

"Watch how you handle him, dammit," Mona said, concerned and angry with the rough way Donny and Mr. Jaspers carried Kirk out of the decimated warehouse. They ignored her, placing Kirk in the limousine without any care. Mona pushed her way past the thugs and slid into the limo next to Kirk, joining her father and his entourage. Within the hour, the limo arrived at the Vaisto estate and Mona exited with a semiconscious Kirk, getting him on his shaky legs.

"Be sure you take care of him," Festus said from the window of the limo parked outside the gate of Kirk's mansion. "We're heading to New York. Going to sort some things out, and then we're coming back to finish what we started."

"You're done with him now, understand?" Mona felt a rage toward her father like she'd never known.

"You've heard the song. You proved the music's got great power. He performed it. That's what you wanted. Done."

"It's a breakthrough. But we need to—how shall I say?—*extend* the terms of our agreement with Mr. Vaisto."

"You can't be serious. He can't play this song again. It'll kill him. It'll kill all of us. Whatever you and Mengele over there have in mind, it's wrong."

Helmut glared at her with eyes looking ready to pop out of his horror face. The mask of shiny, swirly, and scorched flesh made Mona hold her tongue as the former Hitler Youth creeped the bejesus out of her.

"My dear, you've got no idea what we've got in mind. Once you see the light, this'll all make sense."

"You're crazy."

"Always had a soft spot for those rocker-types, didn't you?" Festus smirked. "You really like this guy?"

"I like him just fine, but that's not the point." Mona felt strange, awkward, defending a man for the first time in her life. "You can't use people like tools."

"You should be proud of our family. This Baustone empire is built upon electronics. You probably don't even give a shit about our history." Festus shook his head. "Thaddeus Baustone's patents on crucial electronic parts for the first telephones and radios made our name. My grandpa patented electronic parts for the first automobiles. He went on to patent generators, then car batteries. This all sent us up and away. Your own grandfather produced the first televisions, circuit boards, and electronic operating systems for NASA. You know that? When Grandpa died of a massive stroke back in 1980, I carried on the electronics tradition with microchips and computers. I started that damn record label just to make *you* happy, but you didn't care. Spoiled brat."

"There's lots I don't care about." Mona wasn't impressed with her father. He was right; she didn't give a shit about her family's history or their great wealth. She knew enough about it from her grandmother and what she saw around her while growing up and working for her father. To her it was all a bore. "I definitely don't care about you, Dad. You suck. You're cruel. You should be in prison or fucking dead about now."

"Let me tell you something." Festus spoke with a cold and serious voice. He pointed a large finger at her. "Our family didn't get where we are by being nice. Your great-great-great fucking granddad got the ball rolling. He used everyone possible to make him rich. I maintain our power and wealth by using everyone. I eliminate anybody who gets in my way. I've kicked old people out of their homes and cheated on your mother to seal a deal. I do what I've got to do. Baustones do what it takes to succeed."

Tears welled up in Mona's eyes. Hearing her dad talk about her mother in such a way sickened her. "I'm ashamed to be your daughter. When're you going to put *me* up for sale?"

Festus rolled his eyes. "I've given you everything you could ever want and more."

"You've given me everything. Sure. Except love." Mona tried controlling her voice, but failed. "All the material shit means nothing."

"That's what Grandma was for."

"You make me hate you."

"Hey. Remember, I'll always be your father, hate me or not. Now do as I say and don't cross me. You don't ever want to cross me."

Kirk moaned something and tried to walk as Mona held him up. She looked up, wanting to give her father a piece of her mind, but Festus never gave her a chance as his automatic window rolled up and the limousine took off into the evening.

"Fuck you, Dad," she said to the departing limo. "Fuck you and the horse you rode in on."

Chapter 16
Metal Heart

Kirk woke in his dark bedroom. It looked like the day was turning to night. He sat up, finding himself naked under the sheets. He saw Mona sitting on the edge of the bed, looking down at him with an expression of concern. "What's up?" Kirk's body felt full of sleep, and he ached all over.

"You've been out for a long time. How're you feeling?"

"Exhausted and sore." Kirk began remembering where he'd been before passing out. "That song beat the shit outta me. The visions and the emotions got worse this time. Felt more real. More evil...getting closer. How's everyone else?"

"Who cares? I wish they'd all get abducted."

"The feeling's mutual."

Mona stared at him and smiled. It warmed him, and he reached for her hand. He looked into her curious face. "What?"

"Nothing. Just looking." She bit her bottom lip. "I want to know about you. Tell me."

"Tell you? Okay." Kirk tried to think of where to start. "Well, I was born in Brooklyn in 1968. My parents migrated from Avellino, Italy, as teenagers. They had five kids, including me. They raised us to speak both English and Italian. I'm the youngest. My sibs are ten to fifteen years older."

"How'd you become this godlike guitarist?"

"When I was two, my working-class parents left me in the care of my mother's sister, Mia. Mia's a folk singer and a free spirit who lived with us for a while. During the day, Mia babysat me, and at night she'd play at coffeehouses all over New York City."

"Oh, so you're not the only talented one in the family?"

"Not by a long shot. Mia was and still is an amazing artist. She'd play me Italian and English folk songs on her twelve-string acoustic guitar. The twelve-string was too large for me, but I was undaunted. Did my best to get my little hands and fingers around the neck and work the damn frets."

Mona giggled. "Cute. I like that. Go on."

Kirk squeezed Mona's hand, enjoying the talk. "One morning Mia gave me a miniature, six-stringed acoustic guitar and began showing me how to play. As I was learning the alphabet, I was also playing music on the guitar. By age three, my small fingers built up calluses and fluidity. I surprised the shit outta my parents and Mia when I started playing songs from Mia's favorite albums and songs off the radio, all by ear."

"You were a freaking natural."

"That's what I've always heard." Kirk thought about his evolution from child to Rock and Roll Hall of Fame inductee. "I went from a Brooklyn boy to crossing the bridge and playing Madison Square Garden in a short time, if you think about it."

"Wow, the Garden." She smiled again, wider. "I saw so many killer shows there. Pink Floyd, Iron Maiden, Metallica, Slipknot. I saw you up there, rock star."

"Yeah, that venue was a dream come true. I invited my whole family and childhood friends from my Brooklyn neighborhood when I played my first two sold-out shows at the Garden with Cardinal Slynn." Kirk remembered those unforgettable, life-changing, career-changing concerts. "Y'know, I saw my first concert at the Garden when I was nine. Aunt Mia took me to see KISS. Our seats were cheap and far in the back of the venue, and I was totally blown away. When I finally graced the Garden stage and played my ten-minute solo, I dedicated my spot to the people sitting in the shitty seats of Madison Square Garden. That was where I first felt musical magic. Hell, yeah."

"Your aunt must've been proud of you, huh?"

"Totally. Mia and my whole family. It was surreal. I had tears in my eyes during both of those first shows there. Crying like a baby. The New York concerts at the Garden were a homecoming of enormous proportions. Every time I played New York after that debut, it was a great occasion. My family and friends...everyone saw how far I came. Shit, I just wanted to do something my mom could brag about."

Mona frowned, looking as if her nostalgic spell was broken.

"What's wrong?"

"When you mentioned New York, it reminded about my dad. He and his crew flew back to New York. Dad said they'll be coming back. Sorry."

"Coming back?" Kirk was flabbergasted. "Fuck that. I'm done. I've done everything I was supposed to."

Mona got up, walked around the bed, and climbed in with him, holding him beneath the covers. "Dad and Helmut have gotten a taste of that song's black magic and they're hungry for more."

"What else could they want?" Kirk felt weary. "That music...that song's a sickness. Y'know, if their recordings are intact, they'll be able to listen to it any time they want. My obligations are over."

"He's not going to make it easy. My dad's got something more in store for you."

"Great, I can only imagine."

"I'm sorry he's like this. I'm ashamed and embarrassed."

"Well, he did one thing right." Kirk pulled Mona closer. "He made you."

"Oh, shut up." Mona blushed and kissed him.

"You wanna have a little fun?" Kirk kicked the sheets off his naked body.

"God. Aren't you tired?"

"Not too tired for you." Kirk began kissing Mona's neck.

Mona made little animal sounds before saying, "Okay, let's do this." She got up and stripped out of her two-day-old skirt and blouse before crawling to him and straddling him as he rested on his back. They kissed and explored each other.

"Make love to me." Mona began sliding him into her with slow and deliberate ease.

"I don't know how to make love." He knew this was a true confession, thinking lovemaking was an art for some celluloid heartthrob. He felt himself penetrating her wet heat. "I just know how to fuck."

"Haven't you ever been in love?"

"Not really. I mean, maybe with music and guitars. Never with anyone special."

"Maybe you can learn. Got to start slow."

"I'll try," Kirk said as Mona came down, driving him all the way inside.

Chapter 17
Ticket to Hell

Festus and Helmut sat in a small conference room inside Festus's private jet while it was prepped and fueled at an airstrip near Malibu.

Baustone felt exhilarated, full of hope and also full of foreboding. He and Helmut had just finished reviewing the previous day's video and audio recordings of Kirk's warehouse performance of the Song of Sethis. Festus watched with awe and surprise, seeing Helmut and himself thrash around on the screen. He gasped at the damage done to the equipment and also when the video revealed what appeared as smoky forms of demonic apparitions.

The audio recordings of the baleful guitar music

blared through the surround-sound stereo. The music again filled Festus with terror and lust. He thought he heard tortured cries mixed in the notes and feedback.

When the video and audio material reached the musical climax, the television exploded and the stereo fried. The room filled with piercing white noise and the smell of burnt wiring, forcing the pilot to override the alarm system.

"Good thing we didn't watch this while we were in the air." Festus rubbed his temples. "My God, that was unreal."

"Yes. Amazing." Helmut sounded weak and drained. "It's beyond anything I could imagine. It's the key to Armageddon."

"Armageddon. That's what I keep wondering about."

"Skeptical, Festus? Not after this."

"No, no. The supernatural imagery and forces that possessed us were very convincing. We're dealing with power here, no doubt, but I'm just wondering how this power will destroy mankind and give us the biblical Judgment Day you keep raving about. All I've seen is visions in my head and damage done to guitar gear and a warehouse. Right now the music's only been an apocalypse for high-end audio and guitar equipment."

"These performances are just tiny preludes to what's really in store when this song is played for the entire world. Aknaseth's prophecies mentioned the Song of Sethis—Satan's song—must be played for the entire world to hear. Once Earth is shaken by the music of Satan, Heaven and Hell will be called out to do battle and bring forth Judgment Day."

"How're we supposed to make the entire world hear this at the same time? We've only got one guitarist."

"I'm surprised you haven't already thought of it."

Then it hit Festus and he erupted with laughter. "Of course. We perform the song live, via satellite. My BauStar satellites can deliver televised transmissions to every country, on every goddamn continent. It's brilliant!"

"I've got an idea on how we can set it all up."

"Let me hear it." Festus grabbed a cigar. "Dammit. Don't worry, I won't smoke in here."

"First of all, location's important. We need to have the song performed in Egypt."

"Why there? We could just as well do it in the United States. Like a regular Pay-Per-View concert. Hell, I own some of the biggest arenas in the country. We'll do it at Baustone Arena in Dallas."

"No. We need to do it in Egypt. That's where the power of the music will be strongest. We should have the performance done right on the very site of Aknaseth's pyramid and temple. It's there that Aknaseth envisioned the battle of good and evil."

"Fine by me." Festus thought of more ideas. "I've got an idea how we can pull this off, and we'll look like we're doing mankind a favor."

Helmut laughed. "A favor? Festus, we'll be condemning every mortal soul to death once this performance is complete. You've got a sick sense of humor."

"What I've got in mind is this." Festus got up and pain exploded in his legs as he walked around the table. With a groan, he continued. "I'll unveil Aknaseth's pyramid and temple to the whole world on live television. I'll give the world a firsthand look at a long-lost pyramid no one's ever seen." Festus gestured with his unlit cigar. "All made possible by me."

"You mean *us*."

"Of course I do. I'd never take all the credit." *Nazi bastard*. He wanted to put Helmut in his place, but held back.

"How do you plan on tying the unveiling of the pyramid in with Kirk Vaisto playing the song?"

"It's easy. As part of the live show, Kirk Vaisto will be a special guest who'll perform an ancient song found in the pyramid of Aknaseth—a song no one's ever heard before. We'll offer a new wonder of the world and a live concert to boot. We need to get started right away." Festus moved in pain and bit into his cigar. "I'll get crews together, start setting up a huge stage with lights. Get us a giant, state-of-the-art sound system that'll blow away anything that's been used in concert before." Festus began feeling excitement at the thought of it all. "There'll be a live audience in Egypt. A festival. I'll have cameras and satellite feeds covering every aspect of the performance."

"What about the tests on Vaisto? What were the results?"

Festus walked over to a manila envelope on the conference room table. He opened it and pulled out long, computer-printed papers covered with chart lines.

"I can't make heads or tails of this crap." Festus scanned the notes on the papers. "Doctor Q. explains here that some remarkable things happened in Kirk Vaisto's body when he played the song."

"Like what?"

"Let's see...okay, when Vaisto first started the song, his breathing and heartbeat were cranking up with nervous energy." Festus deciphered Doctor Q's chicken scratch. "His brain idled on alpha waves occurring from seven to twelve cycles per second. Then he immediately fell into super-deep delta waves that read at one to three cycles per second."

"But that's like being in a coma."

"Yeah, that's what Doc says. But as we saw, Kirk Vaisto was playing that song like a maniac." Festus scratched his scalp. "His hands were moving at light speed. I don't know how to explain it."

Helmut appeared to be lost in thought. The raisin-like slits he had for eyelids blinked and he said, "All I know is that the song possesses Kirk Vaisto and takes over his entire body in order to make the music fulfill its purpose. The same could be said for us. When we listened to that song, we lost control of our minds and bodies."

"Says here that Vaisto's breathing slowed to almost nothing. His heartbeats dropped to three or four a minute."

"It would seem impossible, especially with the intense physical activity he produces when performing the Song of Sethis. It's as if his brain works with his heart and lungs in one world, while his hands and fingers are doing their own thing somewhere else."

"I've heard of something similar to this before." Festus took a seat at the table. "I've read about people who've claimed to see apparitions of Jesus or the Virgin Mary. When these people had their encounters, their heartbeats dropped and their brains produced the same kind of delta waves."

"*Ja*. It seems in order for us to comprehend the power and imagery of God or Satan, the human condition must be altered in order for the mortal mind to accept their true forms."

"Hmm, maybe. All I know for sure is we've got a lot of work to do in a short amount of time."

"*Ja, ja.* Like getting Kirk Vaisto to perform our song for the entire world."

"Getting Vaisto to perform won't be a problem. I'll offer him and his agent a mountain of money."

"And if he says no?"

"Then I'll have to get rough."

Helmut ran his pink, unburnt tongue over his bare teeth. "Good."

"I'm going to fly back to New York to get this titanic production off the ground. You're staying in Malibu with Donny and Mr. Jaspers. I've got work for you here."

"Moving fast is key. It has to be done right." Helmut sounded too anxious for Festus's liking. "When do you think the performance will happen?"

"Apocalypse now? Or tomorrow? Won't be long, worrywart." Festus lit up his cigar. *Fuck the crew. I own this goddamn jet.* He blew smoke into Helmut's face and said, "Within days, Armageddon will be televised."

Chapter 18
Speak of the Devil

Kirk and Mona woke up in the early afternoon. Mona had spent the entire night teaching him the difference between making love and fucking, and he'd been happy to learn.

"So what're you going to do now?" He was in a bathrobe, sitting at the kitchen table drinking coffee with Mona.

"A limo's on its way here to take me back to my hotel suite. The first thing I'm going to do is take a nice, long bath. I need fresh clothes. Don't forget, you owe me new panties. I don't like going commando, pal. I ain't Britney Spears."

Kirk laughed. "Sorry I've held you hostage for so long."

"I'm a willing hostage." Mona smiled. "What're you going to do for the rest of the day?"

"First thing I've gotta do is call Grainy, tell him I'm not going to be able to finish my solo album until my studio's rebuilt. I just wish I'd finished before I met Helmut Hartkopff or your old man."

"Sorry."

"Ah, don't worry about it. I trust I'm getting that damage check from your dad, so I'll rebuild. As for the solo work, I'll get it done soon enough."

"What're you going to do when my dad shows up again and wants you to do something else?"

"I'll cross that bridge when I come to it." Kirk sipped his coffee. "I'm calling my agent this afternoon. Gonna tell Yaggerwood I'm not doing any more work for your old man. If I've gotta take legal action, I will. Dear ol' Dad's gotta realize he can't always get what he wants."

"I know, but he'll never see that. He's got blinders on. He thinks he can conquer the world with money."

"Well, he can't conquer me. I'm not gonna stand for any of his bullshit. He can't push me around or buy my life."

"Guess he wouldn't make a good father-in-law, huh?"

Kirk almost spit out a mouthful of coffee. "What was that?"

Mona giggled. "Just kidding. I'm not looking to get married."

"That's good. I'd hate to have your old man after me to marry you. His idea of a shotgun wedding probably involves a nuclear warhead."

"Do you think you'll ever settle down?"

"Shit...not sure. I've been a bachelor so long, I don't know what I'd do with a wife."

"Well, first you've got to fall in love with someone."

Mona smiled. "You still need to learn what that's like."

Kirk smirked. "I guess if I ever tied the knot, I'd do it quick. Vegas style. Though my mother would never let me get away with that. She'd insist on a huge, Italian wedding."

"I envy you. I've never had a real family. My dad's not even good enough to call a friend." Mona sniffled, then tilted her head back as if to contain her tears, but they rolled out of her eyes and down her face without restraint.

"Hey, it's okay, hon." Kirk got up and put his arms around Mona. "You've got me. I promise you that."

Mona smiled and wiped away the tears. "Thanks, Kirk. You're such a sweetheart. I don't mean to lay all this heavy shit on you."

"I'm cool with it. You're a good person. I know you've tried to love your old man. It sucks not getting that back."

"Yeah. Y'know, I try to be professional and help him out so he'll be happy with me. I thought if I worked for him, we'd get closer, but he just uses me. He talks down to me all the time. He treats his secretary better than me."

"That's his loss. If your old man can't appreciate his daughter's love, then he's a loser. The richest man in the world can't see you're his greatest treasure."

"You've got a lot of heart for a rock star."

"I'm full of surprises." He kissed her.

Mona laughed and kissed Kirk back. "Thanks."

"Are you really going back to New York?" Kirk broke the embrace and sat next to Mona.

"Yeah, I was planning on going back today. I need to pack up my office and shut it down. I'm not working for my father anymore."

"What'll you do for work?"

"Not sure. I've got a huge trust fund in my name. I can live off that for the rest of my life. I'd like to either go back to college or do something in the entertainment biz. Either way, I'm breaking away from Dad."

"Well, I'm thinking of dumping my agent. Maybe you could be my personal manager."

"I'd like that. Maybe we can work something out."

"Listen, why don't you hold off on going back to New York? Your old man's not exactly in a sane frame of mind. It might be a good idea if you steered clear of him for a while."

"What do you suggest I do?"

"You can hang with me." Kirk smiled. "I'd like to take a break myself. I can't finish my album on account of my studio being destroyed, and I need some time to recuperate."

"Are you thinking...vacation?"

"What d'ya think about Maui?"

"I love Maui." Mona's face brightened.

"Me, too. What do you say we fly out there tomorrow and stay at a resort for a couple weeks? I'm buying."

"Say no more. I'm in."

"Excellent. I'll call my travel agent this afternoon and get everything booked."

"Wow. I need this. I've got to go shopping, though. I don't have enough clothes or girlie things at my hotel for a vacation."

"By all means, go get what you need. If we book a flight for tomorrow, you'll have plenty of time to shop today."

"Shopping and vacationing. I'm such a lucky girl."

Mona giggled. "What are you going to do?"

"I'm gonna salvage what I can from my studio. Then I'm hanging loose."

"I was wondering something."

"Go for it."

"Are you at all disappointed that you're not playing that song again?"

"Fuck, no. I don't want anything to do with it." Kirk figured he'd rather get the Ebola virus than jam Sethis's tune again. "At first, I was eager to see what the song was like, but it only took the pluck of a string to see the music is diseased. Pure terror. Pure evil manifested in every note and lick. I think I know its purpose now, and that's another reason I'll never play it again."

"Purpose?"

"Yeah." The earlier images rose unbidden in his mind. "The last time I played the song, it all came to me. The music told me everything."

"What?"

"Many things. I have a spiritual and a scientific take on it."

"Give me both."

Kirk set his coffee mug down and collected his thoughts. "Okay, it's like this, and you're gonna have to have an open mind."

"I'm with you."

"First, on a spiritual level, this music possessed my body, mind, and soul. It controlled me, used me to bring itself out into the world. The music took me away and I transcended the human realm."

"There's no way to stop it?"

"Not that I know of. Once I start playing the song, it takes over. I don't think even an exorcist could help anyone once the music gets in the driver's seat."

"Where'd the music come from?"

"Crazy as this sounds, the music came from Hell. Satan wrote it thousands of years ago. The song is his key to walk the Earth, and his tool to destroy it. Earth is actually Satan's domain, but he's not free to walk his property. He's locked down below the netherworld crust until the door opens. In ancient Egypt, Satan was called Sethis. They're both the same dude."

"Wait. Helmut didn't mention any of this?"

"No, it was the fucking song. Like I said, the music showed me all this."

"Why does Satan need to use a song to walk on Earth? Wouldn't he just be able to come up and do his evil work any time he wanted?"

"Doesn't seem like it. The warden's got a different plan. Satan's supposed to be the greatest liar and trickster ever created. He wrote the song and used a weak pharaoh to prepare it for play. Playing the music opens the gate, but the pharaoh failed. Satan's an impatient bitch. He wants his feet on mortal soil. The music can make that happen, once it's blasted loud enough for Earth to hear. Then we all die."

"My grandma taught me the Bible. I know the Book of Revelation mentions seven angels who're supposed to blow trumpets that'll sound and bring forth great devastation upon the wicked people of the world. Maybe that's what this guitar music's going to do, but in Satan's favor."

"If I remember right, only God can set Satan free. This song's a key that unlocks God's hold on the gates of Hell. This music gives Satan his chance to take over the world before God can come down and pass judgment on us all. Satan had an ace up his sleeve when he was cast down."

"You sure you're not a closet Christian?"

"Music's my only religion." Kirk paused, remembering the darkness he'd been forced to face. "This song's shown me terrible things. I see an army of darkness doing battle with an army from the heavens as Satan tries making Earth his own forever."

"Have you seen anything else?"

Kirk thought about how he saw Conquest and War embodied in Festus and Helmut, two horsemen of the Apocalypse riding with Famine and Death, leading the armies of Hell across a global battlefield. Kirk saw himself crucified to a giant guitar. The replays of countless and unspeakable images tore through his mind like a sharp bone saw. He didn't want to share any of it.

"Nothing else I can recall," Kirk said. "Seeing Armageddon's bad enough."

"Do you believe everything the song showed you?"

"What I saw was either some very frightening hallucinations or prophecies of things to come. If what I saw is really gonna go down, then the end of the world's coming. Real or not, the music scared the shit outta me."

"What's your scientific angle?"

"Well, I'd say the damage to the studio, to the warehouse, and the shaking we felt might've been caused by the physics of sound."

"Like extreme sound waves or something?"

"Yeah, somethin' like that. When you snap your fingers, or when I play a guitar chord, that creates pressure. That pressure forces itself against air molecules and creates energy. That mechanical energy's transformed into sound waves in the air. Sound waves move at about 1,100 feet per second in air and even faster in liquids and solids."

"The energy of sound waves can cause the destruction we've seen?"

"I've seen glass break and ceiling tiles fall because the sound waves were so intense from our PA system and amps. In fact, Cardinal Slynn made the *Guinness Book of World Records* for being the loudest band in the world."

"There's an accomplishment." Mona laughed.

"Hey, if you're gonna be the baddest band in the land, you'd better be the loudest. As they say, if it's too loud, you're too old."

"Ah, the philosophy of heavy metal. Don't make me misty."

"Seriously, though, it's all about the power of sound. Sound waves and amplitude could cause the physical destruction of the warehouse and my gear. This strange music generates extraordinary, overdriven amplitude that bombards objects to the breaking point."

"Maybe it's just magic."

Kirk laughed. "That's as good an explanation as I've heard."

"I've got a thought."

"What's that?"

"If music communicates, and it's thought that Satan speaks in many tongues—"

"Yeah?"

"—then maybe this music's another, unique tongue Satan uses to communicate with us."

Kirk thought about the idea. "Cool theory, though it sounds frighteningly like a Tipper Gore/PMRC press release."

Mona laughed.

"I think Satan's made it clear what he wants to tell us," he said.

"I don't want to know."

"Me either." Kirk spoke as a shiver chilled him. "That song's best left alone. If I had those texts and the disc with the sheet music, I'd destroy it all. I won't play it. No one ever should. Festus will have to kill me first."

"I wouldn't let him do that." Mona got up from the kitchen table to sit on Kirk's lap.

"You're gonna be my bodyguard?"

"Of course. I'd hate to have anything happen to your bod." Mona gave him a gentle kiss.

Kirk nibbled on her bottom lip and whispered, "You in the mood for some afternoon delight?"

"Mmmm, I'd love that, but I really need to get going." Mona frowned and stuck out her bottom lip. "I need to get to my suite, then I've got shopping to do."

"You're really gonna quit the old man's business?" Kirk rested his face in the nape of her neck.

"Yep, this is it. I'm not only leaving his business, I'm going to disown him."

"But he's your father. You can't really change that."

"Oh, I will." Mona stood up. "Like I told you, I'm just a collectible to him."

Kirk stood up and walked her to the door. At the gate, the limousine waited and the driver got out, holding the door for Mona.

"When will you be back?" Kirk held her hands, not wanting to let go.

"If you're good, I'll be back sooner than not." Mona smiled and added, "But if you're bad, I'll be back even faster."

"Oh, I'll be bad."

"Expect me with all my bags by tomorrow

morning."

"Sounds good. I'm booking our trip after you leave. I'll try to nail a flight for tomorrow afternoon. I can't wait."

"Me either."

Kirk and Mona kissed and held each other for a moment before saying their good-byes.

Kirk watched her limo drive away. He held strong feelings for her, and knew it was more than just great sex. His heart weighed heavy as he closed the front door and felt alone. Love scared him almost as much as the evil in the Song of Sethis.

Chapter 19
Running From the Devil

Kirk booked the Maui trip and spent the rest of his day in his recording studio, cleaning up and taking inventory of all the damaged equipment.

Once the sun began setting, Kirk went inside his house to clean up. He looked forward to a relaxing evening, hoping to get to bed early.

Kirk was out of the shower, damp hair tied back and wearing black sweatpants. He was tired but wanted to play some guitar before going to bed.

He prided himself with practicing every day, a four-hour workout filled with arpeggios and modes, speed runs, and major and minor scales. He spent half his practice time writing new riffs and playing his own original music. Since Mona, Festus, and Helmut came into his life, he hadn't practiced or played anything other than the satanic music of Sethis. His battered fingers were still healing, but he'd practice, regardless. He felt guilty about missing his daily, six-string routine.

Just as Kirk was about to enter the guitar room, he heard his cell phone ringing. He walked down a vast hallway and picked up the cell in his living room.

"Yeah?" Kirk hoped it was Mona.

"Long time no talk, kid."

"Hello, Rod," Kirk's voice registered the disappointment of not hearing Mona on the other end.

"What's wrong? You don't sound happy."

"Just tired." Kirk took a seat on his sofa. "The past couple of days haven't been fun."

"What've you been doing all afternoon? I've left at least a dozen messages on your voice mail."

Kirk clicked on his large flat-screen television, browsing channels as he talked. "I've been cleaning out the remains of my studio. Didn't have my phone in there. I'm glad you called, though. There are a few things I need to talk to you about."

"Sounds good, kid. I've got lots to talk to you about as well. There are some great things coming your way."

Kirk didn't want to hear about deals or offers. "Rod, I'm not doing anything other than my solo project."

"You haven't even heard what I've got to say."

"Does it involve Festus Baustone?"

"As a matter of fact, it does."

"I don't wanna hear it. I'm done with that fucker. Got it?"

"I thought things were fine between you and Baustone. In fact, he said you've been doing a great job."

"You talked to Festus today?"

"Yeah, we had a nice conversation. That's what I

wanna talk about."

"I don't know what Festus told you, but things aren't good between us. I don't like the guy. He's a lunatic. Got me involved in some dangerous shit."

"Dangerous shit? What the hell you talking about?"

Kirk let out a long breath. "It's a long story, Rod. I'll tell you about it later. For right now, you should act like a real agent and respect the wishes of your client. I'm *never* working with Festus Baustone again."

"I respect your wishes, but it's also my job to keep you rich and famous." Rod's voice became louder. "I just accepted the most lucrative deal of your career."

"What d'ya mean, you accepted a deal? Don't tell me you've signed something new with Baustone."

"Correct again."

"What the fuck, Rod? You can't keep doin' deals without checking with me first. I'm not honoring your arrangements."

"Don't you at least wanna hear the offer?"

Kirk remained silent.

"Baustone offered one million to have you play that Egyptian song on a live television broadcast. It'll be seen around the world." Rod's excitement crackled in Kirk's ear. "He wants you to play that song at a special ceremony where he's unveiling a newly discovered pyramid. It's supposedly the greatest find of the new millennium."

"I don't think—"

"I told him you'd do it, but I demanded another five hundred grand, as well as three percent of any Pay-Per-View or rebroadcasting and residual royalties." Rod talked faster. "He agreed and already wired the money into your account, minus my percentage."

"You fucked up. I'm not doing it."

"Hey. This is the biggest, most important gig you'll ever play in your life. Not to mention the most lucrative."

"No way."

"This is what we've worked so hard for. You've got the fame and the fortune, but this is the one show, the one grand, fuck-all performance that goes down in history. This one gig alone will immortalize you."

"What part of *no* don't you understand? I sound like a broken record. How many times do I gotta say that I'm not working for Baustone or playing that fucking song?"

"It's too late for you to back out of this deal now, kid. Everything's signed, sealed, and delivered."

"Bullshit. Give Festus his money back, including your percentage. I'm not covering your slick ass."

"Can I make a suggestion?"

"What?"

"Turn on your TV."

"It's already on."

"Turn to CNN. Quick."

Kirk clicked his remote control to the twenty-four hour news station. "You've gotta be fucking kidding me."

On the large-screen television, he saw stock video of himself with images of Festus Baustone and a pyramid. The newswoman was reporting that Festus Baustone would be revealing an Egyptian pyramid no one had seen for more than three thousand years. She said Baustone would be presenting the find to every country in the entire world on live television, and as a bonus, Kirk Vaisto would be performing an ancient song in a live concert at the pyramid.

Kirk watched in horror as Festus stepped in front of

a microphone at a news conference.

He spoke with pseudo goodwill, explaining how he'd share his discovery with the world. He said he'd bring the live broadcast and Kirk's performance to the world for free, carried on every network, television station, and terrestrial and satellite radio station he owned worldwide.

It was happening two days from now.

"This is insane." Kirk watched the news clip end. "I don't care if all the stations in the world carry this news flash. I'm not playing one fucking lick."

"You'll get nothing but bad press if you back out of this concert. It's gonna hurt your career."

"What's this?" Kirk was yelling now. "Entrapment? Just 'cause you and Festus dropped my name doesn't mean I'm obligated to do shit. My fans'll understand if I don't do the gig."

"And if they don't?"

"Fuck 'em!" Kirk didn't mean it. He loved his fans, but he didn't like being pushed. "It's my life, Rod, and I'm not livin' it for anyone else."

"If you don't do it, Baustone's gonna fuck us hard." Rod's voice sounded cold. "I won't be able to stop him. He's got lawyers you can't imagine. C'mon, kid, I've known you for too long. I *know* you wanna do this."

The dark melody of the song rang in Kirk's mind. It iced his flesh and nauseated him.

"Hey, we need to talk, kid." Rod's voice sounded panicked. "Baustone's calling me tonight to follow up and make sure you're with the program. When I tell him you're not cool with it, he's gonna get rough."

Kirk laughed. "Yeah, I know you've seen Festus Baustone's mean side. Jack Slynn told me all about it."

"What did you say?"

"You're fired, Rod. I'm done with you and Sterling Stars. You'll get my written notice in the mail."

"Goddammit!" Rod screamed like a hawk into the phone. "Listen to me, kid…"

"Don't call me kid, you money-grubbing asshole. I'm almost forty, for Christ's sake."

Kirk hung up, letting out a loud, "Fuck!" to his spacious living room. He was burnt out, stressed, and longed for the vacation with Mona.

Yaggerwood called non-stop after Kirk hung up on him, and Kirk ended up turning his phone off. His main priority was getting out of California. Tomorrow's flight to Maui wasn't soon enough for him.

How ironic to now be in Jack Slynn's shoes—running away from Festus Baustone.

Chapter 20
Stigmata

Kirk awoke in the middle of the night, startled by a loud noise in his bedroom. In the darkness, he made out the shape of someone standing at the foot of his bed.

"Who's there?" Kirk yelled, trying to intimidate the unexpected guest. The intruder scared him. He jumped up in bed and prepared to fight with only a pillow in his hands. "I've got a gun, you sonofabitch."

"Give us light," a man's voice said in Italian.

The bedroom lights came on, and Kirk saw the intruder: a tall, gaunt man with ragged clothes and a clerical collar. Kirk recognized him as the old priest who had approached him in the bathroom of Vampire Sun days earlier.

"What the fuck're you doin' here? How'd you get in my house?" Kirk wondered why his alarm system hadn't gone off.

The man raised his hands and spoke in English with a heavy Italian accent. "I come on behalf of He who liveth and was dead and whom you will behold as living forever. I mean you no harm. I'm here as a messenger, to give you the tools you'll need to fight your enemies, including Satan."

Kirk's heart accelerated. The man seemed crazy. Kirk decided it best to remain cool while he tried to figure out what the old guy wanted. Kirk wanted him out of the house. "I'll give you five minutes to say whatever you want. If I don't like what you've got to say, then I want your ass off my property. Otherwise I'm callin' the cops."

"I've much to tell you. We have little time."

"Again, you've got five minutes." Kirk sat on his bed and studied the stranger with great unease.

"You've been tricked and manipulated by two of Satan's pawns. Festus Baustone and Helmut Hartkopff have tempted the Beast. They've found you...their key to freeing the locks that imprison Satan and his legions. They'll use your musical talent to unleash Hell."

"But, Padre, I'm not gonna do anything for either of those bastards. I've already made it clear to everyone. I'm not ever working for Festus again."

"It's too late to deny Festus or Helmut. They're already bent on having you do their bidding. They'll stop at nothing until they've used you up for their needs. Helmut Hartkopff is a false prophet who wishes to embody Satan, while Festus Baustone is no different than the Whore of Babylon. Like Babylon of old, Festus is powerful and proud. He's most insolent toward all the people of God. His is a heathen world."

"So is my world." Kirk was unimpressed. "Big deal."

"Like the wicked and deceptive Whore of Babylon who made all nations drink of the wine of her fornication, Festus too clouds the mind and eye with the oppressive media that pumps his wickedness into the world, breaking down all moral restraints. Festus urges all to embrace his vision of a godless world, one that worships nothing but his televised programming penetrating every nation." Zacharelli spoke with fierceness in his voice. "But like the Whore of Babylon, he will be overthrown, and he will be turned to dust."

"Yeah, well, while Baustone's being turned to dust, I'm gonna be soaking up some Maui rays. I'm in control of my own destiny. Understand?"

"The laws of man no longer apply to the situation you're in. The laws of good and evil are dictating your fate. It's all part of God's plan."

"God's plan, huh?" Kirk snorted at this. "What's the Almighty got in store for me?"

"This."

Father Antonio Zacharelli bent down and picked up a thin, black, rectangular instrument case at his feet.

"What's that? A guitar?"

Zacharelli placed the case on Kirk's bed. "This is a guitar from God."

A guitar from God for the God of Guitar? Kirk laughed. This was too much. He wondered who played the joke and where the hidden cameras were. He got off the bed and stood next to Zacharelli. "I've gotta see this. You mind?"

"Please. Acquaint yourself with it. The instrument was made for you."

Kirk opened the case, finding an electric guitar inside. He didn't see anything fancy about it. It was made with a strat-style body and featured a bolt-on neck and pointy headstock. There wasn't a brand name or logo anywhere on the instrument. The guitar didn't look painted or finished. Kirk ran a finger over the sanded wood grain.

He looked at the fixed bridge feeding the guitar strings to the black tuning pegs on the headstock. The guitar also had one no-name black and square humbucker pickup with a single volume knob. A standard, quarter-inch cable jack was recessed into the side of the body.

Kirk studied the fingerboard. It looked ordinary, made of a light-colored wood with twenty-four frets. The inlays caught Kirk's attention. They were shaped like crosses and set into nine individual frets across the board. They looked to be made of metal. Kirk admired the craftsmanship. It was simple and beautiful.

"C'mon. Who really made this guitar?"

"The materials are natural, but the instrument was made by God." Zacharelli remained unmoving at the foot of Kirk's bed.

Kirk smiled. "Right. God made a guitar and Jesus built Al Jourgensen's hot rod."

"This is no time to be blasphemous."

"God doesn't make electric guitars. Why would He do that?"

"He made it for you, so you can deliver the world of man from Satan's fury. Though you're to be used as the key to unleashing pure evil—the Antichrist—upon this world, you're also the one who possesses the power to undo Satan's work. You can send the devil back into the abyss. You alone can conquer the legions of evil with this instrument. By the grace of God."

"With a guitar?"

"Yes, and when you play God's guitar, you will be 'in the spirit', as John was when God spoke to him on the Lord's Day. God will speak to you with a golden clarity that will move you in profound ways, and He will convey His power from Heaven through you, channeling it through this guitar when you have it in your hands." Zacharelli's voice was smooth and gentle. "Like the Ark of the Covenant, this guitar is a testament, a symbol of God keeping His gracious promise to deliver us all from evil. Like the harps of angels, this guitar is an instrument of God because He created it and it will be used in His glory."

"And what exactly am I gonna play on this guitar?" Kirk strummed the instrument.

"You will play a song. A song like the song of Moses and the song of the Lamb, Jesus Christ. You're very much like Moses, as you've been chosen by the Lord to deliver man from the bondage of evil that will arise in Egypt. The music you perform on God's guitar will be Heaven sent."

"Heaven sent? Y'know, I'm really sick of playing other people's shit." Kirk didn't believe what he was hearing. "For fun, say I'm religious. I'm not, but say I am and I believe all of this brimstone. How's a simple axe like this gonna blow away Satan?"

"Don't be deceived by appearances. Tell me, how does it feel in your hands?"

Kirk held the guitar, testing the weight. It felt average, like any other electric guitar. He thought the wood had a different feel, though, and looked different than most guitars he was familiar with. This detail he couldn't explain.

"It feels fine, but I'm not sure what to make of this wood." Kirk examined the guitar with a careful eye.

"Wood for electric guitars is usually mahogany, maple, alder, basswood, or ash. This just looks and feels different."

"It *is* different. That God created the instrument makes it different. The instrument's constructed of palm and cypress, olive and cedar."

"And why would God make a guitar from that stuff?"

"Four pieces of wood make the Holy Cross Christ was crucified on. There's the upright beam and the crossbeam. The other two pieces make the table above the Savior's head and the wooden shelf that Christ's feet rested upon. These woods are palm and cypress, olive and cedar."

"Stop. Don't tell me this thing's made from the Holy Cross. C'mon. The one Christ was crucified on?"

"Yes, that's exactly what I'm telling you. You're holding the Holy Cross in your hands."

"Shit, I've heard everything now," Kirk didn't feel this was worth a laugh or comment. He didn't believe Zacharelli. He looked around the room. Now was the time Ashton Kutcher was supposed to pop out with the camera crew and punk Kirk's ass.

"It's true. The guitar's made from the Holy Cross. The neck is made from the crossbeam. The body is made from the upright beam, which is a symbol for the Divine Ray, possessing the atomic vibration of God. God passes this energy directly down and across all planes." Zacharelli's voice boomed. "Kirk, you shall be a medium, a channel, for this divine power. It will transmit down from God and through you to conquer all evil. As Christ was God incarnate, so shall you be."

"I don't believe you, Padre. My mother's a devout Catholic. She made me go to church every Sunday. I don't remember much from church, but I know the Bible and New Testament never mentioned the original Holy Cross of Christ being made into a guitar."

"In the year 350, Saint Cyril of Jerusalem claimed the Holy Cross of Christ was in the possession of the Roman Catholic Church. Pieces of the Holy Cross were said to be in Cappoacia in the late 370s during the life of St. Macrina, in Antioch in 386, and in Italy and Gaul in 403. Writings in Constantinople give September fourteenth, year of 320 as the date for the discovery of the Holy Cross. But that's not true."

"What's the truth?" Kirk was close to kicking Zacharelli's holy ass out the door. "What d'ya know about the Holy Cross?"

"Everything. The Holy Cross is the most precious relic remaining of the Savior's earthly life. The first Christian Emperor of Rome was Constantine I. In 326, his mother—the Empress, St. Helena—discovered the Holy Cross in Jerusalem. Either by the request of Constantine or by divine inspiration, St. Helena directed excavations on the site of Christ's execution. She uncovered three crosses, as well as the nails that pierced Christ."

"If there were three crosses discovered, then how did she know which cross belonged to Christ?" Kirk felt himself growing more skeptical and weary of all this.

"At first there was no way of telling which was Christ's cross and which were those of the two thieves crucified with Him," Zacharelli explained with broad hand gestures. "The dilemma was solved when the crosses were taken to the bedside of a dying woman. The true Holy Cross was revealed when it miraculously healed her."

"Uh, right. What happened to the Holy Cross after

that?"

"It was eventually taken to one of Helena's palaces, then later hidden in the Church of the Holy Cross in Rome. That's where I went to retrieve the Holy Cross. Now it's your cross to bear...constructed into an electric guitar by God's hands."

"You're a freak, dude." Kirk just couldn't imagine the Holy Cross being in his grip. The most famous relic in the world made into a weapon of riff destruction? He almost laughed. *How absurd is this shit?*

"Tell me, Kirk, what does the Holy Cross mean to you?"

"I guess it's a symbol of Christ. It's definitely the most widely used of Christian signs." Kirk thought about his limited knowledge of the symbol. "I don't know. I'd say it represents the death of God's son?"

"It's an emblem of life over death, of good over evil. The Holy Cross isn't a symbol of the Savior's defeat, but rather of His victory. A symbol of His passing into the divine glory that was His by nature."

"I've gotta tell you again, Padre, I'm not really big on religion. I'm not saying I'm an atheist, but I just don't buy into a lot of Christian stories."

"Do you have any comprehension of faith?"

"Sure. It just depends on what we're talking about." Kirk gave thought to his own beliefs. "I've got faith in lots of things, spiritual and otherwise. As far as a higher power goes, I guess someone or something's up there."

"You must have faith in God. You must believe that Jesus the Savior died for your sins and that He's going to save you. He'll welcome you into Heaven once you leave this mortal world."

"That sounds good, but it's hard to believe."

"Do you believe in atoms?"

"Yeah."

"Molecules?"

"Of course."

"Those are things you don't see, yet they're there. You believe they exist, even though you can't examine them with the naked eye. That's what faith is all about. Molecules and atoms are all around you, and so is God. His presence is everywhere, in the sights you see and in the air you breathe."

"I understand what you're saying, and I wanna believe something created this world and the entire universe. Some force, some great power had to start it all. But I need proof above and beyond what I see around me."

"You *must* believe and you *must* have faith. Once you've established faith within yourself, you can truly embrace the power that God will pass through you and this guitar. Have you ever been baptized?"

"Yeah, not long after I was born."

"Good. Accept God. He's the all-seeing, all-knowing creative force you want to believe in. You want to know what God is and what He looks like, but you'll never comprehend what God truly is until you die. Only then can you grasp His purpose and what He is. That's what the Apocalypse is all about."

"I thought the Apocalypse was all about plagues and death. All that miserable fire and brimstone shit."

"Not completely. Apocalypse is another word for *revelation*. It's an unveiling, a revealing that refers to things that man can never know on his own and which only God can make known to him. Now, as a mortal, you must have faith that He is everything and that He has a very important purpose for you."

Kirk put the guitar back in the case. He looked the instrument over again. He stared at the fingerboard and said, "If God made this, He's quite the craftsman. The metalwork on the inlays is top notch."

"The cross inlays and frets are made from the actual nails that were driven through Jesus Christ. That very metal nailed Him to the Holy Cross."

"Okay, I think it's time you got out of here."

"This holiest of instruments is your ultimate weapon against Festus Baustone, Helmut Hartkopff, and the devil himself. Your lack of belief and faith will turn around. It's all in God's plan."

"Let's talk about *my* plan because I'm getting gone. I'm gonna be on a Maui beach by tomorrow night. I don't wanna be anywhere near Festus, Helmut, Satan, or the boogeyman. God'll have to figure something else out."

"You can't escape the inevitable."

"We'll see about that."

"You need to keep your heart and soul with Christ and also with the music you'll use to deliver man from evil. Fear God. Give glory to Him and worship Him."

"Sure. I'll do it at the Grand Wailea."

"Satan and his henchmen make their demands and threats first, then they'll force you to do their bidding. They'll even try to make you worship Satan and receive the mark of the Antichrist once he's risen." Zacharelli's tone grew louder and his eyes appeared wide and furious. "But you mustn't bow to Satan, no matter what the situation. For God warns, if any man should worship Satan and his image, as well as receiving Satan's mark in the forehead or in the hand, man shall then drink of the wine of the wrath of God."

"Six-six-six?"

"Yes."

"I just won't play the song. If what I know is true, then Satan's song is his key to Armageddon. I won't jam the tune and all will be good in the world."

"It's inevitable, son. There's not a thing you can do about the unthinkable forces already set in motion."

"You really believe God can destroy Satan? I've seen things. It doesn't look like the good guys are gonna prevail here."

"The Lord's power is supreme. He's already taken Satan captive, binding and sealing the beast in an abysmal cell for thousands of years. Satan will never have a moment's rest or respite in his captivity."

"Seems the devil's got ways of doing business from his cell."

"Satan's work goes on, but his activities are kept in check by the bounds God has set. He is but a vicious dog on a leash. He can't personally deceive the nations, so he's reduced to working through others, like Festus and Helmut."

"How'd Satan get put away in the first place?"

"God threw Satan out of Heaven. The fallen angel fell from Heaven into the abyss, to remain imprisoned until God is ready to break the seal of the pit. Evidently, Satan's figured a way to be freed by the unholy music he's created. He tried to get free, thousands of years ago in ancient Egypt, but was unsuccessful. Now he's using Festus and Helmut to liberate him."

"When was God supposed to free Satan, before Festus and Helmut started dicking around?"

"We've no way of knowing when the sentence would have ended."

"Obviously, Satan doesn't want to wait for God to

open the seal, does he? He's got an agenda."

"Satan certainly wants release *now*. He wants an immediate foothold on Earth so he can wipe out mankind and bring Hell to this world with the largest army possible. Satan will gather all his servants and agencies together for a global overthrow and everlasting damnation."

"What about God's original plan to release Satan on His own accord?"

"If God releases Satan, it's written, then all God's people will be brought to Heaven in the Rapture, while Satan and his legions run the Earth for a thousand years."

"And if Satan slips past God?"

"If Satan's released upon Earth now, he'll steal the souls of those who would've otherwise turned to God, and he'll also destroy the Holy Church, which would have normally been protected in God's hands."

"You're talking about Judgment Day, right?"

"I'm talking about a passage of revelation. Good will battle evil in what the Hebrews referred to as Armageddon."

"Isn't that the same as Judgment Day?"

"Some people interpret it that way. The name Armageddon comes from the Hebrew name *Har-Magedon*, which means mountain of Megiddo—the ancient, elevated city in Northern Israel. The Hebrew name of *Harmah* means the place marked for destruction and, when combined with *Megiddo*, is another version of the same name. Armageddon doesn't necessarily have to be in Megiddo. The place of destruction can be anywhere, including Egypt. That's where Satan hopes to make his break, without God's authority."

"And I'm supposed to be the asswipe who busts the devil out of his hole?"

"You can correct it all. As I told you, Satan can be cast back into the abyss, but only if you use the instrument of God. This electric guitar is the only hope. It's salvation."

Six-stringed salvation? Kirk's thoughts turned to blues legend Robert Johnson. Johnson was rumored to have raised Satan by playing guitar at a country crossroads. Legend had it Johnson then sold his soul to the devil in exchange for phenomenal guitar-playing abilities. Kirk conjured up Johnson's lyrical fragments in his mind. *I've done sold my soul, I've sold it to the devil, and my heart's done turned to stone.* "I don't want to be a part of anything that's gonna cause pain and death."

"I understand, but it's all—"

"Inevitable, right?" Kirk sighed. "Okay, if this crazy shit goes down and I succeed in kicking Satan's ass"— Kirk paused, thinking how ridiculous it sounded— "then what will happen on the actual Judgment Day?"

"The armies of Satan will battle the armies of God, and good will prevail. Fire will rain down from Heaven, devouring Satan and his legions. He and his followers will be cast into a lake of fire, the infinite and eternal punishment of the lost and damned"

"What harm comes to those who are good?"

"The fiery punishment of God does not strike, or hurt, or harm the children of God—those who are victorious over the image and mark, immune to the number and name of Satan. Those who believe in Him gain this victory through our Lord Jesus Christ. Satan has no power over them. God will end the world in fire, and Satan and his legions will be tormented for eternity. This is God's final answer to all who say there is no infinitely fearful, painful, and eternal Hell."

"Well, I'm still getting the fuck outta Dodge. I'll consider hitting the big man upstairs for a favor if I get in a pinch." Kirk looked Zacharelli in the eyes, the only part of the priest that seemed alive.

The priest raised a hand and lowered it. Kirk's eyes caught a shiny wetness on Zacharelli's cuff. Kirk stared at a glistening red rivulet of liquid dripping from the priest's sleeve and into the carpeting of the bedroom floor.

Blood dripped from large holes in Zacharelli's wrists. Kirk noticed the priest's shoes and ragged socks were soaked with blood from his ankles.

"I bear the wounds of Christ," Father Antonio Zacharelli said. "It's part of my purpose."

"I told you to get a doctor last time." Kirk was alarmed by Zacharelli's injuries. He set the guitar down and prepared to call an ambulance. "That shit looks bad. You need help."

"I don't need a doctor. I just need to return home. My tasks for the Lord are done for now." Zacharelli walked out of Kirk's bedroom.

"Where are you going?" Kirk shouted and followed the old priest downstairs and to the front door.

Kirk was bewildered as he noticed the front door was locked and the security system was still on. He almost asked Zacharelli how he got in the house, but decided it didn't matter.

"I went to Rome in order to retrieve the true Holy Cross of Jesus Christ from the Church of the Holy Cross so God could create the guitar—your weapon against evil." Zacharelli unlocked the front door and stepped out into the night without the alarm going off.

"My home is at the monastery of San Giovanni Rotondo in Foggia, Italy. I'm returning there until the Lord dispatches me again."

"What kind of priest serves God like this?"

"Every priest serves Him. I've been serving God since 1887."

"Since *when*?" Kirk was sure he heard the wrong date.

"I was born in Pietrelcina on August twenty-eighth, 1887."

Kirk coughed. "But that would make you—"

"An old man. I entered a monastery when I was fifteen. In 1910 I was ordained and entered the monastery of San Giovanni Rotondo. In 1918, after I said Mass at the monastery, Christ appeared to me. Since then, I've borne the wounds of Christ—as a sign that I'm one of His true servants—and I've served Him in every way I can, including my visit to you."

Kirk's inquiries were spent. His mouth opened and provided nothing.

Father Antonio Zacharelli smiled. "Keep light and music in your heart and soul. You will prevail. May the Lord be with you."

"Yeah...you too."

A moth fluttered in Kirk's face. He blinked and swatted it away. Refocusing, he saw Father Zacharelli had vanished, leaving not even a drop of blood. Kirk shivered in the warm night. He went back inside his mansion and locked the door.

Chapter 21
Spirited Away

After Zacharelli's visit, Kirk couldn't go back to sleep, so he wandered around his mansion. Anxious, he turned off his home alarm and went outside, walking and thinking about all things mortal and otherwise.

Bored and cold, Kirk went back inside. The sun was just coming up and he returned to the upstairs bedroom to try sleeping again. He went into his private bathroom. Taking a leak, he thought he heard sounds outside the door. Was it Father Zacharelli again?

Kirk walked out of his bathroom and felt the immediate pain of a hard slap to his face.

"Wake up, motherfucker," a voice said.

Holding his stinging face, Kirk saw the Baustone thug known as Donny standing before him.

"What the fuck are you doin' here?" Kirk said.

Donny grinned. In his tired state, Kirk thought of a

line from a ZZ Top song. Something about a New York brim and a gold-tooth display.

"You're takin' a little trip with us." Donny grabbed Kirk by his shoulders and shoved him hard.

"Fucker!" Kirk blurted as he was slammed into a wall.

"I wanna break you," Donny said. "Real bad."

"Don't hurt him." Helmut stood in the doorway, dressed in some kind of desert camouflage. "We need to keep Mr. Vaisto in one piece. He's our most valuable possession."

Donny frowned and released Kirk.

Kirk faced Helmut. "I'm not doing a goddamn thing for you guys. I'm giving Festus his money back and that's gonna be the end of it."

"We need you more than ever now."

"Tough shit."

"That's too bad, *mein* Kirk," Helmut said. "Donny, hold Mr. Vaisto down."

Before Kirk could think, Donny grabbed him from behind and held him in a tight bear hug.

"What are you gonna do? Torture me? Beat me up?" Kirk wheezed as his ribs were squeezed. "It's not gonna do you any good. I ain't doin' shit."

"I'd love to torture you. It's one of my favorite pastimes." Helmut walked up and grabbed Kirk's face. "But physically hurting you won't get me the results I want."

"Got that right." Kirk gave him a defiant smile.

As Donny held Kirk tight in his arms, he put his face next to Kirk's left ear and sank his gold teeth into it.

"Motherfuck!" Kirk howled as the pain from Donny's bite shot through his head.

"*Ficken!* That's enough, Donny," Helmut said.

Donny let go of Kirk's ear. He grinned next to Kirk's face and continued his arm hold. His teeth were gold and red. Blood dripped off his bottom lip.

"Cocksuckers." Kirk felt blood flowing down his neck. "You need me to play that song. You wanna set Hell loose, but it can't happen unless I open the gate. You're fucked. Nothing's gonna make me do a thing. You'll have to kill me."

"*Ja.* You're tough, Kirk," Helmut said. "But even you must value life. You wouldn't mind if we tortured and killed you for not playing the song for us?"

Kirk realized his escape plan to Maui was a hopeless fantasy now. Unnerved and scared, he was also pissed and remained adamant. "I don't give a good fuck."

"I admire your courage. Though I'd like to hurt you and end you, I'm afraid we can't do any of that. Instead, we're going to kill someone else if you don't cooperate with us."

"What d'ya mean?" Kirk felt something nasty in his gut.

Helmut released a malicious laugh. "Mr. Jaspers, you can come in now."

The large and formidable dark-skinned bodyguard walked into Kirk's bedroom. In his bling-filled right hand, he held a gun Kirk identified as a nickel-plated Desert Eagle .44 magnum. With his left hand, he held Mona by her hair. She was crying and looked roughed up. Her makeup was smeared and dry blood ringed her nostrils. Mr. Jaspers stood a few feet away with his hostage. Mona whimpered as he put the gun to her head.

"Are you outta your fuckin' mind?" Kirk shouted

and tried in vain to lunge out of Donny's restraining arms.

"Such a noble gesture, willing to give up life and limb to spite us. But are you bold enough to let someone else pay for your mistakes?" Helmut said.

"What do you want?" Kirk said.

"A show. Play the Song of Sethis in Egypt. We've already set up a stage for you. Everyone here will be very happy," Helmut said. "If you don't, we're going to pull an Auschwitz on Miss Baustone. She referred to me as Mengele before. Perhaps I can live up to the nickname."

"Fuck you," Kirk said. "When Festus finds out you're threatening his daughter, you're done."

Helmut and his cutthroats exploded with laughter.

"*Mein* Kirk." Helmut was laughing and sounding happy for the first time since Kirk met him. "This was Festus's idea."

Mona cried as Mr. Jaspers lifted her off the ground by her hair with one hand while holding the barrel of the handgun to her temple with his other hand. Kirk watched Jaspers holding her up by a fistful of locks with ease while Mona clung to the enforcer's thick wrist, keeping her scalp from tearing.

"Please, Kirk. Do what they say," Mona cried out in a high voice as she struggled in Mr. Jaspers's grip.

Kirk couldn't stand to hear the painful plea or see the pain in Mona's twisted face. "Okay, okay! I'll play the song. I'll do whatever you cocksuckers want, just let her go."

"*Ja.* I knew we'd reach an understanding," Helmut said. "Okay, Mr. Jaspers. Donny. Let our friends go."

The Baustone thugs released Kirk and Mona and shoved them together. The lovers embraced. Mona sobbed into Kirk's chest while he held her tight.

Kirk glared at the men in the room. He wanted to kill all of them. "What's your plan?"

"We're packing whatever clothing, equipment, and accessories you need. Then we're taking a ride to the airport and boarding a Baustone private jet," Helmut said. "We're making a pit stop in New York to get Festus. He's been busy wrapping up last-minute details to get this concert in full swing."

"The ultimate in asshole promoters," Kirk said.

"Within forty-eight hours, you'll be in Egypt, giving the performance of a lifetime."

Kirk held Mona close. "I'll play the song. Just promise me you won't harm her."

"*Mein* Kirk, do what we wish, and you and your girlfriend won't be harmed," Helmut said. "Now, let's get going. We've got to be in Egypt by tomorrow."

"I'll get my things together," Kirk said.

Releasing Mona, he walked to the foot of his bed. On the floor was the guitar case Father Zacharelli left him. Kirk picked up the case and put it on his mattress.

"Wait a minute. Lemme see what's in there," Donny said.

"Chill out, man," Kirk said. "It's just one of my guitars. I'm gonna need it when I jam in Egypt."

"Don't care. I wanna check it out." Donny tore the case away from Kirk. "I don't take chances. You could have a machine-gun in there for all I know."

Kirk watched as Donny opened the case and picked up the guitar. He didn't look impressed. "Just a hunka wood. Looks safe enough." The enforcer turned the instrument over in his hands before dropping it back in the case.

"Hey! Careful with that," Kirk said. The sight and

sound of a guitar being dropped was horrible to him. He'd never abused a guitar in his life and couldn't understood why some musicians destroyed their gear on stage.

"Fuck you," Donny said, looking at the palm of his left hand. "Damn thing gave me a sliver."

Kirk watched as Donny pulled a tiny splinter out with his fingernails. The enforcer flicked the sliver away and returned to playing watchdog over him.

"That guitar isn't necessary," Helmut said. "I've already got the instrument you're playing in concert."

"What do you mean?" The sudden thought of not being able to use the God guitar alarmed Kirk.

"I had a customized electric guitar made for you," Helmut said. "I hired a manufacturer to make it to my specifications. You will play this in Egypt."

"No way, man. I need my main axe for the concert." Kirk knew Helmut and Festus were up to something. He wondered why they would go through the trouble of having a guitar made.

"This is a special occasion, and we want you to play a special guitar made just for the unveiling of the pyramid. You *will* play what I give you," Helmut said.

"I can't wait to see it." Kirk lied and tried sounding casual. "Look, I really need to bring this guitar with me so that I can practice. Plus, I need it for backup. It goes everywhere with me. I'm sure you'd like to have me properly prepared for such an important performance, no?"

Kirk looked over the God guitar before closing the case. He was concerned. If Father Zacharelli was right and the God guitar was indeed a weapon against evil, then Kirk wanted it with him more than anything.

Helmut sighed. "Fine. We'll bring your precious

guitar. Only for practice and backup. Just be a good boy and cooperate with us, otherwise I'll use your guitar for firewood."

"No problem." Kirk felt relieved. "If you don't mind, I'd like to get dressed."

"Don't worry about that right now. You can get dressed later," Helmut said. "Just grab extra clothes. Quickly, now. We're leaving."

Within the hour, Kirk, Mona, and their captors arrived at the airport. They boarded a Baustone private jet and flew to New York City.

During the flight, Mona explained how Helmut and the two bodyguards had kidnapped her in her suite after she returned from shopping and threatened to torture and kill her if Kirk didn't play the song. She mentioned being disgusted, but not surprised, when she found out her father had given his blessing to use her as a hostage.

Once they landed in New York City, Festus Baustone joined the group while the private jet refueled.

"I'm glad to see you're all together and in one piece," Festus said, boarding the jet with an unlit cigar in his mouth. "How's my prized musician doing?"

Kirk was silent. He gripped Mona's hand and stared at Festus, wanting to drop the fucker on the spot.

"I see my daughter's taking care of you." Festus smiled at Kirk. He turned to Mona. "How are you, my dear?"

"Fuck off," Mona said.

"Hostile, as always." Festus smiled wider.

"You've stooped pretty low in your time, but this is a new one," Mona said. "I can't believe you're willing to let these bastards torture and kill me if Kirk doesn't play that song. I'm your daughter, for Christ's sake."

"Yes, you're my daughter. You're also the greatest asset I've got to ensure that this deal goes down."

"You make me sick," Mona said.

"It's just business, darlin'." Festus winked.

"This isn't business, fuckwad." Kirk was growing angrier with each passing second. Pointing a finger in Festus's face, he said, "This is kidnapping. International shit. Extortion. You're going to prison when this is over."

Festus stared at Kirk and giggled.

"We need to go over the plans for tomorrow's concert." Helmut interrupted Festus's fun. "What's going on in Egypt?"

"I've already got the entire stage, sound system, guitar backline, and lighting set up out there, with an army of engineers to go with it all," Festus said. "I've got two dozen crews out there, handling all of the filming, satellite feeds, and broadcasting. The entire show will be broadcast live on every continent and in every country around the world tomorrow night, Egyptian time. All regularly scheduled programming will be put on hold. Every major network, including my own, and all my cable television and radio stations are picking up the live broadcast. You don't know what this cost me. Wasn't easy. Thankfully, the FCC's in my pocket."

"Will there be a crowd at the event?" Helmut asked.

"We estimate twenty thousand," Festus said. "Locals, foreigners, Egyptian soldiers. We expect a large draw out of Cairo alone. Maybe the Taliban will show up. The concert will look great."

"Security?" Helmut asked.

"I'm using Egyptian soldiers everywhere." Festus

turned to Kirk. "I've even hired a handful of extra-special men to keep an eye on you, Mr. Vaisto."

Kirk detected something sinister in Festus's words. "What're you talking about?"

"To make sure you don't get funny ideas, I've got three of the best snipers in the world waiting for you in Egypt," Festus said. "The snipers will have you and Mona in their sights the entire time. They'll be equipped with two-way radios. If I give 'em the word that you're not playing what you should, or if they see you fucking around, they're gonna put a bullet through my daughter's head, then yours."

"You're a sick fuck." Kirk couldn't believe this madness was happening. *What kind of psychopath does this?*

Mona spat in Festus's face. "Hate you. *Hate you!*"

Festus wiped his face and shook his head.

The pilot's voice came over the intercom, informing everyone it was time for takeoff.

"Looks like it's time to go." Festus took a seat next to Helmut, across the aisle from Kirk and Mona. "I'm going to be right here the whole trip with Helmut. Mr. Jaspers and Donny will be in front of and behind you. So, if you need anything, just ask."

"I wanna see you go to Hell," Mona told him.

Festus smiled. "Daughter of mine, if things in Egypt go the way we hope, Hell's coming to us."

Chapter 22
The Root of All Evil

Hours later, as the jet flew toward Egypt, Kirk and Mona fell fast asleep and Festus soon followed suit. Helmut remained awake with the enforcers. Donny was looking through a porn mag, while Mr. Jaspers did nothing at all.

Helmut moved with quiet and deliberate ease from his seat, not wanting to wake Festus. He strolled to the back of the plane where he had stowed his personal carry-on cases, including the one containing the coffin texts of Aknaseth. He sat by his cargo and shuffled the cases around. He opened one small case, gave a cautious look around, then examined the golden uraeus placed inside. It was the authentic one found in the sarcophagus of Aknaseth. Helmut knew it was solid gold and made for the immortal commander of Satan's army.

He then thought of another uraeus. This headpiece was an exact replica of the unholy original, except it was made out of aluminum covered in gold leaf. He'd made the dummy back in Egypt, right before he flew to New York City. The replica was now in the possession of Festus Baustone the Third.

Helmut closed the case, locked it, and set it down. He moved on to another, larger case and opened it. This was a guitar case. Resting inside was the guitar he wanted Kirk to play. Helmut didn't know anything about guitars, but he knew what specs the guitar needed.

Helmut had hired an independent guitar manufacturer to make the instrument in just two days. More than ten thousand of Festus's dollars were spent to make the guitar that quickly. The instrument was now finished and ready to be played.

The guitar was a strat-styled, neck-thru guitar Helmut modeled after one of Kirk's own signature-model ESP guitars, retaining the same body style, hardware, and pickup configurations. This one, however, possessed additional and unique features.

Helmut ordered the fingerboard made from a piece of Aknaseth's original instrument found at the excavation site. The fingerboard, neck, and inlays were bound in solid gold. Every gold inlay was in the shape of an inverted cross or an inverted Egyptian *ankh*.

The other custom feature was the paint job. The entire guitar and neck were finished in a dark red color. The instrument looked like some kind of skinless animal. Helmut had sent the paint to the guitar manufacturer in a half gallon can. When the guys in the custom guitar shop asked Helmut what kind of paint he gave them, he said it was a natural Egyptian coating for staining wood.

The luthiers found the paint difficult to work with. When it jammed up their spray guns, they added thinners. Helmut, intolerant and concerned only with the job he paid for, ordered the guitar craftsmen to save their petty problems and get the fucking job done. He instructed them to shut up and apply as many coats as possible to the instrument. The guitar shop did as ordered. The paint dried, and the guitar was strung and shipped. It was ready to be played. Though the craftsmen warned a guitar made this fast could have serious issues later, Helmut was pleased with the results.

He never mentioned how the paint was made from human blood. He knew the true origin of the pigment wouldn't sit well with the guitar makers and would implicate him in murder. They never seemed to suspect anything, only referring to Helmut's choice of coatings as shitty and cheap.

Now Helmut thought back to when he was inside Aknaseth's pyramid. He thought of how he took the archeologist, Barkley Simms, and introduced his victim to a boot knife. The pig didn't put up much of a fight. Barkley screamed for a moment before the knife went to work. When Helmut withdrew the blade, all was quiet.

Helmut had almost decapitated Barkley when he cut the pig from ear to ear. It was a messy job. Hot blood sprayed and covered Helmut's face and clothes as he did his handiwork. As the blood shot out, Helmut used an empty canopic vessel to collect as much of the pumping fluid as possible.

He mixed the blood with specific chemical agents until he was satisfied he had a perfect batch of paint.

All for Sethis, Helmut thought. *All for you, Great Satan. And all for me. Thank you, Professor.*

It was the professor who first told Helmut of the legend of Aknaseth and the Song of Sethis. Helmut remembered the day Durban mentioned discovering a rare artifact: an Egyptian vase from the Armana Period engraved with hieroglyphics telling the story of Aknaseth's strange and horrific life. The vase was the only direct relic of Aknaseth and Sethis discovered at the time.

Many years later, Festus Baustone made finding Aknaseth's pyramid possible for Helmut. He had used Baustone's money toward sophisticated and customized ground-penetrating radar. The machinery could find almost any object underground, from a bottle cap to a cargo plane. Within two weeks of implementing the radar, Helmut located the lost pyramid. He felt a slight excitement while reliving the moment.

Now, Helmut felt even greater excitement. Knowing the legend was all too real, he realized the music would be heard by every living soul worldwide, just as Aknaseth had written it should be done.

Egyptian music was important. So important, it was known to have influenced the Greeks. The Greek biographer Plutarch said the Egyptian god Thoth invented music and all stringed instruments. Helmut knew Plato studied in Egypt and extolled the excellence of Egyptian musical standards. The Greek philosopher Pythagoras also investigated music theory in Egypt. Ancient Greeks thought music and the human soul were both aspects of the eternal and stimulated each other with powerful scientific precision, thanks to the essential kinship of the two.

Helmut remembered learning how the ancient Chinese took the Egyptian and Greek theories regarding the power of music a step further, believing music was the basis of everything. Human beings, the Chinese said, were molded from the music inside each of us.

Helmut never cared to be a musician. He held no musical talent or ability, but he understood the magic music possessed. He believed music held emotional power, giving a sublime experience that transcended the human world and connected to something greater. As a key to the human soul, he felt music was the most potent instrument available for man's enlightenment.

Helmut wasn't using music as a tool for enlightenment, however. He wanted to exploit Aknaseth's satanic music for a more sinister plan.

He fingered his blasphemous guitar. He had worked hard and done everything possible to ensure Hell would be unleashed on Earth, and he couldn't wait to be rewarded for his efforts. Thoughts of the upcoming event wore on him night and day. He didn't eat much and hadn't slept in more than forty-eight hours, but he didn't care. Deep in his septic heart, he knew after tomorrow passed, there wouldn't be any more tomorrows, and he'd never need food or rest again.

Chapter 23
Pre-show Jitters

Kirk sat inside a trailer parked behind the concert stage at the site of Aknaseth's pyramid and temple. He had arrived early in the morning with everyone else on the Baustone private jet.

An Egyptian army escort took them to the site where Kirk and Mona were ushered into separate side-by-side trailers for safekeeping. He watched Mona shooting him one last unhappy glance before Mr. Jaspers pushed her inside.

Soldiers walked amongst the trailers. Donny guarded Kirk inside as Mr. Jaspers watched Mona within the neighboring trailer—ensuring no escape. Food was brought to Kirk upon request, and Festus and Helmut made frequent visits to him.

Kirk sat on a leather couch he had slept on earlier. He heard the sounds of many voices outside the trailer.

He also heard a distant, reverberating voice testing the PA system. It sounded like thunder.

The couch Kirk sat on was deep and comfortable, and he found the trailer to be a cushy jail cell. It was carpeted and clean, with brand-new appliances and furniture. A giant LCD TV took up an entire wall. Kirk watched old footage of himself performing live in bygone concerts on a high definition CNN feed. Donny sat in a recliner with his shades on and a golden grin on his face.

"Today's your big day, huh?" Donny said.

"I guess."

Donny muttered and rubbed his left hand. Kirk noticed it was bandaged, the fingers swollen and black.

"What happened to your hand?" Kirk asked this with no real concern.

"Not sure. I think it was thatsliver in my hand from your fuckin' guitar." Donny wore an expression of pain. "Been a mess ever since."

"Looks bad." Kirk saw the bandage was soaked with red and yellow fluid.

"Yeah, well, I'm not trustin' some dirty Egyptian to touch me. I'll have it checked out when I'm back in the good ol' U.S. of A."

"Suit yourself." *That's what you get for biting my ear, asshole.*

Kirk got off the couch and walked toward the bathroom in the trailer.

"Hey, where the fuck're you going?" Donny jumped up.

"Gotta piss. Okay with you?"

"Make it quick."

Kirk walked into the bathroom. Above the toilet was a window, and as he relieved himself, he looked out and saw Mona's trailer.

As Kirk looked out the window, Mona appeared in a window. She looked out and met his gaze. He smiled and she smiled back. He zipped up his pants and mouthed the inaudible question, "Are you all right?"

Kirk read Mona's lips. She nodded, gave an okay sign, and mouthed, "Yes, I'm fine."

He blew her a kiss and she returned one. Then she flashed him her breasts and he started laughing.

"Hey, what the hell you doin' in there?" Donny shouted from the other end of the trailer.

"Nothin'. Just thought of an old joke."

"Quit fucking around and get your ass back in here."

"I'm coming." Kirk blew Mona another kiss.

He read her lips one more time. "I love you."

A fluttery feeling hit Kirk in the stomach as her words registered. He was surprised she said that, but he was also happy she did. It felt good.

"I love you." Kirk mouthed the words back to Mona. They waved goodbye as he turned away. Kirk walked back into the trailer's living room. Despite the circumstances, he began feeling better.

Inside the living room, Helmut waited. "Donny, walk our star to the stage for a sound check."

"Where's my guitar?"

"Here." Helmut handed a guitar case to Kirk.

Kirk set the case down on the couch and opened it. "This isn't my guitar." Kirk cringed at the sight of the blood-colored instrument.

"*Ja*. Remember, Kirk, I told you I already have a guitar for you. Made just for this concert. You will use this instrument."

"I remember, but I wanna know where the other

guitar is, the one I brought for backup. I haven't even had a chance to practice with it. It's important I have it handy. Okay?"

"Don't worry. We've got it on the side of the stage."

"Well, let's go do this sound check then." Kirk shrugged his shoulders and walked out of the trailer with Helmut and Donny.

Kirk was in awe of the production. He guessed the stage was half the size of a football field, with enormous PA speakers and monitors across the front and on the sides. A huge lighting rig hung fifty feet overhead. He was impressed by the backline, which consisted of towering racks full of amp heads, and guitar-system equipment. An immense wall of Mesa-Boogie speaker cabinets filled the rest of the stage. This was all topped off by an immense backdrop of fabric, airbrushed with artwork depicting a pyramid with the Eye of Horus above it and numerous inverted cross-like ankhs below it.

Pretty evil. The Bible Belt's gonna love seeing that.

A large and expansive area opened up in front of the stage to accommodate the thousands of people expected to attend tonight's performance. At the moment, Kirk only saw the hundreds of people who made up sound crews, television crews, and Egyptian soldiers walking and working through the concert area.

A large partition about one hundred yards in front of the stage was where the mixing board and the lighting board for the show were located. Beyond that, dozens of semi trailers and television trucks with satellite dishes pointed toward the sky. Festus had explained that the dishes would beam the live broadcast from Egypt to all the Baustone satellites circling the planet. From there, the satellites would broadcast the live show to every television set and radio in the world. The concert would also stream live on the Internet.

As Kirk stood on the stage, he felt as if he were back at Britain's Wembley Stadium or on the main stage of the last concert he'd played at UK's Download Festival. Kirk felt both exhilarated and terrified to be there.

He locked a strap to Helmut's instrument and slung it on while a couple of stagehands plugged the guitar into the racks of gear. His fingers were no longer sore or achy. He took a few moments to check the tuning of the guitar, then fiddled with the tone of the amps until he was satisfied with the sound.

Kirk played a few power chords and speed runs. The soundmen operating the PA and stage monitors tweaked the sound and pumped the volume up. The entire stage shook. He figured the pyramid and temple, along with the red sands of the surrounding desert, all shuddered with the amplified fury of his playing. Kirk couldn't help feeling powerful while producing such an audio bombast. He couldn't deny loving this. The soundmen and Kirk gave each other the thumbs-up, satisfied with everything. Kirk took off the guitar and put it on a stand.

"How does it feel?" Helmut said.

"Not great," Kirk said. "The action and intonation isn't to my liking. Where's my real guitar?"

"Over there." Helmut pointed.

The God guitar rested on a stand on the left side of the stage.

Festus approached from stage right. He said, "Wow. That's some powerfully loud music. It's going to be great. Think?"

"I think you should go smoke a dick," Kirk said.

Festus frowned. "You and my daughter make a great couple. You speak the same language. Now, I've got a couple things to show you."

Festus put an arm around Kirk and pointed. "You see those three towers beyond the satellite trucks?"

From the stage, Kirk saw a tall tower to the left, one in the middle, and one to the right. On top of each tower was a platform, and on each platform the silhouette of a solitary man.

"Yeah, I see 'em. So what?"

"You see a man on each one?"

"Yeah."

"Those would be my snipers. I just wanted you to see 'em. A reminder not to get stupid. They'll have their crosshairs on your head and Mona's head during the whole show. So, Johnny Be Good, eh?"

"You won't have any trouble from me." Kirk imagined ending Festus's life.

"Now, if you look to stage right, you'll see where my insurance policy is."

Kirk saw Donny and Mr. Jaspers holding Mona on the side of the stage. He gave her a smile and hoped it would comfort her.

Mona nodded with wide, terrified eyes.

"Just in case you get squirrelly and the snipers can't nail her, Donny and Mr. Jaspers have their orders. They will, how shall I put it? Fuck her up."

"Congrats. I think you just made Father of the Year," Kirk said. "Now, take your fucking arm off me, *Dad.* I wanna puke."

Festus released him. "I'll leave Helmut to explain technical things you'll need to know."

Kirk watched Festus walk to the side of the stage where Donny and Mr. Jaspers were holding Mona. He said a few words and they all moved away except for Donny, who stayed behind to watch his every step.

Helmut brought Kirk to the front of the stage. "You see the teleprompter?"

A twenty-five inch television screen filled with snow was sandwiched between two stage monitors.

"Yeah, I see it." Kirk studied the screen.

"You'll use that teleprompter for reference. It's going to run the music for the Song of Sethis across the screen, just like the computer."

"How much longer until show time?"

"About three hours. Are you worried, Kirk?"

"I'm not looking forward to seeing what's gonna happen once I play this music."

"Ohhh," Helmut said, moaning, "it's going to be beautiful."

No. It's going to be horrible.

Chapter 24
Showtime

In his trailer, Kirk tried passing the time by playing the guitar Helmut gave him. He didn't like it. It didn't play great and it gave off bad vibes every time he held it. The deep red paint felt tacky, as if it wasn't dry enough. He set it down on the side of the couch and left it alone. He missed his personal guitars, so far away and locked up at home.

Kirk turned his thoughts to other things. He sat around contemplating what was going to happen once he hit the stage and kicked into Satan's international hit.

He knew the concert area was filling in. Kirk heard the sounds of people everywhere. Voices boomed over the PA system and two-way radios crackled throughout the backstage area. Kirk heard the drone of helicopters flying overhead and Helmut barking orders in English, German, and Arabic.

Kirk looked over at Donny. The bodyguard was pale and sweaty. "What's wrong with you?"

"My hand's getting worse." Donny took off the bandage. "Damn, check it out,"

His hand was now black and swollen to twice its normal size. All of the fingernails had fallen off and thick, yellow matter oozed out of a hole in the palm of the hand.

"Holy shit." Kirk was almost glad to see Donny suffering. "That looks bad."

"Yeah, all fucked up. How can a little sliver of wood do this to my hand? It must've been infected with somethin'. It just gets worse. I bet that fucking old priest did this to me somehow."

"Old priest?" Kirk was now interested in Donny's words.

"Yeah. This old Italian priest shows up outta nowhere the other day. Me and another bodyguard took him out back to ruin his day. The old prick killed my partner and shoved my .357 right up my ol' pucker." Donny's jaws clenched into a gold grimace. "I don't know who the old fucker was, or how he moved so quick, but I'd like another shot at him. No one does that to me and gets away with it."

Kirk imagined the scenario and didn't want to picture it. He couldn't fathom Zacharelli doing such a thing, but then again, the Lord moved in mysterious ways. "Sounds nasty."

"Yeah, it was. And I'm feeling meaner than usual. You might wanna keep that in mind."

"I'll do that."

Kirk was about to rest on the couch when Helmut

entered the trailer dressed in bright, silky-looking robes. On his burn-scarred head, he wore a red headdress. His disfigured face, along with the headdress, gave Kirk the impression he was staring at a three-thousand-year-old mummy dug fresh from the sands and reanimated.

"It's time to go," Helmut said. "The world awaits your performance."

Kirk didn't want to get up, but knew he had no choice. He was walking toward the door to go on stage when Helmut said, "Wait. You're forgetting something."

"What?" Kirk said.

"The guitar I gave you. You must have it for your performance, Kirk." Helmut pointed at the guitar leaning against the couch.

"Oh yeah. Forgot about it." Kirk retrieved it and walked outside into the night air in the company of Helmut and Donny. Kirk wondered if what Zacharelli said was true.

I don't have the holy guitar, Padre. Will all be lost now? The eyes of the world are on me and I feel completely hopeless and helpless.

"This is going to be a momentous occasion," Helmut said. "Your talents finally used for their true purpose."

"Yeah, that's great." Kirk was feeling sick again. He started to gag.

"Control yourself, *mein* Kirk. This isn't the time to lose your composure." Helmut put a leathery hand on his neck to keep him walking.

Kirk got himself in line and continued toward the stage. Then he was startled as he heard a sudden, loud, violent howl from Donny. Kirk turned around with

Helmut. Donny was hunched over, holding his arms to his chest.

"What is it?" Helmut said.

"It's my fucking hand," Donny yelped. "It...fell off."

Donny stood straight up and extended his left arm. It was true; the hand was missing, leaving only a meaty stump with maggots wriggling out of it. Kirk looked down, seeing Donny's disconnected hand lying on the ground like a decomposing baseball glove.

Kirk watched as all of Donny's flesh turned pale, then a dark, rotten color. Donny let out a small cry and collapsed on his back. The Baustone bodyguard twitched for a moment, then became still. His golden teeth created a dead man's grin.

Helmut yelled something at some men who stood nearby. They ran up, talking amongst themselves as they huddled around Donny. The men carried his body away along with the rotten hand.

"Looks like a disease of some kind." Helmut pushed Kirk to the stage. "Gangrene or leprosy can do that."

No, the power of the Holy Cross can do that.

Kirk was ushered to stage left. The stage was now filled with lights and electrified gear. Kirk saw the God guitar resting on a stand. He was glad to see it, though it seemed a million miles away.

Stagehands ran around making last-minute adjustments. A CD of Egyptian music played over the PA system as thousands of people crowded into the concert area. Television crews, reporters, and Festus Baustone's own camera crews filled in every space not already occupied by soldiers or general onlookers. Thousands of camera flashes went off like fireworks.

Kirk now stood next to Helmut and Festus. Looking over his shoulder, he found Jaspers behind him, an arm hooked around Mona, keeping his handgun placed on her ribs.

"Are you all right?" Kirk asked her.

"Aside from this asshole holding me hostage, I'm okay." Mona gave Mr. Jaspers a dirty look.

"I'm so glad to see you," Kirk said.

"Me too." Mona smiled.

Festus walked between Kirk and Mona. "I don't want you two getting too close right now. We've got a show to do, and we can't have you messing up."

Festus was also dressed like Helmut, wearing a fancy robe, his head adorned with a golden headband and red headdress.

"How do you like my outfit?" Festus said.

Kirk, looked at Festus and Helmut. "You make a great couple. Why don't you go fuck each other?"

Festus chuckled while Helmut remained silent and glared at Kirk.

The music over the PA began to fade out and the stage lights dimmed. A man in a purple tuxedo walked onto the stage and spoke into a microphone.

"That's the emcee." Festus moved in fast and excited circles. "Things are rolling."

Kirk turned his attention toward the stage.

"Ladies and gentlemen, welcome to Egypt!" the emcee said. "Tonight you're going to witness an unprecedented televised event. Imagine a lost Egyptian pyramid full of treasures and tales not seen for thousands of years. Imagine a lost song, full of mystery, that's never been heard by mortal ears. It will all be seen and heard tonight!"

Kirk watched as the live audience roared their approval.

"I wrote that, you know." Festus produced a proud

grin and popped a fresh cigar in his mouth.

"This entire discovery was made possible by a great and unselfish man." The emcee spread his arms and embraced the crowd's applause.

"Gag me with a spoon," Mona said.

Kirk kept quiet, experiencing an extravagant joke unfolding in front of him, but finding no humor in any of it.

The emcee continued his intro. "Let me introduce you to the man of the evening. The magnificent, the gracious, the one and only Festus Baustone."

"That's my cue," Festus moved onto the stage with Helmut walking alongside. Festus stopped fast. Grabbing Helmut, the rich man said, "Where do you think you're going?"

"This is my greatest discovery. I'm the one who found the pyramid and Satan's music," Helmut said. "I'm going to present it all to the world with you."

"I don't think so." Festus held Helmut back on the side of the stage, looking him up and down. "No one's going on stage and on TV except for me and Kirk Vaisto. No one wants to see your ugly face anyway."

Kirk watched with surprise as Festus gave Helmut a hard push, knocking the old Nazi on his ass. Festus walked out onto the stage, waving at the cheering crowd and at the cameras beaming his image to the world. Kirk thought of how, at that moment, billions of people were watching Festus on live television or tuned into him on radio stations and Internet streams. The live event could make the entire planet stop as the world's eyes and ears were focused on this Egyptian show.

Kirk watched from the side of the stage while he warmed up with the guitar Helmut had given him. He glanced over at Mona and wanted to be with her on the other side of the planet. She remained in the clutches of Mr. Jaspers. Kirk was sick of feeling so helpless.

He turned back and watched Festus explain the history of the pyramid and temple of Aknaseth. He talked about how it was all discovered under the desert sands of Egypt, along with a unique and ancient song now unearthed for the world to hear.

Festus took full credit for everything and Helmut appeared pissed as he swore under his breath and shook his head in disgust. Kirk was amused.

Trouble in paradise.

Festus went on to explain how the pyramid and the temple were among the greatest discoveries of the twenty-first century. Kirk listened as Festus spoke about giving the history-changing discovery to the entire world on this day. He also wanted to introduce everyone to a unique pharaoh, Aknaseth, whose talents gave the world the music of the gods.

"The music you will hear tonight was written thousands of years ago. I call it the Song of Sethis, as it was written by Sethis, the god of the underworld," Festus said. "No one's ever heard it before. When I found the song, it was in the form of strange musical hieroglyphics. Once I deciphered the cryptic writing, I knew I had an important piece of music here."

Helmut stomped his feet with rage as Festus stole his spotlight.

"Once I realized the song was meant to performed on a guitar, I hired the best guitarist in the world to help me transcribe it," Festus said. "You all know who I'm talking about. The God of Guitar—Kirk Vaisto!"

Festus applauded and smiled as he turned to Kirk.

Two stagehands plugged a cable into Kirk's unholy guitar and hooked him up to the amplifiers.

"You're all set," a stagehand said. "Get out there."

He turned to Mona, but Mr. Jaspers was quick to shift his aim to Kirk. "Take it easy. I just want a good luck kiss."

Mr. Jaspers was silent. He kept the gun on Kirk as the guitarist talked to Mona.

"Wish me luck, okay?" Kirk said.

"I'll be waiting for you after the show." Mona gave him a long kiss. "I love you."

"I love you, too."

He turned from Mona and walked onto the stage. Spotlights blinded him and the crowd roared. Kirk figured he had played more than three thousand concerts during his career, always with a jacked-up, excited, adrenaline-filled happiness. Now, for the first time in his life—in his career—he prepared to perform with nothing but pure dread.

Chapter 25
Raising Hell—The Armageddon Chord

Kirk walked to the center of the stage, where Festus stood with open arms. The man tried giving him a hug, but he brushed off the fake embrace. He stood in front of the microphone stand while Festus walked off the stage.

Kirk looked out at a sea of faces. The crowd was loud, cheering, and waiting for him to deliver music to their ears. On the other side of the barricade separating the stage from the crowd, he saw women in the front flashing him.

Damn, there are even groupies in the Egyptian desert. He looked down at dozens of bare breasts.

Kirk looked over the crowd and the concert area. He saw thousands of civilians and soldiers, the camera crews, the PA partition, and the satellite trucks. A beautiful, clear, bright night sky with a full moon added a nocturnal clarity to the show. He blinked at the three tall and foreboding sniper towers. They were an ugly reminder he was to get on with the show and play the song.

He stepped in front of the microphone and spoke to the throngs attending the concert in Egypt and to the billions watching and listening around the world.

"I guess you all wanna hear a song," Kirk said.

The crowd gave a deafening reply. Some people yelled out their favorite Kirk Vaisto songs.

"Sorry, I'm not playing any of my own songs here. I'm here to play you a real hot number from ancient Egypt." Kirk glanced over to the side of the stage where Festus and Helmut glared at him.

Kirk looked away from them. He stared at the teleprompter wedged between the two stage monitors in front of him. The unholy music was ready to run across the screen as soon as he gave a nod to the stage techs.

"This will be the riff heard 'round the world. I just wanna say to all the people of Mother Earth that I'm sorry if this music...should hurt you in any way."

Kirk glanced over at Festus and Helmut again. They looked angry and signaled for him to shut his mouth and start playing. Mr. Jaspers put his handgun to Mona's head. Kirk looked into her eyes and saw terror. The sight made him weak.

"God forgive me," Kirk spoke in a whisper. He nodded to the techs on the side of the stage and the teleprompter started.

The music took on a life of its own the second Kirk performed the first measure. His hands became a blur of motion as the music inhabited his soul.

In his mind, Kirk saw unmentionable visions straight from every circle of Hell. He also viewed the mortal realm on a global level, around the planet, people going into trances, falling into violent seizures as the music he played infected them. He experienced billions losing their minds everywhere. Young and old, inside houses, cars, and stores; on streets; anywhere a television, radio, or computer hosted Kirk's live performance. Countless accidents, injuries, and deaths caused by the music, all of it occurring on a simultaneous international scale. Dark musical forces owned the minds, bodies, and souls of the world, no matter where they were.

Within the Egyptian concert grounds, Kirk's mind's eye saw everyone affected by the music. All those unfortunates without ear protection went mad. The thousands of people in attendance looked like a giant orgy, their bodies writhing together in violent convulsions.

He entered the minds of Festus and Helmut; these men didn't share the visions of the world. These guys wore earplugs. Kirk looked through their eyes, seeing the madness before them from their point of view. He felt their astonishment and hatred for one another, along with their excited anticipation as they awaited immortality and the unholy rewards the music promised.

Kirk's attack on the guitar was more frightening than ever. His hands moved across the fingerboard so fast it seemed as if time was standing still only for his fingers. Blood flew from his fingertips and smoke puffed from his guitar pick as it burned against the strings. With every note of each new run, the sinister-sounding music rocked the planet as the entire world listened.

Kirk's mind was full of the imagery he'd experienced before. Himself crucified on a giant guitar planted in the middle of a battlefield. The Paradisio's army of angels and the Inferno's legions of demons and damned souls charged each other as God and Satan did battle. The forces of good and evil were fighting for the sake of Earth and for every mortal soul. This, Kirk knew, wasn't a mere nightmare; it was a preview of what was coming to all in moments. The End Time was at hand, and he wasn't the only one who saw the images on the inbound storm. Those under the influence of the music also shared his distorted visions of an Egyptian-Biblical Armageddon.

Five agonizing minutes later, Kirk performed the final measure of the song. His body had become spastic and out of control as the music became more intense. Earth trembled as the sonic fury of the music sent tremors through the planet and in the desert. He gasped as the ground opened up in front of the stage, swallowing the twenty thousand-plus people gathered in the concert area.

With a hard stroke of his hand, Kirk ended the song on a power chord, and this time, the last riff blared and ripped through the levels of Earth, Heaven, and Hell. The ringing power chord induced a global shockwave, causing chaos and devastation worldwide.

Kirk observed this damage with an international eye. By his hand, fault lines cracked and tsunamis formed. Countless buildings toppled and he bore witness as mankind's foundation of civilization was thrown back to the primitive. Planet Earth shuddered from the sonic, guitar-blasting detonation he created.

The camera gear and satellite trucks in Egypt and the BauStar satellites orbiting the planet all exploded as the chaotic and destructive signal of the satanic music nuked the electronic components. On every continent, every device amplifying the Song of Sethis exploded as the Armageddon chord rang.

Kirk felt the roar of it all dying, and he knew the live broadcast was canceled as all electronic transmissions went black and were silenced. Still, the Armageddon chord rang on across every inch of the world's veneer. Unthinkable damage had been done.

Kirk collapsed on the stage. His head throbbed and ached with unbearable pain. Blood ran from his mouth, nose, and ears as he got up on his hands and knees and vomited. He heaved and his eyes fluttered. He caught sight of the entire PA system and the hundreds of guitar speaker cabinets making up the backline of the stage. Everything containing a speaker had exploded. It looked as if a giant bomb had gone off, filling the world with a great boom, leaving the hum of chaotic feedback in its aftermath.

Kirk finished retching. He looked around and saw debris scattered across the stage. Smoke drifted in the air and he smelled electricity along with burnt plastic and wiring. The confused voices and screams mixed with the sounds of Egyptian soldiers yelling orders.

Mona. Mona? Kirk looked to his immediate left to find Mona curled in the fetal position next to Mr. Jaspers. The pair was without ear protection and now lay unconscious.

Kirk crawled over with Helmut's guitar dragging from his shoulders. Festus and Helmut ran past him without acknowledgment. They seemed more concerned about something going on in front of the stage, where the concert crowd once gathered.

"Hey, are you okay?" Kirk gathered Mona in his arms. She was bleeding from her head.

Mona stirred. She groaned and coughed, then said, "God, I feel like shit. I guess I'm all right."

"Good." Kirk kissed her forehead.

He heard a voice groaning and saw Mr. Jaspers moving with a gun in his hand.

Kirk leapt to his feet and stood tall. Mr. Jaspers's sunglasses were missing and the two men made eye contact. As Kirk looked in his dark, gray eyes, Mr. Jaspers smiled and pointed his gun.

"Fuck you." Kirk swung Helmut's unholy guitar by the neck. As hard as possible, he nailed Mr. Jaspers in the head with the body of the instrument. Mr. Jaspers let out a small squeal as the guitar connected and split his skull open. He lay on the stage, motionless.

Kirk grabbed Mona by her arm and lifted her up onto her feet. "Come on, you gotta get up."

"I feel bad. Dizzy." Mona struggled to stand. Once on her feet, she took a moment to get a grip. "Okay, I'm good to go."

"Let's get the fuck outta here." Kirk got them walking.

Halfway across the giant stage, Kirk and Mona stopped as they looked out at the area where thousands of people had stood watching Kirk's performance. The desert and concert area were lit up by the full moon. All those people were gone. There was nothing there but a massive, deep, black hole.

"Where'd all the people go?" Mona asked.

"They're down there." Kirk pointed toward the darkness of the giant pit. It scared him. "The hole...ate them."

The only signs of life were soldiers and some of the remaining technicians standing around the perimeter of the hole. Festus and Helmut stared into the chasm from the stage.

The scene made Kirk think of an epigram Jack Slynn plucked from philosopher Friedrich Nietzsche for use in a Cardinal Slynn song: "Beware of staring into the abyss, for the abyss begins to stare back."

Festus and Helmut continued to look over the edge. Kirk watched them fidget, as if they expected something big. He pulled Mona across the stage. "I say we get the fuck out of Dodge while your old man and that Nazi bastard are occupied."

"Okay, just slow down—"

Her voice cut off as Kirk heard a wet sound behind him like a water balloon bursting. He stopped and turned. Mona stood in front of him, looking down at her chest. Blood spread across her white blouse, dyeing it red. The blood bubbled up through the fabric.

Mona looked up at Kirk and said, "Hey?" before exhaling and collapsing on the stage.

"*Noooo!*" Kirk knelt beside Mona's limp body. He ripped open her blouse, exposing her blood-covered breasts, applying pressure to the hole in her chest to stop the bleeding. It was useless. He knew the wound was too destructive. In seconds, she turned white and cold.

Kirk screamed for help, but no one came. Festus and Helmut didn't even turn around to see what had happened. Kirk got up, full of rage, and charged at Festus and Helmut as they stood with their backs to him. He was only a few feet away from tackling them when he heard a sleek whistling sound cutting the air followed by a hot, sharp pain in his right shoulder. The force spun him around and he fell. He now saw a smoking hole in his shirt. The opening was black for a moment, then it turned red with blood. He looked out to see where the shot came from and knew.

Squinting, Kirk saw the silhouettes of the men on the sniper towers, their figures black against the clear and bright nighttime sky. The assassins must have worn ear protection, as they were still standing. *They did it. They really did it.* He couldn't believe the bastards shot him and Mona.

Another bullet whistled through the air, hitting the stage next to Kirk's left hand with a loud snap.

These snipers suck. Kirk crawled as flat and close to the stage as possible.

He tucked the pain of the bullet wound away and continued to crawl on his belly, toward the front of the stage, until he was right behind Festus and Helmut. If the snipers wanted to get him, they'd have to take out one of the other two first.

Lying flat, he looked between Festus and Helmut's legs. A glance into the giant hole in the desert told him why Festus and Helmut found it so interesting.

"Oh, my fucking God." Kirk stared at an orange light with red and black smoke erupting from it. It looked like the smoke from a steam engine, but it was different, not just in color but also in the shapes it created.

The smoke spewing from the pit possessed a life of its own. It didn't dissipate, but rather built upon itself like multiplying bacteria and held its form.

Hell-smoke, Kirk thought, watching the otherworld spume taking on skeletal and demonic forms. Apparitions joined together and rose up in a large and impious mass of writhing damnation.

"Praise Sethis!" Helmut shouted in a joyous tone with his arms raised. "Praise Satan!"

"I don't see the devil." Festus sounded unimpressed. "Where is he?"

As Festus spoke, the Hell-smoke erupted and whirled from the pit, transforming into a single, gigantic form. The shape like a Rorschach blot with bat wings seemed to thrill Helmut and Festus, but chilled Kirk to the core of his being. It hurt his eyes to look at it. The giant blot pulsed and rippled like a living geyser of red and black liquid rather than smoke. Kirk watched the large mass rise high in the air, glowing in palpitating oranges and reds. An inky umbilicus extended from the bottom of its form and coiled down into the dark fissure. A dreadful presence—pure evil— exuded from it in waves and washed over Kirk.

"Satan." Kirk felt scared and nauseated to utter the name.

All around him, surviving soldiers and civilians came unglued. Some ran for their lives and some committed spontaneous suicide with firearms and rocks to their heads or anything they could find. Some cast themselves into pit. Still others began uncontrollable wailing. He saw men and women begin rabid fucking and panicked people falling to their knees in prayer as the liquid shape rose from the Hellhole and loomed over the stage like a blanket of airborne crude oil.

Kirk choked as evil emanated from the shape like a thick, piety-killing stench. The epitome of anti-Christianity swirled and formed a face. Kirk looked into eyeholes now. The noxious and deep orbits glowed bright with a red-yellow fire. Imperfect features bloomed and a liquid maw opened large and wide.

Satan's voice oozed in, filling Kirk's mind. It was the voice of a billion years, a thousand tongues. The voice of pure dread.

"I am free of His abysmal shackles."

Helmut began chanting something in an ancient Egyptian tongue. Kirk realized Helmut was talking to Satan.

"What're you doing?" Festus asked in a confused and angry voice.

As Helmut continued, Kirk watched the Egyptologist remove his red headdress and drop it to the stage. Then, reaching into his robes, he pulled out a solid gold uraeus and placed it on his head.

With the uraeus in place, Helmut began shouting at the form. "I wear the original uraeus, Great Satan. I wear the authentic one you gave Aknaseth. I'm the one who freed you. I'm the one who delivered you from the abyss so you and your legions may rise against God and His armies of light."

"Wait a minute, asshole." Festus began grabbing and clawing at Helmut's robes.

Helmut pushed Festus away and retrieved the unholy guitar Kirk had played. "Look," Helmut said, holding the instrument up for Satan to see. "I'm the one who used this guitar and your song to release you. I'm the one who took your musical key and opened the abyss. The song, the true uraeus on my head...see that I'm the chosen one. I am a horseman. Your commander!"

A long, swirling tendril shot out of Satan's inky form and hit Helmut in the face, wrapping his head like caramel on a candy apple. Kirk watched the tendril lift Helmut up and off the stage by his head, sensing this virulent tentacle was injecting an unimaginable darkness into the old Nazi. Then the liquid member released Helmut and dropped him back onto the stage.

Kirk tried running away. One glance at Satan's form was almost enough to turn him into a gibbering lunatic, and he wanted to be far from it. Bolting from the stage, he looked over at Mona. He had been unable to save her, but he thought he could save himself—if he ran fast enough.

Just as Kirk neared the side of the stage, a bullet pierced his chest. Another sniper shot hit him and this time it was bad. The mere sight of Satan in true form drove most mortals mad, but these snipers seemed unaffected. Kirk realized they were steady with their aim, true to the code of one shot, one kill, one way. He feared they'd do their job no matter what faced them.

Another sniper shot Kirk and caused him to do a running-stumble as the bullet exited his body. He fell on the stage and rolled. He came to a stop on stage right, out of the sniper's sight, but not out of trouble. He was bleeding a fountain. The sniper round had entered his chest right above the heart and entered his left lung. He was on his way out of the mortal world.

As he began dying, Kirk saw Helmut and Festus near the front of the stage. Helmut was on his back, thrashing around as if having an epileptic seizure. Festus took a few cautious steps back, looking bewildered and terrified of Helmut's current condition. Kirk watched on and wondered if Festus still thought immortality might be attained.

Kirk focused his fading vision toward Helmut. He watched the Egyptologist bucking in violent fits with his backside slamming into the stage floor. Helmut came to an abrupt stop, then rose in the air. He floated several feet straight up before tilting and floating back down to the stage like a feather. He landed on his feet and began to tremble with a vicious shuddering. Helmut screamed and began removing his clothes.

As Helmut stripped off his robes, Kirk gazed at the old and disfigured man, seeing his entire body covered with vicious burn scars. Helmut stood naked, wearing only the unholy uraeus on his fire-seared head. Kirk heard Helmut mutter something that wasn't part of any human vocabulary. Helmut spoke the inhuman speech and began transforming. Kirk witnessed the aged and flawed body taking on a new shape.

Kirk found it difficult to watch Helmut and Festus. It took all his strength just to keep his dying eyes open. He turned away from the men and said one last prayer. As he asked God for forgiveness, he looked to the side of the stage, spying the one thing in the world holding any goodness or hope for him: the God guitar.

The guitar Father Antonio Zacharelli gave Kirk rested on a guitar stand, sitting there all day for backup. It rested a few feet away, waiting for him, and he wanted to feel it one last time.

Kirk used his remaining life's strength to crawl to the holy instrument. The guitar was the only thing in the world he wanted to feel before he died. It was the one thing he loved more than anything else.

Crawling, Kirk heard strange sounds that made him turn his weak head around. Helmut transformed like a caterpillar into a butterfly under high-speed camerawork. Nasty cracking and gurgling sounds emerged as Helmut's spine stretched and his vertebrae elongated with his limbs. Helmut was now several feet taller, his fingers and toes transformed into claws. Kirk watched with a pinch of wonder and revulsion as Helmut's melted skin turned from white and tan to a deep, dark, desert-sand red. Helmut's flesh flexed and sprouted instant scales that glistened under the night sky.

Kirk heard more sickening and hideous pops and crunching noises as Helmut's head widened and stretched with his lower jaw jutting out into an obscene set of chops full of large, twisted and sharp teeth poking out of the gum line. Helmut's eyes rolled back into his skull, then rolled back again as black, soulless spheres. His burnt flaps of ear cartilage fell off, leaving crocodilian ear holes.

Obvious to Kirk, Helmut was no longer human. Kirk watched the last traces of Helmut's human qualities excreted onto the stage as Helmut-demon squatted and shit out his soul in a steaming pile of flaming, tar-colored waste. The stench smelled like a thousand deaths.

Kirk believed Festus's sane mind departed as the rich man watched with an expression of terror as Helmut metamorphosed into a monster. Festus was in a full-blown rage, screaming about immortality and trickery.

Helmut-demon looked up at Satan and spoke in English with a voice that sounded as if it came through a throat full of mud. "I serve to lead your legions across the world of man. We conquer the mortal realm. We own the realm of God and all of His light. I swear this upon—"

"Wait a minute." Festus was stomping and shouting in a hysterical voice, a uraeus in his hands. He twisted it into a ball before throwing it at Helmut-demon, screaming, "Aluminum? You gave me a fake? You tricky Nazi motherfucker!"

Helmut-demon ignored Festus and continued to

praise Satan.

"What about me?" Festus screamed, desperate and enraged. "I'm the one who paid to make it all happen. We had a deal. Make me immortal!"

Helmut-demon growled something incomprehensible. Then, with human words formed with an alien tongue, Helmut-demon said, "Shitmonger. You'll never be anything more than a dung beetle in Hell."

Helmut-demon muttered something alien and as Kirk watched, the demonized Nazi slapped Festus hard across the face with a clawed hand. Festus's face sprayed blood, and he was knocked to the stage floor as Helmut-demon turned his attention back to Satan.

Life drained from Kirk. He reached the God guitar. It felt like it took him years, his hiccupping heart and lungs losing power. His blood loss was massive and it would be a mere moment before he succumbed to the bullet wounds.

Grasping the bottom of the guitar stand with his hands, he pulled the guitar and stand down on top of him. On his back, he held the guitar close to his chest. He hugged the instrument, his blood soaking into the wood, slicking the fingerboard.

As Kirk curled around the God guitar, a voice in his head asked, *Do you believe Christ died on the Holy Cross for your sins?*

"I do." Kirk spoke weak words to the air.

Do you have faith enough to let Him into your heart and into your soul so you may do His work on this day?

"I do." Tears trickled from the corners of his eyes and ran over his temples and ears. "Oh, God, I do."

"Then rise and let the power of God and the power of the Holy Cross guide you."

Electrifying warmth filled his body. All pain and weakness disappeared. He was healed and felt his soul becoming one with the God guitar as the bullet inside him melted away along with all of his wounds. His scars and everything else unhealthy in and on his body vanished. His mind, his body, and his mortal soul possessed a divine clarity. He felt like a new being, reborn and stronger than ever.

He stood up and strapped the God guitar onto his body. He picked up a long guitar cable and plugged the God guitar into the racks of amplifiers and guitar gear that had fried up with the hundreds of exploding speaker cabinets. As soon as he plugged into the giant guitar rig, the blown and toasted equipment came alive with lights and a healthy hum.

"The power of the Holy Cross," Kirk said to himself.

He possessed the confidence of a god. With his guitar—the Holy Cross—in his hands, he turned to face his enemy.

Chapter 26
The God of Guitar

The unholy guitar, with its inverted-cross inlays and its body painted with the blood of an archeologist, was lying on the stage when Festus picked it up. He grabbed the instrument by the neck, holding it over his head as he screamed and charged at Helmut-demon like some kind of Fortune 500 gladiator.

"Trickery! You fucking tricked me." Festus ran up behind Helmut-demon and beat him with the unholy guitar. "I helped raise Satan. I'm supposed to be immortal, you fucker!"

Helmut-demon turned on Festus with a guttural roar and picked the multibillionaire up with his clawed hands. The unholy guitar fell from his grip and hit the stage with a clang as Helmut-demon grabbed Festus's head and lifted him. Helmut-demon hissed at Festus and opened his mouth in a wide, hyperextended yawn.

Kirk waited, watching with no emotion as Festus screamed and Helmut-demon bit down on his former employer's head. The long, sharp teeth of Helmut-demon's twisted jaws bit through Festus's scalp and sank into his skull with a violent crunch; his body jerked and wriggled as teeth pierced his brain.

Helmut-demon's mouth and face dripped from the eruption of Festus's blood. He took his claws off Festus and held his head with his mouth for a moment. Kirk continued to wait, biding his time while Helmut-demon finished. He observed Helmut-demon using his new, large, clawed hands to yank off Festus's arms and legs, tearing the rich man limb from limb.

Helmut-demon kept Festus's head locked in his jaws. Convoluted brain matter hung out of the hole in Festus's dome like coils of gray rope. Helmut-demon swallowed a mouthful of Festus's head and brain before slamming the dismembered torso onto the stage.

The red and scaly penis dangling between Helmut-demon's legs moved like a snake. It rose up and pointed at Festus. Helmut-demon stood over Festus's mutilated body while the penis spit a stream of urine on the billionaire's remains.

Kirk decided he'd seen enough and began his move.

"By the grace of God, and by the grace of all that is light and good in His power," Kirk yelled his words across the stage, "I send you and your legions back to the abyss."

Kirk, with the God guitar strapped on, was ready for battle and approached as Helmut-demon continued pissing on Festus's dismembered carcass in the middle of the stage.

Helmut-demon's mutated head snapped and spun á

la Linda Blair at the sound of Kirk's voice. Helmut-demon let out a long, drawn-out screech and leapt across the stage at him.

Kirk turned up the volume knob on the God guitar and hit a heavy and distorted barre chord, stopping Helmut-demon in midair. The chord froze the Egyptologist-turned basilisk, suspending him above Kirk's head, just a foot away from making contact.

Kirk looked up at the motionless Helmut-demon for a moment. His claws were outstretched, the lips of his large mouth drawn back and frozen in a sharp-toothed snarl, his black, soulless eyes focused on Kirk, his reptilian penis erect.

"Body of Christ." Kirk spoke and hit an ear-piercing, mind-shattering harmonic that obliterated Helmut-demon where he floated.

Helmut-demon exploded and showered the stage with bits of gory shrapnel. The old Kraut wouldn't command anything more than a broom and dustpan now.

Kirk walked to the middle of the stage and stood over the lifeless body of his lover, Mona. He knelt down and touched her with the God guitar, hoping the Holy Cross lived up to the hype. For a moment nothing happened, then she stirred.

"What happened?" Mona looked up at Kirk.

Kirk smiled. His heart blossomed as he looked down at her. "You're beautiful." He stood up and brought Mona to her feet.

Mona stood next to him, looked herself over, and then looked around the stage. "Hey, wasn't I—"

"Not now," Kirk said. "I'll explain everything to you later. Just get behind me and hold on with everything you've got. We're getting into a fight."

He walked to the front of the stage with Mona holding tight to his waist. They stepped over the remains of Festus Baustone. The mutilated torso and unattached limbs lay in a heap of piss-soaked gore.

The pit loomed before him, the evil flowing from it. He saw Satan's red and black inkblot and bat-winged form rising up from the Hellhole. Satan loomed over the stage while countless armored locusts filled the air and unholy legions of unspeakable shapes poured forth from the abyss. The survivors in the concert area fled in vain from Hell's minions, but Satan's unstoppable swarms devoured everyone.

Kirk and Mona stood at the front of the stage and the killers in the sniper towers had him in their sights once again. The shooters hadn't deviated from their mission, even with literal Hell breaking loose. He felt the snipers' determination to kill their human target, a target who seemed to have nine lives.

The snipers fired. Bullets from the left and right snipers came at his head while the bullet coming from the middle traveled through Satan's form and went for Kirk's chest.

The bullets hit home but flattened into harmless lead mushrooms against Kirk's head and chest.

The snipers looked through their scopes at Kirk still standing and moved, looking to reload. He turned up the volume knob on the God guitar and hit three high-pitched harmonics that blasted from the amps and across the desert.

The divine power resonating from the God guitar incinerated each of the snipers on his platform. As Kirk watched, they ignited and exploded into yellow and red fireballs. Flames consumed them, and the sniper towers erupted in flames, looking like the burning platforms of three distant oil refineries.

Kirk turned his attention to Satan. A higher power in his hands, his head, and his words. "By the glory of God, I compel you to retreat back into the abyss from which you came. You shall stay there until the day you're to be released by His divine hand."

Clouds rolled in over the desert, and the clear night sky turned into a tenebrous blanket, matching the color of Satan's diabolical form. The glowing orifices burned bright as Satan's inky face bent down on a long, sebaceous neck and hovered in front of Kirk and Mona.

"What is *that*?" Mona asked.

"You know what that is. Close your eyes now and hold me tight. Don't open them until I tell you it's okay."

"Okay. My eyes are shut. God, Kirk, I don't want to see it."

Satan's reek cut through the lovers like an immoral and frozen wind. Kirk faced Satan and said, "By the power of God, and by the power of Christ, I command you to leave this world and re-enter the abyss."

"His power isn't enough to stay me," Satan said.

"It was by His power that you were imprisoned, and it's by His power that you'll be put back in your place until He's ready to free you for the Judgment Day to come."

"I am here, and here I will remain to make this world my own. Where is your God now?"

"He's here, in me. I'm sending you back to Hell."

An explosion of ominous hatred ripped into Kirk's brain, trying to corrupt his soul and his faith.

"You? Chosen by Him? No. Christ was a weak man whose failure on the Cross proved God's frailty."

"The triumph of the Holy Cross shall send you

back."

Ink red and black tentacles erupted and extended from Satan's form. They covered the stage and surrounded Kirk and Mona.

Kirk watched Satan's dark form engulfing him and Mona.

"What's going on?" Mona's voice bordered on a scream.

Satan's form covered the lovers, cutting off the sights and sounds of the outside world. Kirk hoped Mona's eyes were closed. She shook with uncut terror.

"Don't worry." Kirk spoke in a calming, gentle whisper as the liquid evil surrounded them. "Be calm and have faith."

Kirk stood still as Satan's swirling face hovered in front of him. A long, black, liquid tongue rolled out of Satan's mouth like a glistening, fiery snake. The tongue slithered up, down, and around Kirk and Mona without touching them.

"Like you, I'm also a musician." Satan blurted this fact with his liquid tongue curling. "But my music doesn't give pleasure to the masses—it condemns them. My music is created to *un*create. To destroy all He has done and to destroy those who worship Him."

Satan's tongue flickered out and licked the God guitar. Kirk bore the blast of an indescribable scream as Satan shuddered, repulsed by the virtue and power of the Holy Cross, now in guitar form.

"What instrument is this?" Satan bellowed the question in a thousand voices. His shape oozed away from Kirk and Mona, receding like a pool of motor oil going down a drain.

Kirk turned up the volume knob on the guitar. A steady hum of restrained power filled the stage.

Satan roared as his inky form rose and grew larger. "Priests, popes, saints, and angels have faced me, and I've conquered them all. You're no saint. You're a foolish man bent on your own destruction."

"No. You'll be conquered this day. The power of the riff compels you."

Kirk hit a power chord on the God guitar. It shook the ground, sending massive vibrations through all stratum, mortal and otherwise. Satan's glowing and cloudy form repercussed backwards, as if punched by a mighty and invisible fist.

"Stop!" Satan's otherworld voice shrieked with a piercing, inhuman register. Numerous tentacles and tendrils shot out of the inkblot shape, threatening to strike.

Kirk ignored Satan's menace. *Stay focused and open your heart.*

He closed his eyes and began playing the God guitar.

At the sound of the first notes, a ray of celestial light burned through the dark sky, bathing Kirk in brightness like a spotlight from Heaven.

As the guitar music erupted from the amps, Satan tried attacking Kirk, but there was no damage Old Scratch could do. His efforts were useless. Kirk knew he and Mona were untouchable, protected by a divine force.

Satan's liquid tendrils whipped and lashed out with fury but burned to instant ash as soon as they touched the holy light.

Kirk played a couple of improvised technical measures, keeping Satan at bay and feeling the immediate presence of a higher power moving through his body like high voltage.

Kirk's mind, already opened with a pure clarity when he became reborn through the Holy Cross, now upgraded with an enlightenment seen only through the eyes of God. He felt himself becoming a channel, the purest channel in existence conveying power from above. This power ran through his body and through the divine guitar in his hands.

Kirk played the God guitar as a man possessed, but this time it wasn't an evil musical entity in him. He felt overcome with something pure, reinforced by something holy and powerful.

Kirk submitted and entered into a trance. His heart and mind opened to the energy and power channeling through his body and soul. He played the guitar as if his fingers were making love to the fingerboard. His digits moved across the inlays and frets made from the crucifixion nails. He performed with the grace and essence of God.

He heard himself playing guitar music with no diabolical or sinister-sounding notes or passages. Deep in his subconscious, Kirk knew he played notes unlike any form of manmade music. His riffing sounded like a million angels singing, as if the universe itself were crying in every note. He embraced supreme power, atomic energy from God, in the form of celestial guitar riffs and hooks. This was music with the power to rock worlds and destroy all evil.

Satan roared and lashed out again and again at Kirk, but his efforts were futile. Satan said something over the guitar music in a inhuman language to the voracious hordes of Hell pouring out of the pit and across the desert. Clouds of armored locusts and armies of misshapen and unspeakable things began attacking the stage.

Kirk played on. Every note drove Satan's legions back into the Hellhole. He watched as the heaven-sent guitar music caused the entities a pain far worse than the agonies of Hell. The hordes withdrew their attack on Kirk. The music he channeled from the heavens and through the God guitar was like holy water or the sign of the Holy Cross being inflicted upon evil. Audible exorcism against the Antichrist.

As the music Kirk played became more intense, the beam of light upon him grew brighter and he felt lighter, rising and floating several feet above the stage with Mona. She grabbed him tighter, and he assumed she must feel the sensation of rising. He hoped she'd keep her eyes closed through all of this.

In the air, Kirk watched as the locusts combusted and Satan's legions retreated and slithered back into the pit. The numerous evil beings were unable to bear the sound and agony caused by God's voice—in the form of guitar music—blaring through the amplifiers.

Satan's lava-like form shrieked, cursed, and spread out over the entire stage. Kirk watched the satanic mass blanketing everything aside from the beam of God's light. With mouth agape, Satan vomited fire upon the stage and ignited it, but Kirk remained undaunted, hovering in the air and continuing his furious performance as the stage became an inferno.

The amplifiers and speakers were surrounded and licked by flames but remained unharmed. With divine protection, every piece of guitar gear maintained the musical assault and blasted Kirk's guitar music.

"I am Set. I am Sethis. I am Satan. I'm all He despises, but without me He cannot exist. He needs me." Satan's words boomed at Kirk before the underworld voice took on a neutral tone. Satan almost sounded like Kirk's maternal grandmother. "I sort bad from good. This world is mine while God's children reside in His kingdom. Discard your guitar. It's God's plan. You can't change anything with your music."

Kirk ignored Satan's voice as it tried to besmirch his focus. He played on, harder and heavier, feeling the music beginning to beat Satan down. Satan continued to vomit fire, but it didn't matter. Satan failed to stop The God of Guitar.

"Look." Satan's voice sounded more desperate as he pleaded with Kirk and the surrounding desert. "God made man in His own image. He also made *me* in His image. I'm as virtuous and good as any man or creature made by God. I'm a brother to Christ Himself."

Kirk's eyes remained open and clear as he floated in the beam of celestial light. He continued playing the music, never stopping; the notes and chords ran through him like his own blood. All around him was fire and the sound of the guitar music. Then, through the walls of fire, he saw a blasphemous sight in front of him.

Satan floated in front of Kirk, but now in a new guise. Satan transformed from a liquid, bat-winged blot into the form of a man. He was now Kirk's size, naked, and looked like Jesus Christ.

Kirk looked at Satan-Christ, a thin, frail man with legs bound together by rope and with his arms outstretched in the form of the ultimate martyr. Satan-Christ's skin was white and flames from the stage fire licked at his feet, legs, and penis without harm. The hair of the fake Savior was long and a crown of thorns wrapped his head. Kirk looked into Satan's Christlike face. It was pale, with a beard and mustache and eyeless sockets holding nothing holy or human.

Eyes are the window to the soul. This thing has no soul. He found the empty holes devoid of sympathy, kindness, or warmth. They were as hollow as a dead tree. Only a faint, red light illuminated the sockets from somewhere within the pseudo-human head.

"Can't you see?" Satan-Christ spoke as black tears rolled from the empty eyeholes. "I'm part of God. I'm Christ's brother. You don't want to harm me. Put down your guitar so we can exist in harmony, His way."

Kirk's fingers blazed across the God guitar. "I order you gone from this world in the name of the Father..." Kirk spoke while downpicking hard and hitting power chords.

"No!" Satan-Christ screamed as the music from the God guitar split his human shell from the neck down to his genitals. Red and black ectoplasm oozed out, feeding the hungry flames below like grease on a grill.

"In the name of the Son..." Kirk spoke louder and again hit another power chord. This riff produced a powerful quake through the ground and leveled Aknaseth's pyramid and temple.

"How dare you?" Satan-Christ's raging and screeching words were drowned out by the blessed metal din.

The ringing chord summoned a bolt of light that burned down from above and entered Satan-Christ's head, baptizing him in holy brightness. Kirk watched with satisfaction as beams of pure light blasted out from Satan's hollow eyeholes, mouth, and gutted midsection.

"And in the name of the Holy Ghost..." Kirk's words were a roar now, and he spoke not for God, but rather *with* Him, through Kirk's body and the guitar.

"Amen."

Kirk struck a final power chord. The strength, intensity, and heaviness of the massive riff cleansed the globe and burned away the dark skies above. The surrounding desert opened up to a brilliant and bright sky. The atomic energy of the God guitar entwined with sonic power of divine music and obliterated Satan's Christ-shell, blowing Satan back to the giant pit as he screamed in a thousand harmonized tongues.

The final power chord rang out with eternal sustain and Kirk looked out, seeing Satan in his original inkblot form again. The burning, bright light from above pummeled the Antichrist. Kirk saw forms, beings of light, flowing down from the sky and through the celestial rays bombarding Satan. The bright and beautiful forms owned winged, humanlike shapes. Kirk watched as they began attacking Satan.

Angels, Kirk thought, watching good fighting evil. Satan lashed out to fight, but the Lord of Darkness was overwhelmed by angelic forms of light swarming and subduing him. More and more angels raced down from the heavens, like brilliant twisters funneling from the sky and into the pit.

Satan cursed and roared in human and inhuman voices, but his words held no power. The angels ripped his liquid form apart, casting his pieces into the bowels of the abyss. Kirk watched Satan being driven down and shoved back into the prison where God put him before time began.

A voice—God's words—like thunder rang through the air and through Kirk's mind. *"Evil forever beneath my feet as a snake crushed by my weight."*

With those words, a massive bolt of light blasted down into the pit and unleashed an explosion of light and fire, like a detonated atom bomb.

The explosion filled all of Kirk's senses and consumed his surroundings, yet he was unharmed. He closed his eyes and when he opened them, the light had vanished and the pit was sealed. The ringing chord also stopped when the light disappeared. Kirk and Mona fell to the ground, lying side by side.

Some time passed before Kirk spoke. "It's over," he said, God guitar in hand. He crawled over to Mona. "You can open your eyes now."

Mona opened her eyes and looked up at Kirk. She smiled and hugged him. "Are we dead? What—?"

"Satan tried to sucker-punch God and failed. It's over. The evil is gone. Satan's back where he belongs."

"My dad, Helmut...all those other people. All dead?"

"I'm afraid so." *God's plan?* It gave Kirk little comfort. He wiped dirt from Mona's cheek and said, "We're alive. That's all that matters now."

"This is a fucking miracle, huh?" Mona began sobbing and laughing at the same time.

Kirk smiled. "Yeah, it was definitely a miracle."

Mona's eyes widened as she looked past Kirk. "Behind you. What's that?"

Kirk stood up and turned around. Standing before him was a bioluminescent human form. The form radiated with a bright glow. White, fiery wings stuck out of its back.

Kirk took a step back and Mona stood up, clinging to him. Kirk held the God guitar out in front of him. The face of the angel looked familiar to Kirk. "You're Father Zacharelli, aren't you?"

The angel took the guitar from Kirk and spoke. "I'm a servant of God, like you. You've performed wonders today, and God blesses you. Your work is done here. Now you can rest. Now you can live."

The angel touched Kirk and Mona on their foreheads with a glowing hand. Zacharelli the angel was the last thing Kirk saw before he blacked out with Mona on the desert sand.

Chapter 27
Aftermath

"That's it. We're all done, man!" Kirk said to his studio engineer, Grainy, as they sat at Kirk's studio mixing board.

Kirk was happy to learn Grainy was busy hiking in the Canadian wilderness with a young lady when Kirk performed Satan's song for the world. The studio engineer missed Kirk's entire performance and avoided any potential harm since he didn't hear it, though Grainy admitted he and his companion were thrown to the ground when the Earth shook.

"Sounds great. I'll take the recording to the mastering facility tomorrow." Grainy stood and began packing up the master digital discs and hard drive containing Kirk's new album.

Kirk finished the solo album he'd started before

getting mixed up with Festus Baustone and Helmut Hartkopff. Four months had passed since he and Mona walked out of the intense heat of the red desert without sunburn.

He thought of those first several weeks, when the entire world knocked at his door, wanting to know what happened at the pyramid and temple of Aknaseth. Every worldwide power grid fried out. Every television, radio, and computer in the world was destroyed by the greatest and freakiest power surge on the planet. No video footage or any other recordings existed to prove what had happened. The globe turned to Kirk and Mona for explanations.

Kirk thought of how he and Mona had become newspaper and tabloid front-page favorites. The paparazzi had never been worse. The lovers were questioned and interrogated. They were given lie detector tests and were subpoenaed to testify about what happened in Egypt. Every federal agency and the leaders of every nation demanded answers, but in the end, they got nothing. Kirk and Mona maintained they didn't know what happened. The polygraph tests they were forced to take concurred. The agencies and foreign countries gave up their inquiries, yet Kirk and Mona remained under the suspicious eyes of the U.S. government and public. Kirk smiled at that.

Thousands of people around the globe had died and many more were injured from the accidents and natural disasters brought on by the cataclysmic Armageddon chord in Satan's song. Kirk knew he ended up saving the world and almost all life on Earth with the holy guitar, but he also knew he'd never shake the guilt of knowing his hands were responsible for the mass death and chaos he'd first created, under duress, on stage.

The truth and the things Kirk and Mona knew were never discussed again. Even as they lay together under the sheets of Kirk's bed at night, naked and intimate, they never talked about what happened in Egypt.

Kirk wanted to leave it all behind, knowing there was nothing back there anyway. The site of the concert, where Aknaseth's pyramid and temple were uncovered, was now nothing but a desolate, scorched piece of desert. After the Armageddon chord rocked the world, the United States and Egyptian military surveyed and dug up the entire area. They found nothing but sand.

Archeologists and scientists from around the world went to the Aknaseth concert site to analyze sand and soil and also to take atmospheric and radiation readings. The numerous scientists never produced evidence to explain how a pyramid and temple and just over twenty thousand people in the desert all vanished without a trace.

The Egyptian Incident joined the mysterious lore of the Bermuda Triangle and the asteroid that hit Tunguska, Siberia, in 1908. Everyone had theories about what happened, but no one would ever know the truth, since Kirk Vaisto wasn't talking.

Grainy came back into the control room and handed Kirk an envelope. "Some guy delivered this while I was taking off."

Kirk took the envelope and looked at it. There was no return address on the outside. Inside, the letter read:

Dear Kirk,

Congratulations on a great performance in Egypt. I caught the first minute of the show before I lost my mind. My TV blew up with all the other crap in my entertainment center.

I don't know what happened to you out there, but I want to thank you for getting rid of Festus Baustone. A weight's been lifted off my chest. I feel free. No more looking over my shoulder. I might even come out of hiding. Who knows?

Anyway, you take care of yourself. Maybe we'll get the old band back together for a reunion tour...

Your thankful Beef Kitten,

J.S.

P.S.: I can't believe you and Mona are a couple. There's a lot of things I'm sorry for, and the way I used and abused Mona is one of the biggest....for so many reasons, amigo. On that note, I really wish you the best.

Kirk smiled. *Welcome back to the world of the living, Jack.* He folded up the letter and put in his back pocket.

Kirk's cell phone rang as he sat in the studio control room. "Hello?"

"Kirk, it's me."

He was silent for a moment. "What do you want, Rod?"

"Just touching base with you. Seeing how you're doing," Rod said. "It's been a while since we've talked."

"Yeah, there's a reason for that. I fired your ass, remember? You're not my agent anymore."

"Hey, c'mon, kid. We've got a helluva history together and you can't just throw all that away."

"Cut the bullshit. I know you're not just calling to be my pal. You've got something else in mind."

Rod sounded drunk. His snicker crackled over the phone. "Okay, I've got deals on the table that could make you lotsa money."

"I've got plenty already, thanks."

"Yeah, but this could really set the record straight about what happened to you over in Egypt." Rod launched into his sales pitch. "Whatever went down over there is one of the biggest mysteries of the new millennium."

"I got nothing to say about that."

"Oprah's willing to pay you five million for a one-hour interview, and the *Enquirer* is talking about fifteen million for the exclusive story of the Egyptian Incident."

"You've always had a fucking hearing problem, Rod. I've got nothin' to say about the so-called Egyptian Incident. I should kick your ass for getting me involved with Festus Baustone. I damn near lost my life because of your bullshit."

"C'mon, kid, you know I've always looked out for you and I've always seen your future in my eyes."

"No, you've only seen fucking dollar signs in your eyes."

"So, it's no?"

"That's right." Kirk emphasized the firmness in his words. "Besides, I've got a new manager."

A hard laugh came over the phone. "Bullshit. Who? Q-Prime? Concrete Management?"

"No. Someone new."

Just then Mona walked through the studio door. She smiled and gave Kirk a kiss as he pulled her onto his lap.

"Someone new, huh? Tell me."

"Here, I'll let my manager introduce herself." Kirk handed Mona the cell phone.

"Yes? Who's this?" Mona said.

"This is Rod Yaggerwood. Who the hell are you?"

"Yaggerwood?" Mona said. "Never heard of you."

Mona hung up on Rod Yaggerwood and she and Kirk burst into laughter.

"Old Rod's steaming right now. He can't stand it when people cut him off." Kirk loved it.

"That's the music biz. Gotta be tough." Mona giggled away.

"Fuck that guy. I'm so glad to be getting on with my life." Kirk held Mona tighter. "I'm done with plastic people and all the other bullshit in this industry. I'm doing things my way, for myself."

"Oh, really? Does this mean 'The God of Guitar' is going to settle down?"

"Let's just say no one's gonna tell me what to do anymore, other than a higher power."

"Do you really want me as your manager? Isn't that a conflict of interest or something?"

"Hey, if Ozzy and Sharon Osbourne can do it, why can't we?"

"You've got a point."

"I've never had a decent manager. Never even had a woman I could call my own. I'm sick of being used and using people. I want something real."

"I'm real." Mona spoke in a dreamy tone and began kissing Kirk. "And I'm all yours, babe."

"Really mine?" Kirk kissed her neck.

"I am. Forever."

"And I'm all yours." Kirk kept his lips on her neck while unbuttoning Mona's blouse.

She straddled Kirk as he sat on the chair. As he undressed Mona, he looked over her shoulder to see Grainy pop his head in the control room.

"Whoops," Grainy said. "Sorry to interrupt you lovebirds. Forgot my phone."

Kirk and Mona laughed at the intrusion.

"No problem," Kirk said. "Just kill the lights on your way out."

"Will do." Grainy hit the lights.

In the darkness of the recording studio, Kirk and Mona made love like there was no tomorrow.